Praise for
Blacktip Island

"*Blacktip Island* is fun and funny, its characters vivid. Take your time and dive into this adventurous story." – *Portland Book Review*

"Another winner from Tim W. Jackson! Protagonist Blake Calloway is in way over his head in this humorous adventure in paradise. *Blacktip Island* rocks!" – Award winner Kathy Brandt, author of *Swimming with the Dead*

"Five Stars. *Blacktip Island* will make you laugh and keep you guessing. The storyline gets readers hooked, and the characters add laughter, suspense, romance, and everything in between to take this book to another level." – San Francisco Book Review

"Beautifully written with a thriller-like pace, *Blacktip Island* will keep you guessing 'til the very end." – Bonnie J. Cardone, author of the *Cinnamon Greene Adventure Mysteries*

"*Blacktip Island* is a fascinating, well-written story . . . with a hero attempting to avoid detection, eco-terrorists trying to stop construction of a new airport, a beautiful bartender keeping her own secrets, and hunts for pirate treasure each overlapping the other. But the story is less driven by the plot than by the characters and the idyllic setting . . . which makes good fiction." – David K. McDonnell for *Reader Views*

"Ever wonder what's going on behind the scenes at your favorite dive resort? Thanks to *Blacktip Island*, we now may know, and it's way more entertaining than you could have ever imagined. Two fins up!" – Greg "The Divemaster" Holt, *Scuba Radio*

"Escaping to paradise to be in the dive business is a dream for those who catch the bug. For others it's an escape from problems they don't know how to handle. Jackson has woven a mystery about a guy who had the bug and then has problems that press him into needing to go now! A good read that will keep you turning pages!" Jerry Beaty, Associate Publisher, *Dive Training Magazine*

"Jackson has a strong voice that makes for an entertaining read from beginning to end. The characters are well-crafted and bold. *Blacktip Island* is a fun adventure with a motley crew that can easily become addictive." – *IndieReader*

BLACKTIP ISLAND

A NOVEL

TIM W. JACKSON

Devonshire
House

Devonshire House

Devonshire House Press
P.O. Box 195682
Dallas, TX 75209

ISBN: 978-0-9910332-8-7

Library of Congress Control Number: 2016908369

Book formatting and cover design by www.ebooklaunch.com

Acknowledgements

Thanks to the many people who helped with this one along the way:

To Bob Bowie, Lisa Gallagher and Gretchen Hodges, beta readers extraordinaire.

To Randy Warsarger for his insight into the bond business (and my sincere apologies to him for any inaccuracies – any/all mistakes are mine, not his).

To The Blacktip Times' faithful readers for all their enthusiasm.

To Kay Russo, again, for her phenomenal editing.

To Dane Lowe for his hand-drawn cover art.

And, of course, special thanks to my wife, Jana, for always believing.

Jessie was a dog.
Casey was a cat.
The beleaguered runway is/was real, though vastly exaggerated here for dramatic effect.
The rest is pure imagination.

"There are ways out of almost every conceivable scuba emergency if you have been trained in what to do and you can keep your head. But the man who just puts on the gear and shoves off is asking for trouble."

The New Science of Skin and Scuba Diving, Association Press: New York. Third Revised Edition, 1968.

1

Blake Calloway had really done it this time. Here he was trying his damnedest to blend in with the scuba tourists until he could stash the bricks of money he wasn't supposed to have, and now everyone on the boat was watching him. It couldn't be helped, though. The bonehead had needed rescuing.

The *Barjack* rolled to port, revealing waves breaking over the reef, and beyond the calm turquoise of Eagle Ray Sound. The blinding-white beach lay across the sound and farther up the wooden resort buildings sat low on their stilts under the palm trees.

The boat rolled to starboard and the island was gone. Blake bounced off the scuba cylinders, shielding the unconscious diver from the spray. He kept his fingers against the man's throat, straining to feel a pulse through the engines' thrum.

"You sure you've proper training?" Lee, the divemaster, kneeling opposite Blake, yelled above the engines. Lee's face was pale beneath a shock of red hair stiff with salt.

"Do you?" Blake snatched the oxygen mask from Lee's hand, turned it 180 degrees so it covered the unconscious man's nose and mouth properly. It was Lee's fault he was in this jam. With luck, though, the divers would remember the incompetent little divemaster, not Blake.

Lee glared, cinched the elastic straps holding the oxygen mask to the diver's face.

Someone draped a pink Eagle Ray Cove beach towel over Blake's wet shoulders. Great. Something to make him more conspicuous. He pulled the towel over his head. Maybe they'd remember the towel instead of his face.

The boat rolled again. Blake focused on the faint throb under his fingertips, reminded himself to breathe. The island doctor would be at the dock. Then Blake could be anonymous again. Get to his room and make sure the maids had honored the 'Do Not Disturb' sign on the door. Set up an account now that the banks were open.

The boat rose on the next swell, turned toward the reef, and raced ahead of a green wave rising head-high. The engines roared. The boat surged forward, and the wave crumbled behind them in a white boil. The *Barjack* shot between the channel markers and into the sound's calm water. The engines slowed, quieted.

The man's pulse beat obvious now, though he still stared unblinking. Lee still glared at Blake. Dive guests watched Blake, admiration in their eyes. Just his luck. But he couldn't have let the man die.

The boat bumped against the Eagle Ray Cove pier and men in firefighter shirts and a woman in scrubs swarmed aboard. They rolled the man onto a backboard and rushed him away.

Blake sat back, adrenaline draining. For all his volunteer divemastering, he'd never had to rescue anyone in a real emergency.

Someone put a hand on his shoulder. Blake pulled the towel off his head.

"Thanks." Marina the captain smiled down at him, then gave Lee a disgusted look. "Get our oxygen bottle back."

"Didn't need his bloody help." Lee jogged after the medical team.

A man stepped onboard, massive as a circus bear. The resort's dive manager. The boat rocked from his bulk.

"How'd you get sucked into this,…?"

"*Blake* jumped in when Lee froze," Marina emphasized the name. "Can we trade Lee for him, Ger?"

Ger held up a hand to silence her. He threw a trunk-sized arm around Blake's shoulders and yanked him to his feet.

"Hell of a vacation, hey, Son? Let's get you back to it."

He hauled Blake onto the pier and half-dragged him up the boardwalk. Blake tripped on a wooden plank. Ger held him upright.

"You done that before." There was no question in Ger's voice.

"Stumble?"

Ger made a rumbling sound that could have been a chuckle. "Marina's right. You ever get tired of making money, you got a job here."

Blake forced a laugh, ignored the looks from resort guests. Lee scurried back toward the boat, oxygen cylinder under his arm. He looked venom at Blake as he passed.

Blake tried to break away at the path to his bungalow. Ger's arm tightened, steering Blake, pink towel still draped over his bare torso, to the resort's center.

At the thatched bar, the bartender turned to greet them, setting her gold earrings dancing. Green eyes large over high, faintly freckled cheekbones. Her black hair flowed over tanned shoulders and red tank top. More gold flashed on her fingers and wrists. She raised an eyebrow at Ger.

"Mal, you know… uh…?"

Ger had already forgotten Blake's name. Good.

Mal's gaze shifted to Blake. Blake's mouth went dry, choking off any words.

"Hero of the day," Ger continued. "Kept a guest alive. How 'bout we get him a beer."

Mal set a green bottle on the tile-top bar, adjusted the bottle and coaster so they were centered on a square tile.

"Gotta check on our guy," Ger said. "I'm at the clinic, anyone asks." He pounded Blake on the back and stomped away.

Mal's eyes dissected Blake.

"Ger Latner doesn't just call people heroes. Or buy them drinks…" Her voice trailed off, questioning.

Blake sipped his beer to wet his mouth. He needed to get to his room. But he couldn't afford to look suspicious. And Mal's look was intoxicating.

"Blake." He pulled the towel tight around him. "A diver panicked and embolized. I saved him."

"How's his family?" Mal said.

Guests stopped talking, stared at Blake. Blake's stomach rolled. He was bragging while a man lay in some backwater island clinic. The man's friends were sitting here. Remembering everything about Blake.

Mal spun away to mix margaritas. Her khaki shorts rode low on her hips. Blake looked away. She was beautiful, but he had no business gawking. He would be back with Tess in two days, with her none the wiser about why he'd made this last-minute trip.

"So what do you do when you're not sticking your foot in your mouth?" Mal was back, talking at Blake while she watched other bar guests.

"Crappy bonds trader," Blake heard himself say. Idiot. Was he trying to get caught?

"False modesty?" Mal's eyes were on him again. Hint of a smile.

"Ugly reality. Dyslexia's a harsh mistress." Blake had never seen eyes so green.

"Dyslexic bonds trader. Ha! No such animal."

"Sure there is. I make a ton of money." He needed to shut up, but with Mal looking at him like this… "Computers do the math. I just schmooze the clients. Helps when it's your dad's company, too."

"But you know how to turn money into more money."

"In theory." Blake pushed his beer aside. He had to get to his room.

"We need to talk."

"Sure. Hey, where's the nearest bank?"

"Bank?" Mal laughed. "A hundred people on Blacktip. Not worth a bank's effort. You need cash? The drink's on Ger."

"No. Nothing like that." Blake kept his voice even. What the hell kind of place didn't have a bank? "I'm just… I'm in finance. I wanted to take a look."

"Uh huh." Mal gave him a measuring look. Did she suspect? How could she?

"Look, I need to get cleaned up." Blake flapped the pink towel, as if Mal hadn't noticed it.

Mal lifted his barely-touched beer from the bar, still studying him. Blake retreated for his room, making himself walk slow.

Inside, his daypack was still wedged behind the corner armchair. Blake unzipped the bag, pulled out the hardbound *Chapman's Piloting* boating manual, and opened the cover. The six stacks of $100 bills lay untouched inside the hollowed-out book, a bigger problem now than they had been that morning. He couldn't park cash in an island bank if there wasn't a bank. But what to do with it? His only experience with this sort of thing came from movies.

The resort office had safe deposit boxes, but he could only leave the cash there while he was at the resort. There was nowhere he could hide it that it wouldn't be found. He'd have to fly to Tiperon, the big island, where they damn sure had banks, open an account there, build up some off-the-record interest to cover his shortages. He would take tomorrow's flight and be rid of it then.

It had started with a small mistake, a misplaced decimal point, and he'd moved money from another account to temporarily cover the shortfall. Then, when the second account was due for an audit, he moved money from a third account to cover that. Then a fourth account to cover that. Then a fifth. In the process the total had grown. Blake had converted it to cash so he could win back the difference at the Seminole Bingo casino. The blackjack tables had dug his hole even deeper.

Blake stuffed the *Chapman's* back in his pack, told himself to calm the hell down. There was nothing he could do until the daily flight the next morning. He would stay out of sight until then, not draw any more attention to himself. Hope his dad, or anyone else at Calloway, Olivetti, and Nieves in Tampa, didn't stumble across the encrypted files in his office computer.

Blake stayed in all afternoon, watched the palms sway outside his window, his stomach too nervous to eat. After the sun set, though, the bungalow seemed to shrink around him, cell-like. This was no good. He wandered out to the tiki bar, found a chair at the deck's farthest corner where he could sit in the shadows without being drawn into a conversation. He was better in the fresh air, torches guttering behind him and the white noise of voices giving the illusion of fellowship.

"Here you go, Mr. Wall Street." Mal set a cold beer in front of him. Gold rings winked in the torchlight.

"I didn't order that."

"They think you earned it."

At the bar, a couple from the boat raised their glasses. Blake nodded his thanks. Great. Now he was someone's vacation highlight.

Mal glided back toward the bar, grabbing empty bottles and glasses as she went. Her red top rode up, revealing her tan waist with every reach.

Blake downed half the beer. Focused on the stars. Willed his nerves to settle. The crowd thinned as guests went in to dinner. Then swelled again with latecomers. He finished the beer, too fast on an empty stomach.

A hand on Blake's shoulder. Mal. With a second beer.

"You gotta be kidding," he said.

"It's free." Mal pointed to smiling guests he didn't know. "I see why you're such a crappy bonds trader."

Mal walked away. Blake, angry with himself for gawking, shifted his chair to face away from the bar, out across the beach and the darkness of Eagle Ray Sound. Tiperon tomorrow, then back to Tampa for damage control. With Calloway, Olivetti, and Nieves, and with Tess.

He pictured Tess, smiling and bright in their early days. Tess lying warm next to him in the dark, rain pattering on their cottage's tin roof. Mornings in bed with coffee and croissants. She had her own place now. And he had his. While they sorted things out.

Palm fronds rattled in the breeze, sounding like faint rain. More stars than he'd ever seen brightened the sky. A half-mile across the Sound, unseen waves boomed crashed on the fringing reef. Blake finished his beer, felt his stomach unclench. The voices behind him faded. The bar lights snapped off, leaving the deck lit only by the torches.

"Stay as long as you want." Mal circled the deck, blowing out torches. She ran a hand across his head as she passed.

"What was that for?" His scalp tingled where she'd touched him.

"You looked like you could use it, Blake Jr."

Mal's eyes smoldered, unfathomably deep. A slight smile that could have been inviting. Or predatory. Blake shivered. He glanced behind him. Nothing but the darkened grounds. A low moaning rose and fell, like far-off voices calling.

"What the hell?"

"Wind. In caves." Mal's teeth flashed again as she circled him. "Island's shot through with them. Locals say it's duppies. Island spirits, you know?"

The torchlight caught in her eyes. She tucked a stray strand of hair behind her ear, blew out the next torch.

Blake's heart jumped. Mal was flirting? No. His imagination was running wild.

Mal stepped toward him.

"This guy, I like. The one who watches stars instead of my ass."

Idiot. And of course she had noticed.

"You get a better view on the dock." Mal blew out the last torch, started down the boardwalk. "The Southern Cross should be nearly up by now."

Blake followed. This was stargazing, nothing more.

The pier's end was lost in blackness. Waves slapped at the pilings below, winking blue and green with bioluminescence. Heat lightning flickered on the horizon, too far away for its thunder to be heard.

Blake's head spun from the beer. He couldn't tell where the pier ended, or where the flickering water stopped and the starry sky began. To his left hung a triangle of three stars, the lowest, most westerly glowing orange on the horizon.

"Other two not up for another hour." Mal was so close the hair on his arms stood on end with shared electricity.

Blake nodded, knowing Mal couldn't see the nod. Grateful the darkness hid his hot face. Cave wind came louder over the water. Dock planks creaked behind him.

"So why the thousand-yard stare?" Mal's voice was a caress in the darkness.

"Multiple messes. Back home."

"So relax. You're on vacation."

Blake leaned toward the lilac scent, barely breathing. He didn't dare touch her. But he wanted her to touch him.

Movement beside him. Dock planks creaked again. Mal was walking away.

"Enjoy your stars," she said.

Blake's throat tightened, as if something had been ripped from him.

"Is… the view better from the beach?" It came out too fast. Great. With one cheesy line he had ruined… whatever this was.

The creaking stopped. He couldn't see Mal but could feel her eyes on him.

"One way to find out," she said.

Footsteps creaked again on worn planks.

Blake shuffled after her, heart pounding. Just a walk on the beach. Just talking.

Mal stopped even with the sound of waves shushing on the sand below.

"Wooden steps lead down," she said. "Here."

Blake shuffled toward her, tripped, reached out to catch himself. His hand met air, then Mal's fingers, slim and warm.

"Careful." Mal led him down a half-dozen rough steps to the moist sand.

Blake barely felt the sand. What was he doing? He was here to hide money, not chat up beautiful women. And beautiful women didn't go on nighttime beach walks. Not with him, anyway.

Mal dropped his hand, walked away, her silhouette a gap in the sequined sky. Blake stepped after. To his right, heat lightning pulsed in time with his racing heartbeat.

"You hate your job, why not quit?" Mal's voice drifted back.

"You never met my dad."

"He rather Junior be happy or suicidal?" Beside him now. Like she could see in this blackness.

"Suicidal. He'd kill me himself." And still might. "I'd rather be a divemaster."

"You're a mess."

"I'm a Calloway. Weakness is frowned on."

They walked in silence. Blake's eyes adjusted to the dark. Ahead, boxy shapes, rooflines, loomed above the beach.

"Houses?" he asked.

"Vacation cottages," Mal said low, to herself. "Occasionally staff'll rent one."

She stopped so abruptly Blake bumped into her.

"Blake Jr., you need to have some fun."

Blake's heart skipped. He reached for Mal.

She was gone, her footsteps hissing faint in dry sand. Walking up the beach, toward the cottages.

"Where're we going?" he whispered.

"I've always wanted to see inside…" Mal's arm swung in a broad arc against the sparkling sky, "… that one."

Her arm stopped at the cottage farthest to the right.

"Who lives there?"

"One way to find out." A schoolyard dare.

Blake paused. The place was empty, or Mal wouldn't suggest entering. She wanted a reaction, to see him loosen up. Fine. Blake stepped toward the cottage. Cut between two barely-seen palm trees.

Something pressed against his thighs. Blake stumbled, raised his hands for balance. His fingers tangled in netting. He tumbled forward. The webbing wrapped around his face and shoulders, snatched him off his feet, flipped him headfirst into the sand, held his feet in the air. Blake flailed, near-panicked, trying to keep quiet. What was this place?

Hands clamped on his shoulders, held him still.

"Dude. Hammock." Mal whispered, fighting back laughter.

She pulled him upright, freed his hands, then flipped the netting off his head, still stifling laughter. Was this the joke?

Mal led him up to the cottage. They crept across the cement patio and peered in a window. More darkness. No telling what Mal could see. Or how far she'd take this.

Mal tiptoed to a glass-jalousie door. Faint metallic squeak, then a click as the door latch slid back.

"Last one in's a rotten bonds trader," she whispered.

Mal eased the door open on sand-gritted hinges, stepped inside. Blake followed, not about to quit before she did.

One step into the utter blackness. Then another. Light exploded, blinding. An overhead fixture snapping on. Blake spun, expecting an angry homeowner armed with who-knew-what. White walls. Black-and-white floor tiles. Refrigerator. A kitchen. Someone laughing. Mal. Hand still on the light switch.

"Relax. It's my place," she said.

"You have a vicious streak." Blake's pulse boomed. He should've known.

"You have no idea." Mal, teeth bright, pointed to the next room. "Sit. Relax."

Rattan couch with floral-patterned cushions. Matching armchair and coffee table. A wooden chess set on the table, lacquered pieces frozen mid -game.

Mal joined him then with a straw-wrapped bottle of Chianti and two glasses, settled into the couch other end. Blake downed his glass. Mal raised an eyebrow and refilled his glass.

"You do want to see stars, don't you?"

Blake laughed, too quick and too loud. Mal lit a candle in an empty wine bottle.

"Who were you playing?" Blake nodded at the chessboard.

"Victor Korchnoi."

"He work at the resort, too?" Blake asked, alert for an angry Russian boyfriend.

"Soviet grand master. Long dead," Mal laughed.

Blake picked up a pawn. Smooth as glass, and heavier than it looked. Mal snatched it from him, centered it back on its square.

"It's been in the family for generations," she said. "Painted lead junk, but it's got sentimental value. You play?"

"About as well as I sell bonds." With Mal standing so close, he couldn't help himself. And who would she tell, anyway?

"Tell me about that."

Blake talked. Bonds, the brokerage, the stupid mistakes he got away with because he was a Calloway. His wine glass emptied. Mal refilled it.

A warm glow spread through Blake. Mal was the most beautiful woman he had ever met, and she was hanging on his every word. Mal flashed her hint of a smile again.

"What?" How long had he been babbling?

"So, if I had money to invest, you could make me rich, huh?"

"I... Depends on how much money. And what you call 'rich.'"

"Not a ton. But some."

"You have a bank account? On Tiperon?" Blake sat up straight, eyes locked on Mal. Could he park his cash under Mal's name, have it work for them both? He barely knew her, but still...

"Again with... Oh. Tell me you didn't." Mal shifted to sit face-to-face with him. "Tell me there's not a pile of cash in your room."

"No. Why'd you say that?" It came out as one word.

"It doesn't work that way, you know." Mal laughed again. "It takes months, and stacks of paperwork, to get a Tiperon bank account. And your Treasury Department keeps tabs on all of them."

"Hey, I'm in the business. I'm not stupid."

Blake fought down panic. How had he been so stupid? But he couldn't have researched that without raising red flags.

"So the cash you don't have, we talking fifty grand? A hundred grand?"

Blake tried to keep his face blank as the couch tilted.

"More? Dude, seriously?" Mal tapped her wine glass against his. "You're definitely the guy I need to talk to."

Blake imagined himself and Mal wallowing in $100 bills. He leaned toward her. Mal turned away, filled their glasses.

"What's her name?"

"Who?"

"The woman you're not talking about."

Blake choked on his wine. How had Mal known?

"Doesn't matter."

"Sure about that?" The odd smile again.

"Tess." At least Mal wasn't asking about the cash. "She couldn't break free."

"She know why you're here?"

"Dive trip."

"Right. She think you're two-timing her?"

"She knows me better than that." Blake studied the chessboard. Black queen poised to gut a pawn chain. "But she has someone else on the hook, I'm pretty sure."

"You need to sort that out," Mal said.

"Oh, I left things good and sorted." Wine on top of beer had been a mistake.

Mal smiled, gathering everything good and happy and exciting about the evening into the space between them.

Blake leaned toward her again, eyes on her lips. He reached to set his wine glass on the table. Let go too soon. The glass dropped, shattered, sent Chianti across the table.

Mal ran for towels while Blake picked up broken glass and chessmen.

"I'm so…"

"It happens," Mal snapped. She took the chess pieces from him, wiped off the board, the table, then took the glass shards to the kitchen.

Blake dried the chess pieces. A black pawn rolled smooth in his hand. Then heavy in his pocket before he realized it.

Then Mal was back, taking the pieces from him and smiling her odd smile.

"I'll clean the rest myself."

"I ruined a great night, huh?" Blake tried to laugh.

"You drank too much." Mal led him back through the kitchen and onto the porch. Her eyes were on his under the porch light. "Timing's everything, you know?"

Blake nodded. He was a drunken idiot.

She leaned close, kissed him, her lips warm and soft on his for a moment. Then she stepped inside, closed the door.

Blake ran his fingers across tingling lips. What had just happened? He raised a hand to knock on the door. The porch light snapped off, then the inside kitchen light, leaving him in darkness.

He started back down the beach. Mal was right. Timing was everything. And if he felt like this around Mal, that meant he and Tess were through. He had to go back, break things off.

He had to take the cash back, too. Stash it with the rest. Figure out some other way to cover his lapped accounts. The *Chapman's* didn't hold enough money for him to disappear forever. He would fly out the next day, hope Customs didn't stop him in Tampa.

In the morning Blake finagled a seat on the off-island flight, then joined the other passengers outside the shed that passed as the terminal. On the wall hung a Tiperon Islands Department of Tourism poster depicting a dark-haired woman in a rope hammock strung between two palm trees, white sand beyond her giving way to a turquoise sea and an azure sky dotted with cotton-puff clouds. It could've been Mal's hammock.

A red soft-top jeep barreled up the dirt roadway, dust billowing behind. It pulled into the terminal's dirt lot and stopped. The dust settled and the driver climbed out. Mal. Blake went to meet her. She saw him, stopped. Pressed her sunglasses tighter to her face.

"How'd you know I was leaving?" Blake said.

"Small island." Her eyes were hidden behind dark lenses. "Coconut telegraph."

Mal stepped behind the jeep, out of sight of the other passengers. She saw his daypack and her eyes widened.

"You dumb ass! You're gonna get caught putting it back?"

Propellers roared overhead before Blake could reply. A twin-engine Islander, the inter-island shuttle, skimmed the tree line and bounced down on the gravel strip.

"Thanks," Blake said. "For talking sense to me." He handed her an Eagle Ray Cove business card and a pen. "We stay in touch?"

Mal hesitated, gave a tense smile, then scribbled something on the card.

"If you can stay out of jail, we do still need to talk business," she said.

A half-dozen passengers crawled out the Islander's hatch, blinking in the bright sun. The pilot motioned for Blake and the others to board.

At the plane, Blake took a last look at Mal. She was by the terminal now, hugging an older man in slacks and a dress shirt. That explained her surprise. She'd come to greet her dad, not say goodbye to Blake.

At the international airport on Tiperon Island, Blake bought a postcard version of the hammock poster, taped the Eagle Ray Cove business card on the back and tucked it in his bag. He pulled Mal's pawn from his pocket, rolled it between his thumb and fingers, smiling at its smoothness. He would stay in touch. Even if it was from a jail cell.

2

The Customs agent in Tampa barely glanced at Blake, a sunburned, Hawaiian-shirted tourist among all the other sunburned, Hawaiian-shirted tourists coming back from the Caribbean. On the tram from the airside to the main terminal, he silently rehearsed his speech for Tess. It was his fault. He hadn't been there for her. This trip to the islands had opened his eyes. A knot tightened in his gut. He didn't want to hurt her, but this had to be done.

The tram doors opened and the other passengers swept Blake into the central concourse. The crowd dissipated. A familiar woman stood to one side by a planter. She was watching the arriving passengers. Tess. Paler than he remembered. Blonde hair hauled back tight in a bun as if she had come straight from work. Her blue eyes searched the arriving passengers, then locked onto him. How had she known he was coming back? And on this flight? She stepped to meet him, eyes cold.

"You bastard!" Her slap knocked his head sideways. "You think I'm that stupid?"

"Tess, I can explain…" How had she found out about Mal?

"No! It's bad enough you have all that money - I don't want to know where it's from - and to not tell me. But to sneak it overseas?"

"What money?" Blake pulled Tess aside, whispered. How did she know about the money?

"Wads of hundreds. In your dive bag. That isn't there anymore." Tess yanked her arm free. "I stopped by to get some of my things, Blake. A mini-vacation in the Tiperons, out of the blue? You son of a bitch!"

"No, Tess... I still have the cash." Blake tried to get Tess to whisper, too.

"And that makes it okay? People go to jail for things like this. And I'm not going to jail with you! We're through!" Tess slapped him again and stormed off.

Blake watched her go, numb. Nearby travelers eyed him, trying to act like they weren't. What had they heard? What blanks had they filled in? Were any of them cops?

"*What?*" Blake yelled at the man nearest him.

The man stepped away. Other travelers did, too. Blake staggered through the crowd, fumbling for his car keys. Bumped into people. Barely noticed. He needed to get away, lose himself in the crowd, in traffic.

Blake drove to his condo in a daze, barely seeing the cars around him. He stuck to the speed limit, though, used his turn signals, made complete stops. The last thing he needed was to get pulled over, have his car searched.

It shouldn't have surprised him Tess found the money. She had always been a snooper. But why would she expect him to tell her about illegal cash? She didn't want to know - she had said that herself. And they were about to split up, anyway, whether they'd admitted that to themselves or not. There was no way he could have told her.

It wasn't his fault, their failure. Not completely. But with her pulling the trigger first, it felt like it was. That didn't matter, though. What mattered was she hadn't turned him in. Not yet, anyway. What mattered was making sure no one at Calloway, Olivetti, and Nieves was onto him.

At home he re-stashed the cash with the rest of the money, showered, and headed to work. At Calloway, Olivetti, and Nieves, Blake caught a few questioning looks from his coworkers. He'd been scheduled off all week, but no one cared enough to ask him why he was back. Blake closed his office door, scanned the room. Papers on his desk were as he'd left them. Computer files seemed untouched. Good. He was back to square one, though, on how to replace the cash he'd lost. And spent.

The door swung open, and Blakely Hugh Calloway, Sr. walked in.

"Glad to see you gave up on your scuba nonsense, Son," Blake's father said. "I about had Jo Nieves step in on some accounts of yours. These new ones, too. You need to get on these today, duck on a June bug."

He dropped a stack of folders on Blake's desk and left.

Blake gripped his chair's arms, waited for his pulse to slow. He'd come back just in time. He thumbed through the folders. Straightforward stuff, despite the big numbers involved. Blake plowed through them, barely seeing figures he typed into spreadsheets while his mind sorted through options for replacing the missing money. He didn't have enough personal cash to cover the difference. Any side investments he made would leave an obvious trail. He could cash out his personal investments and retirement accounts, hope no one asked why. But would all that be enough? He needed to get home, ransack his personal files for every cent he could find. And hope Tess wasn't mad enough to expose him.

Blake took Mal's chess piece from his pocket, set it next to the computer, propped the hammock postcard against it. A warm glow seeped through him, feeling the pawn's solidity and thinking of Mal. The panic receded. He would inventory everything he had, from finances down to garage sale stuff, and see how much he could come up with.

At day's end Blake filed the papers his father wanted and headed home. After a quick meal, he dialed Tess to make sure she wouldn't rat him out. Or if she meant to, that she'd give him enough time to replace the money now that he had a plan. The call went to voicemail. Blake hung up. He couldn't leave all that as a recorded message. But he should leave some sort of message, hopefully soothe her temper. He redialed. Hung up again. What if she were screening calls? If someone was with her? The way he'd been with Mal. No. He was making himself crazy.

But he needed to talk to someone about things with Tess. His friends were more Tess' friends, though. His brother Adam would laugh. His dad would tell him to stop whining. Next to the phone lay the Blacktip Island postcard. Had the peacefulness of the island been only twenty-four hours ago? Mal would be working now. Something fluttered inside him. He tapped out a quick message, upbeat, thanking her again for setting him straight. Telling her he and Tess were officially done, without giving details. Mal wouldn't reply, but typing it soothed the tightness inside.

Blake pored over his personal accounts, his I.R.A. If he liquidated it all, added that to the cash in his closet, he could replace most of the missing funds. He had to do it soon, though, then smooth over any electronic traces that might give him away. And it had to be done on the Calloway, Olivetti, and Nieves computer. When other staff wasn't around. Early tomorrow, after he'd crashed for a few hours. Exhausted as he was, he'd make an even bigger mess if he tried to do it now.

His phone buzzed. A message from Mal.

"You're a great guy. Things'll be fine. Worst case, you can run off and be a divemaster. Haha."

Just like Mal. And she cared enough to respond. That was good. Blake leaned back on the couch, fell asleep where he sat.

Blake slipped into the office before dawn, closed the door, clicked on only the small desk lamp. He hunched behind his oak desk, alternating between his office computer and his personal laptop, transferring funds, covering his tracks as best he could. It wasn't perfect, but unless someone had reason to look closely, it should be fine. Blake propped his postcard against the lamp's base. Willed his pulse to slow. He needed to calm down. Now. Everything would be okay.

Voices sounded outside as people shuffled in to work. Blake worked quick, double checking figures to make sure he wasn't transposing numbers. Once he was done with this, he could move the cash back in small chunks over the next few days. Voices outside settled into the normal hum of Calloway, Olivetti, and Nieves, sounding strangely like Blacktip Island's duppy caves. All was good.

Then came slamming doors, raised voices. Thunder rolling ahead of a squall. His office door crashed open, and Blakely Hugh Calloway, Sr. stormed in, face red above his spotless suit. He slammed a pile of papers on Blake's desk. The work Blake had churned out the day before.

"You notice anything odd about those numbers?" There was no 'Son' in Blakely Hugh Calloway, Sr.'s voice.

Blake glanced at the papers. Ice shards shot through him. He'd scrambled figures. Shifted decimals. Bought thousands of bonds without checking his math. Sold thousands more.

"You have any idea how much money you cost this company?" Blakely Hugh Calloway, Sr. roared. "'Bad with math,' my ass! You know what 'bankruptcy' is? You know what an S.E.C. investigation is? I'm through smoothing over your screw ups!"

"Dad, I..." There was no air in the room. Only blackness crowding tight around Blake. Smothering. He felt his chest with numb hands, sure his pounding heart had broken ribs. "I just need to finish up..."

"You get the hell out, *now*, I'll spare you a security escort!"

Blakely Hugh Calloway, Sr. stepped between Blake and the desktop computer.

Blake snatched his laptop and postcard and staggered from the office. There was no way to get to the work computer now. And without the work computer, there was no way to alter or delete the incriminating files. It would take Jo Nieves a while to break the encryption, but she would, sooner rather than later. And when she did, Blake would go to jail for a long time. He had to get away. Get somewhere. Somewhere with air.

Blake sped down Bayshore Boulevard in pounding rain, weaving through traffic to get home quick as he could, wracking his brain over what to do with the cash. He couldn't give it back, not without turning himself in. Could he leave a note and the cash in his condo and run? No, the cash in his closet was the only money he had left. He had to take it, all of it, until he found a way to make things right. He had to get out of the country. Mexico was the closest border. That would take, what, twenty-eight, thirty hours driving? And then what? He didn't speak a lick of Spanish.

At home he poured a tumbler of scotch, forced himself to stop, breathe. He had time. Folks at the brokerage would be scrambling the next two, three days to undo the damage he'd done yesterday. Then it would take them days to break the encryption on his lapped accounts. He needed to calm the hell down and think.

Blake stepped onto his balcony. Below, smears of red and white, traffic on Bayshore reflected on wet asphalt. The low shush of tires in the rain drifted up. Beyond, wind-driven waves crashed on the breakwater, sending spray over the balustrade. Trawlers' lights bounced far out on the bay. Shrimpers, making their way in from the Gulf. Could he escape by boat? No, that was more farfetched than driving to Mexico. Wind sent more rain across the balcony, stinging his face.

Blake stepped back inside. His postcard, the Eagle Ray Cove business card lay on the coffee table facing him. A vision of Mal, the reef, the palms. A quick call to the resort would help. He wouldn't have to talk. He'd just listen to a cheery-voiced receptionist, or to the breeze rustling through palm fronds in the background. He could escape, if only for a moment. Blake punched the numbers into his phone with shaking fingers. The international line crackled, gave a series of double beeps. A familiar voice.

"Ger Latner, Eagle Ray Divers."

Blake's heart jumped. Why would Latner answer the main resort phone? He should hang up. But Latner would just ring him back.

"*Eagle Ray Divers!*"

"Ger, this is… Hugh Calloway." He hated his middle name, had always hated it. But at that moment, he hated 'Blake Calloway' more. "I was there a couple of days ago… helped with a guy who got hurt…" Not sure what to say.

"Hugh! Why the hell aren't you down here?" Latner's voice boomed in Blake's ear. "You're quick! I had to axe a divemaster not two hours ago!"

"No… I didn't…" Latner didn't remember Blake. He had forgotten Blake's name on the dock as soon as he had heard it. He had Blake confused with someone else. Named Hugh. Who was job hunting.

"Hugh, I've seen you in action. You're good. You get here by Saturday, the job's yours."

"Uh… sure."

"Hew-Cal-o-way," Latner enunciated, writing down the name. "See you Saturday." Angry voices in the background, someone yelling about being double-charged for rental gear. Latner hung up.

Blake stared at his phone. Took a deep, shuddering breath. Had he just agreed to move to a Caribbean island? In two days? That was crazy.

Or was it? He'd disappear. To another country. From there he could work out a deal to return all the money, plus interest and penalties. He might never be able to come back to the U.S., but he could make things right. And Blacktip Island was a beautiful place to hide.

But could he get the cash - all of it - through Customs a second time? He had no choice. If he tried, he might get caught, but if he didn't try, it was certain jail time.

An odd calm settled over him. The room, his life all snapped into crisp focus, like he was seeing everything for the first time. He had been hiding for years in the familiar, the comfortable. There was nothing left for him here. A new world waited, so fresh and clean it made his eyes water. His divemaster card read 'Blakely Hugh Calloway.' He could be 'Hugh,' create a new life among 100 people who knew nothing about him. He couldn't fake his death, but 'Blake Calloway' would be dead to the world. If he could escape the U.S.

He had until the weekend, maybe, before the Calloway, Olivetti, and Nieves staff discovered the lapped accounts. So long as Tess didn't do anything hasty, that meant a day and a half to create a false trail, send the authorities searching for "Blake" while "Hugh" went unnoticed in the Tiperons.

With Mal. She had said she wanted to see him again, once he sorted things out with Tess. He would start over with a new name, with a gorgeous woman beside him under palm trees and blue skies. He barely knew Mal, but he couldn't get her out of his mind, even with life falling apart around him. They were great together, and he would make sure he didn't screw things up this time.

Who had Latner fired? It had to be Lee. Blake felt bad but not guilty. Latner, and Marina, knew Lee was incompetent long before Blake had stepped in. And Blake had proved he could do Lee's job.

Blake dug out the Dremel and hollowed out his hardbound *Annapolis Book of Seamanship* the same way he'd hollowed out his *Chapman's*. He stacked the remaining cash inside - all older $100 bills with no foil tape for scanners to pick up - and put it in the daypack with the still-packed *Chapman's*. A hardbound book filled with paper had slipped through security scanners before. Hopefully two books would do the same.

He needed a fake passport, but Blake had no idea where, or how, to come up with one. Instead, he would have to muddy his tracks as best he could. Blake called a dozen dive resorts across the South Pacific, hoping to hide his call to Blacktip Island among the other calls. One resort, in Papua New Guinea, he called three times, reserved three weeks lodging and diving, then charged a round-trip flight to Port Moresby to create an obvious trail. During the layover in Costa Rica, he'd leave his phone on the plane for the authorities to trace, then walk out of the airport, pay cash for an overnight bus to Managua, then cash again for the next flight to the Tiperons. The last-minute ticket cost a small fortune, but it wasn't like he'd be around to get the credit card bill. It was the best he could do on short notice.

Next Blake ran to the drug store for electric shears, blond hair dye, and non-prescription glasses to change his looks as much as he could. When he was done, he put his dive gear and a change of clothes in a carry-on bag beside the daypack and fell into fitful sleep on the couch.

Dawn. A phone ringing, rattling the end table. Familiar area code, but unfamiliar number. And damned early. Blake answered.

"Have you lost your mind?" Mal's voice, crackly with a bad connection. "You are *not* to come back here!"

"I…'S your idea." Blake rubbed his eyes. How had Mal found out? And why was she so angry?

"Figure of speech, Blake. Me making nice."

"But we…"

"There is no *we*, Blake. We hung out for a few hours."

"And it was great! You said if it weren't for Tess…"

"You broke up." Mal's voice was calmer now, soothing. "You're in no state to make major decisions."

"I'm kinda out of options." His voice shook. Blackness massed as he said it. Panic. Overnight, Latner's offer had become Blake's only hope. His crystal vision wobbled, soap bubble thin. "My dad just fired me, and I've got to go somewhere."

A long pause, then, "Blake, you can't just run… you bringing your backpack?"

"No!" Blake made himself breathe. Mal knew too much. She might turn him in. Or demand a cut. It didn't matter. He had to drop off the map as quick as he could. The worst Mal could possibly do was better than ten years in a federal prison.

"One of my chess pieces get mixed up in your stuff when you were here?" Mal's voice came lacquer smooth.

"Of course not!"

There was silence so long Blake thought he had lost the connection.

"I can't stop you coming, Blake. Ger's set on this. But *if* you get here, there is *no* romance between us. If you're coming back for me, don't."

"I'm not."

"I don't believe you, Blake." Mal hung up.

Blake's hand shook. It would be okay. It had to be. Mal, he and Mal, it would work itself out. How could it not? He had surprised her, was all. Blake closed his eyes, breathed deep. Told himself for the hundredth time to calm the hell down, trust himself. He'd set something in motion now, and he'd land wherever the inertia took him.

That evening Blake sat in the passenger seat of his convertible, top down, death-grip on the seat and door handle, barreling toward Tampa International. His brother Adam drove, tearing through traffic on I-275, laughing like a kid on Christmas morning.

"She handles nice, bro!" Adam yelled over the wind and traffic. "I'll take good care of her!"

"Don't wreck it! I'm back in three, four weeks," Blake shouted back.

"You're batshit, you know that? New Guinea?!"

"The distance'll clear my head. So will the diving." Blake had made sure Adam was full of bogus information, knowing his blabbermouth brother would share all of it with anyone who would listen.

Adam swerved between a limousine and a delivery van, downshifted, and stomped on the accelerator. The car shot forward, slipped past a pickup towing a ski boat, and fish-tailed around a cloverleaf, tires squealing.

Blake clutched the seat. No use trying to talk in the eighty miles per hour hurricane swirling around the windshield. This was the end of his life in Tampa, whether he made it to the airport alive or not. His worldly possessions, his entire existence, now consisted of a carry-on crammed with dive gear and a daypack stuffed with cash. Scary. Yet freeing. If he got away with it.

"Dad get my latest mess sorted out?"

"Doubt it, Bro." Adam grinned, swerved between two rock trucks. "You screwed the pooch majorly this time!"

"If Dad asks, you don't know where I went."

"He won't ask."

Blake winced. It was true, but Adam shouting it hit him like a two-by-four in the chest. Adam slapped him on the leg to get his attention.

"Mom know?"

Blake winced again. He had forgotten. He could call her from the airport. No. He couldn't risk tipping off anyone who might be monitoring his phone.

"You tell her I'll be back... soon?"

"I'll have to," Adam said. "No way she's breaking the twenty-year silence with Pops. She won't even come to this side of the state."

Blake watched the traffic blur past. He would get word to his mom somehow. Adam slapped him again.

"What if you get eaten by a shark? Or go batshit in the jungle?"

"I go batshit in paradise." Blake tried to sound nonchalant, but his voice cracked. Then, quietly, "And at least I'll enjoy it."

"Getting eaten, or going bat shit?"

3

Humid air washed over Blake when he stepped from the Tiperon Airways jet. He stuck close to a tour group, a dozen people with identical luggage tags crossing the tarmac, pretending to be one of them. The daypack bounced on his back. He prayed his luck would hold. If U.S. authorities had raised the alarm, Tiperon Immigration could put him on the first States-bound flight.

"Hugh Calloway," he announced to the Tiperon Immigration officer. His pulse throbbed in his ears. The name was as foreign in his mouth as it was on his luggage tags: 'Hugh Calloway, Eagle Ray Cove, Blacktip Island.' The officer stamped his passport, waved him through with a bored half-smile.

An hour later he re-crossed the tarmac, squeezed into the high-winged Islander's hatch for the hop to Blacktip Island. He half-crawled onto the middle of three bench seats. A woman, mid-thirties, climbed onto the bench next to him.

"Here, hold this a sec." She dropped her shoulder bag on his lap. Bottles clanked in the bag.

"Ow! What's in there?"

"Duty free. Watch'a got in yours?" She eyed his daypack. American accent, deep South. She clawed windblown brown hair from her face. Smoothed her blue skirt. A nervous smile. "Gawd, we're packed like a charnel cart."

"What the hell are you talking about?"

"I hate small planes, is all." She took back her clanking bag, gray eyes darting from window to open hatch. Her fingers tugged at a cross-and-dove pendant at her throat.

He ignored her, stared out what passed for a window at the propeller. He didn't have the energy for a nervous flyer. Or a lunatic.

The hatch snapped shut. Air in the cabin pressed close and warm, despite the fans. The Islander taxied, lifted off quick in the gusting wind. The window was cool against his forehead. The mangroves beside the airport blurred, fell away in a wash of green. A bright fringe of beach, the turquoise-and-black of reef water over the shallows, then, in a line as distinct and abrupt as the shore, the dark blue of open ocean where the reef plunged thousands of feet in a sheer underwater cliff.

An ache in his chest at that, like something had exploded. He had severed himself from everything he'd known as surely as if he had stepped off that cliff and was falling, with no bottom in sight. He couldn't have stopped this free fall, whatever this was, even if he wanted to.

The airplane climbed into the clouds and there was only the gray window, the dark, close cabin air, and the engines' drone. Wrapped in semi-darkness, he imagined Mal in the Blacktip Island sunlight. He pushed that thought aside. He'd make up with her. His new name would help. "Blake" had screwed up. "Hugh" could start fresh. A couple on the bench in front of him sat with their heads together. The ache inside him sharpened.

A half hour later the Islander dropped from the clouds into bright sun. The woman beside him started praying in what sounded like French. "... que je mette votre lumière..." he made out at one point. She kept it up until they bounced down on Blacktip's dirt airstrip. Bits of gravel, kicked up by the tires, flew eye-level past his window.

Hugh squeezed from the stifling cabin and into the light. He paused, absorbing the sights and scents as if for the first time.

"Get me off this damn thing!" The blue-skirted woman nearly knocked him over as she shoved past, bag clanking.

Resort vans idled at the terminal shack. No Mal. No Latner. His own fault, flying in under the radar. An orange-vested baggage handler pulled luggage from the plane, piled it onto a cart, wheeled the cart to the terminal. Passengers snatched luggage, hauled bags to the waiting vehicles. The nervous woman hoisted a massive duffel over her shoulder, climbed into a green van marked 'Blacktip Haven' and was gone. No Eagle Ray Cove van. Could he bum a ride before the parking lot emptied?

The Islander turned, throttled up, slung a cloud of sand across the parking area. Hugh crouched in the prop wash, shielding his face. The airplane taxied away. Dust settled. Hugh wiped his eyes, spat sand, brushed himself off.

"Hugo! Hugo!"

A gray-stubbled man pushed through the dwindling crowd, waving like he was meeting a long-lost relative. Hugh spun to see who the man was hailing. No one behind him.

"You Hugo Calloway!" Soft Tiperon cadence. *Col-uh-WAY.* The man's stomach strained against a faded teal 'Eagle Ray Cove' polo shirt tucked into khaki shorts. Sockless penny loafers kicked up dust as he walked.

"Hugh." The name still felt strange.

"Yeah! Seen your face last night. Floating on the sea while I was fishing. Knew I had to come for you. Your daddy loves you, y'know."

"What about my dad?" The panic he had left in Tampa gripped him again. Had Ger Latner called Calloway, Olivetti, and Nieves for a background check? Spread the word about

Hugh? If this odd man knew about Hugh's father, the whole island probably knew. "Who the hell are you?"

"Antonio!" The man grinned, tapped his chest like Hugh should know him. "Antonio Fletcher! Your ride to The Cove!" He pointed to the logo on his shirt. The last car pulled from the parking area.

"What'd Ger tell you?"

"Gerry don't even know you're here. Got that myself." Antonio leaned close. "I'm psychic that way, y'know."

Antonio recrossed the dirt parking area without looking back. Hugh didn't move. Antonio stopped. Grinned at Hugh's distrusting look.

"Like old times, Hugo! Shipmates together again!" He walked on to a white-and-rust sport utility vehicle.

"What old times?"

"Sailing before the mast. Past life." Antonio wrenched open the passenger door. Crusted hinges screeched. "She's not the *Bounty*, but she'll get us there."

Hugh looked from the deserted terminal, to the deserted parking lot, to Antonio. He could take the ride or walk three miles to the resort in the afternoon heat. What the hell? He was here for an adventure. Hugh climbed in.

Hinges screeched again as Hugh yanked the door shut. Antonio started the car. It coughed, spat, then settled into the steady '*bwop-bwop-bwop*' of a six-cylinder engine hitting on five. The transmission crunched, ground, caught, and they loped onto the dirt roadway, yellow dust swirling behind. Antonio swerved to dodge an iguana running across the road. Tree limbs slapped at Hugh through the open window.

"Look, now," Antonio yelled above the car's racket. "Reason I picked you up, you need a place to stay. I got a place. Nice place. Perfect for you."

Antonio faced Hugh as he spoke, nudging the steering wheel to the right. The SUV careened across the road again, sideswiping a clump of mangroves. More branches scraped across Hugh's arm and face.

Hugh nodded, poker-faced. Heart skipping in time with the jeep's engine. He tried to raise the window. It wouldn't budge. Great. Here was his adventure: bouncing through shrubbery in a deathtrap driven by the island psychic. Who wanted to rent him a house.

"If you're psychic, you already know if I'll rent or not."

Antonio waggled a finger at Hugh. "Future's cloudy sometimes. Got a new girl interested. Sandy Bottoms got new people, too. But I seen you living there."

They veered back toward the ditch. Leaves flapped across the windshield, caught in the bladeless wiper arms.

"Place's back in the bush, up safe from storms." Antonio seemed oblivious to the brush accumulating on and in the car. "Good people out there."

"Yeah. I'm, uh, have to check with Ger about housing." A pothole sent Hugh bouncing, whacking his head on the doorframe. He fumbled for the seatbelt, found the clasp rusted shut.

"Safety belts don't work on Blacktip," Antonio said. "You'll like my place."

The brush beside the road thinned. A beach spread to their right, and Eagle Ray Sound glistened with the afternoon sun. Soon Eagle Ray Cove's stilted bungalows appeared. Antonio stopped in the sand parking area and grinned. Hugh kicked open the door and jumped out.

"I see you tomorrow, Hugo, right before lunch."

"Hugh." He left Antonio with the shuddering vehicle, jogged for the resort office. He'd visit Antonio's place right after hell froze over.

Inside he found neither Mal nor Latner. The receptionist's face was blank at "Hugh Calloway." Hugh stepped out, cut behind the dining room to get to the dive shop. Panic crept up.

What if Latner had hired someone else while Hugh detoured through Central America? He stopped, breathed deep, then walked on whispering, "Calm the hell down!" He took a deep breath to steady himself and stepped into the dive shop.

"No, I don't know anything about missing fertilizer!" Ger Latner yelled into the office phone. "I run a dive op, not a farm!"

Latner saw Hugh and slammed the phone down.

"Hugh! Wondered if you were gonna get here!" Ger Latner lumbered across the shop to greet him, gave Hugh's blond hair a puzzled look.

"Hugh. Yes." Relief washed through him. "Antonio gave me a ride."

"Good for him! You meet Casey? He'll be training you."

A divemaster with a mop of dark hair and black hooded sweatshirt, despite the heat, scowled from behind the computer. The man had to be sweltering.

"What's this one running from?" A Beatles accent. Reek of cigarettes, and an earthy smell, like the man had been hauling decaying mulch through a swamp.

"I... nothing." Hugh looked to Latner. "What've you been telling people?"

"Everyone on Blacktip's running from something." Casey turned back to the computer. "We'll see if he lasts any longer than the others."

The darkness pulled at Hugh. This was his trainer?

"I don't tell no one anything they don't need to know." Latner loomed over Hugh, his voice a warning growl. "Now, the welcome rum punch party's starting. Let's get you introduced." He grabbed Hugh's shoulder with one paw and propelled him out the door.

"Marina can't train me?"

"Casey's your man." The threat returned to Latner's voice. His paw was vise-tight on Hugh's shoulder.

"I need to drop my bags…"

"Later."

"… and get cleaned up."

"You need to get into the mix."

Hugh walked on rubber legs, carry-on bag in one hand, daypack clutched to his chest. He needed quiet, a chance to exhale, and here he was trotting toward a crowd of strangers, arm half-numb from Latner's grip.

Fifty guests crowded the tiki bar, sipping pink rum punch from plastic cups. More packed in behind Hugh and Latner. Mal stood behind the bar, red tank top so tight it could have been sprayed on. Rings flashed as she poured punch from a plastic jug into neat ranks of cups. Hugh dropped his carry-on bag, breathless. He could have been seeing Mal for the first time.

A slender man with a microphone stood at the bar's end, badgering the crowd.

"Is everyone having a great time?"

A smattering of applause. A few 'yeses.' Some general nodding.

"I said, *'Is everyone having a GREAT time?'*" The man yelled into the mike.

Loud applause. Whoops. 'Hell, yeah!'s. Hugh caught Mal's eye. She turned away, kept serving punch. She was still angry with him? A pale-haired man in a green Eagle Ray Cove t-shirt helped her serve.

"I'm Mickey Smarr, the resort manager." Mr. Microphone was relentless. "My staff and I are here to make sure *all* of you have the best vacation *ever!*"

Mal flowed from guest to guest, ignoring Hugh.

"Now, you all know about our great staff, our great food, and our great amenities. But you're all here for the diving, right?" Mickey paused for the cheers to subside. "Well, here's our dive manager to tell you about that!" Mickey waved toward Latner, who shouldered through the crowd.

Mal, her back to Hugh, served a group of divemasters across the bar. Lee, in the middle, stared hard at Hugh. Latner hadn't fired him, then. Lee's eyes lit with recognition.

"Thanks, Mickey." Latner didn't need the microphone. "First, I'd like everyone to meet the newest member of the Eagle Ray Divers team. Hugh Calloway."

Two hundred eyes focused on Hugh. He raised a hand, got a smattering of applause. The divemasters across the bar studied him. Lee looked puzzled, mouthed 'Hugh?' to Marina. Mal overshot a row of plastic cups, sloshed pink punch across the bar. Lee and Marina jumped back to stay dry.

Latner launched into a well-rehearsed speech. The *Barjack*, *Skipjack*, and *Blackjack* were the resort's dive boats. Two dives in the morning, one in the afternoon. Please tip your dive staff. To Hugh, the speech, the crowd blurred. The resort felt different. Staff faces weren't welcoming. Mal was angry. Coming back had been a mistake. Hugh needed his room. He backed away. Bumped against a post supporting the bar's thatched roof.

A woman in a dive flag t-shirt asked where he was from, shoved one of her two rum punches at him. Hugh said he didn't drink. Blake would've downed the drink in a heartbeat, but Hugh was too new to the world. He'd promised himself that on the trip down.

"Calm the hell down, idiot," He whispered to himself. "Calmthehelldown."

"They usually don't talk to themselves until the fourth week." An older woman in a floral sundress, bleached hair, and caked-on make-up sidled up to him. "You'll fit right in on our little team. I'm Kitty." She stood close, eyes on Hugh's. He tried to back away. The post stopped him. At the bar, Ger Latner grinned. Mickey glared, doing a fair imitation of Lee.

"You… work here then?" Hugh's pulse raced. He needed to run. Couldn't. Lashing out didn't seem appropriate.

"Mickey and I run the place." Kitty rolled her eyes. "Or keep it from crashing. New faces are always good."

The crowd shifted, pressed Kitty against Hugh. Her hand on his chest. "You don't have a drink!"

"No, I… don't drink."

"Oh, I never trust a man who doesn't drink. You *are* trustworthy, aren't you, Hugh?"

Mickey shoved between them. "Hugh! Mickey Smarr!" A glare at Kitty. "I see my *wife* has introduced herself."

Hugh fought down panic. What kind of island was this? In less than an hour he had been hustled by a lunatic, insulted by his supervisor, and now had been sucked into a domestic squabble. He should have stayed in Tampa. Up there he was the only crazy one.

The Smarrs, nose-to-nose, spat insults. Hugh clutched his daypack tighter, eased sideways, bumped into someone. Black hair, red curves, lilac scent.

"Here's your drink, Mickey." Mal reached past Hugh, waved a green beer bottle in Mickey's face. Mickey blinked, nodded thanks before rounding on Kitty again.

Mal pulled Hugh away. "Let me get you something from the bar. *Hugh.*"

A warmth rushed through him at her touch.

"No one knows we spent time together," she hissed in his ear. "You *will not* speak of it."

The warmth vanished.

Mal sat him on a low-backed barstool near the wall, slipped behind the counter. She set a beer in front of him.

Hugh shook his head. Hugged his daypack tight to his stomach.

Mal raised an eyebrow. "Bottle of water? Soda?"

Hugh nodded, concentrating on sitting quiet and still until his heart slowed and the world came back into focus.

"You have to watch out for Kitty." Mal slid a glass of soda in front of him. "Always prowling for fresh meat. Mickey loves to catch her. She loves to get caught."

Hugh took a swallow of soda. Everything would be okay if he stayed calm.

"Subtle." Mal nodded at the daypack. "Holding your bag like a little granny."

"Everyone on this island crazy?" He wanted his room, but Latner had wandered off.

"It's Blacktip," Mal said. "Normal people don't move here."

"You seem okay."

"Don't rush to judgment on that."

The sky deepened to the pink of rum punch. With the speeches finished, guests wandered in to dinner. Across the bar, Lee still scowled at him. Hugh needed to clear the air.

"Time to meet the other lunatics."

"*Sit!*" Mal's voice was so low only Hugh could hear. Her eyes blazed.

"I was just going to…"

"You are *not* to talk to them. I'll introduce you."

Hugh sat. Mal addressed the dive staff.

"Okay, folks, the new guy's kinda road-weary, so what say we keep intros brief?" Mal's voice went sugar-sweet.

"The long-haired guy chatting up the two girls? That's Gage."

Gage looked up, laughed.

"The redhead behind him's Alison." A quick nod from a younger divemaster.

"Marina you know. And Lee." Her voice hardened. "And that's Casey."

The black-clad divemaster had stepped onto the deck, his arm around a resort guest in her twenties. He ignored Mal.

"Casey's training me."

"Is he? How fun for you."

Mal stood in front of Hugh to rinse glasses, dunking the glasses three times each, then setting them upside down in precise rows to dry. Blocking his view of the dive staff. Or their view of him. She was embarrassed he was here?

"We did nothing but talk. Before." Hugh studied his glass, not looking at Mal.

"On Blacktip, that's as good as screwing." Mal whispered. "Spreading rumors is a sport on this little rock. First rule of Blacktip - you sneeze at the Tailspinner, somebody at the Ballyhoo'll say, 'bless you' before you can wipe your nose."

Still no sign of Latner. Across the bar, Alison started to cross to Hugh. Mal stopped her with a look.

Mal was protecting him? Or herself? Whatever was going on with Mal, it was too much, too fast.

"Hey, when's Ger coming back? I really need sleep."

Mal froze, mouth open. "You've been waiting for Ger? That's *just* like him! He's gone. He never sticks around at the Dumb Punch party."

"The front desk give me a room key?"

"Uh uh. The resort's packed. I *know* he didn't set you up here." She studied the divemasters across the way. "And you *won't* stay with any of them. Not tonight." She walked to the cash register, punched numbers into the phone.

Wind gusted through the open bar. Hugh remembered rope hammocks on the beach. He could sleep there. Like the postcard. Just windier. Fly to some other island tomorrow. At least that'd make it harder for the cops to find him.

He didn't want to leave the bright-lit deck, though. As soon as he did, the darkness would take him. What had he done with his life?

"Tough luck, boy-o. No housing to be had tonight." Mal stood in front of him again, rinsing highball glasses. She raised one to the light, pretended to look for spots, and lowered her voice. *"Tonight only,* you sleep on my couch. On two conditions."

Hugh's heart jumped. Mal was angry, but she was helping him. He nodded to his glass, as if lost in thought.

"One: No one knows."

He nodded again.

"Two: You go now. Down the dock like you're looking at stars or whatever, then cut down the beach."

Hugh gazed up, pretending to examine the rafters. A dozen questions rolled through his mind. Mal walked away before he could ask any of them. That was okay. He wouldn't have to sleep outside. He'd be with Mal. That alone would keep the darkness at bay. Hugh grabbed his carry-on bag, left the lights and the crowd. He strolled down the wooden walkway, as amazed as before by the stars. On the beach, flickering wavelets washed across his feet. Heat lightning still pulsed beyond the horizon. Were storms always looming around this little island? Small lights, like candle flames, danced in the underbrush around Mal's place. Fireflies?

Hugh let himself in to Mal's cottage, settled on the couch where he had sat before. The chessboard was set up for a fresh game, an empty square where the final black pawn should be. A guilty pang. The pawn in his pocket pressed heavy against his thigh. It was odd being here without Mal. Odd, her sending him here alone if she wanted nothing to do with him. Did she plan to steal Hugh's cash while he slept? To extort it from him? To keep him secure while she shopped around for a reward?

The kitchen door scraped open and Mal stepped in. She drew the blinds and cut the overhead light, leaving only the dim glow of a table lamp.

"I had to shut the rumor mill down. Hard." Mal's voice came sharp. "Lee was amping up. Nice hair, by the way."

"I can't talk to my coworkers? That's got to happen eventually."

"After *we* talk."

"You weren't ashamed of me last week."

"Are you that naïve?"

"No, I'm a 'great guy.' Remember?'"

"Don't start, Blake. Or Hugh, or whoever. That's really weird, by the way."

"Ger got 'Hugh' stuck in his head. I let him. It's a new beginning, and…"

"Whatever. Rumors are *still* flying. Why do you think all the staff was watching you? Watching *us*?"

"So this *is* about you and me?"

"This is about that ditty bag grafted to you. That gang'd booze you up and pump you dry of every secret in an hour. Here you're under wraps."

"Ah. A shakedown, then."

"Not even close." Her eyes flashed. "With me you're safe. Some of that crew, not so much." Mal took a deep breath. "Look, Blake… Hugh… I don't know how you got down here with that thing. Twice. God really does look after fools. But you gotta to be less obvious. You already have the sharks joking about what's so valuable in your bag."

"These two bags are all I have. I don't want either one to walk off, is all."

"Dude, we are so beyond that." A smile played across Mal's face. "You sure you don't know where my pawn went? When we were cleaning up?"

Hugh shook his head, felt his face flush. The pawn in his pocket burned hot as his face. Mal studied him for what felt like forever.

"Damned Ritchie must have it," she said to herself.

"Who?"

"So. You bolted for good?" Mal said.

"My dad fired me. My girlfriend dumped me. I need a break from… everything."

"With enough cash to live comfortably?"

"It's not like that. It's… complicated. I just need to be a divemaster for a while. Why'd you bring me here?"

"You are a good guy. A babe in the woods, but a good guy. Even if you did ruin my chess set. You don't deserve to be thrown to the sharks your first day. But we do need to keep our contact at a minimum for a while."

"To help me hide or to squelch rumors about us?"

"Both. Rent one of these. Tomorrow." Mal handed Hugh a bar napkin. "Only places available if you don't want a roommate. And you don't."

'Southpoint Cottage,' 'Parrett's Nest' and 'Antonio's' were scribbled on the napkin.

"I may need a little more to go on."

"Parrett's Nest's a mile north, inland." She pronounced it 'Pah-ray.' "Southpoint Cottage's two miles down from here, on the water. Antonio's place is a little past Southpoint, up the bluff."

"That's it?"

"Small island. Other resorts have new staff house hunting, too, so don't waste time. Antonio's your best bet."

"Antonio thinks he and I sailed on the *Bounty* in a past life…"

"Oh, he's nuts. Everyone here is, remember? Important thing, he's harmless. And honest, by Blacktip standards."

"And the places?" Hugh imagined cottages like Mal's. Watching sunset from his porch, wine in hand and Mal beside him, more beautiful, more understanding than Tess had ever been. A twinge at that.

"They're quirky," Mal said. "Everywhere is. Your buddy Casey lives on a boat. Worst case, rent a dump for a month or two 'til something better opens up."

"There a car I can use?"

"There's a scooter you can have. Beside the house."

Hugh nodded. Tess would laugh at the thought of him without a car.

"So, there a reward out for Blake Calloway?"

"No, no. Nothing like that." Hugh's pulse quickened.

How much had he told her? Her guesses were close enough to make his life miserable. But if she wanted the money, she would have already made a play for it. This was about him, not the cash.

"How about I don't say a word about us if you don't say a word about me?" Hugh said.

"Now you're thinking."

Mal's eyes shone. She was a rescue line, a bright, shining rope stretching down into the black pit that'd formed around him the past days. She stood, stepped to the bedroom. Hugh's heart raced. A moment later she was back with a pillow and a light blanket, stepping closer, more beautiful by the second.

Mal dropped the pillow and blanket on his lap.

"Sleep well, you." She walked to the bedroom, closed the door. The lock snicked into place.

Hugh stared at the door. Idiot. Why couldn't he control his imagination when he was with her? He unfolded the blanket, turned off the lamp.

Darkness. Stifling air. Hugh took the pillow and blanket outside, lay down in the hammock with the daypack on his stomach. It was better in the onshore breeze. Stars arched above. Fireflies, or whatever, flashed in the underbrush. Waves hissed faint on the sand. Low sighs from the distant caves.

Hugh stretched, relaxed. In the morning he would find a beach cottage of his own. He slept sounder than he had in years.

4

Next morning Hugh sputtered down the limestone road on what was left of Mal's motor scooter. It was obvious why she had given it away. Its original color was lost under years of rust. The engine grumbled like an overworked lawnmower. The headlight hung useless over the front tire. And a cloud of blue exhaust spewed from its tailpipe, surrounded Hugh and set him coughing. The scooter was small, too, and Hugh felt like a circus clown riding a miniature tricycle. It beat walking, though the scooter's top speed was barely more than a fast walk. It was registered as Mal's, too, which was good. No "Calloway" on a vehicle registration or phone account or utility bill made Hugh that much harder to find. He would ride the scooter until it fell apart and make do without a cell phone.

His pack hung on his back. No matter how suspicious Mal said it was, he didn't dare leave it behind. He scratched at his leg. Mosquitoes, something, had gnawed his calves and shins raw while he slept. The morning ground fog from the road cooled the itching.

To his left the island's southern bluff loomed 200 feet above, at its base a riot of sea grapes and gumbo limbo scrub. The strip of land between the bluff and the water narrowed to barely a hundred feet. The sea to his right was the flat blue of polished gunmetal. Hugh could have been the only person on a new world, bouncing through some primeval jungle on a coal-fired machine.

He stopped at a pale pink, tin roofed cottage that had to be Southpoint, sitting on a rocky point at the sea's edge. The owner, an older man with a deep-tanned and sun-lined face, introduced himself as 'Coptin Vic.'

"Mal say you'd be coming." His voice was rough, as if from years of shouting above wind and waves. "You a friend of Mal, you good people."

Captain Vic walked Hugh beside the cottage and onto a back deck of graying wood. Fifty feet beyond, the sea lapped at ironshore, a dark limestone pocked and cratered by wind and tides into an impassible moonscape.

"No sand here. Or sand fleas." Captain Vic nodded at Hugh's legs, eyes crisp under his wide-brimmed straw hat. "On the beach at dusk or dawn, they do eat you alive."

Hugh remembered pulling the blanket over his head that morning to block the rising sun. Exposing his legs. Legs now burning like fire.

The lack of beach was a letdown, but the jagged shoreline had its own rough beauty. Hugh could see himself sitting on the deck in the evenings after work. Mal stopping by.

"Calm, leeward coast, here on the west side." Captain Vic said. "Most weather from the north or northeast. Away from the new runway, too, and all that noise."

"What runway?"

"Paved one. Bring in jets. More people." Captain Vic shook his head. "A few folks on this island with all the money, and they do want more. South End here, though, is old Tiperon."

Captain Vic led Hugh through a sliding glass door and into the cottage. The air was thick, almost liquid. A musty smell, as if a wet dog had whelped on the couch.

"The air conditioning work?"

"Oh, don't need air con. She gets a nice cross breeze when she's opened up. Built old Tiperon, you know."

Hugh paused, eyes adjusting to the gloom. Thin shafts of light streaked in from small, high-set windows. Hugh scanned the room for places he could hide his cash. The lower portions of the walls were darker than the rest.

"Old wainscoting?" Hugh said.

"High water mark," Captain Vic laughed. "From the storm. All fixed now, though."

"You said storms didn't hit this side."

"Oh, a point like this, it does get some weather now and then."

"And the water gets this high?" Hugh gazed at the flat sea.

"Only in big storms," Captain Vic said. "Every four, five years, y'know. Storm last year, so you got a good four years with no worry. You just keep your TV up on a table. About so." He waved his hands waist-high.

What was Mal thinking, sending him here? Hugh thanked Captain Vic, promised to get back with him, walked as calmly as he could out the front door, into the fresh air and sunlight.

"Captain Vic?" On the doorstep stood the woman from the flight the day before. Still fidgeting with her necklace. Her gray eyes darted from Hugh to Captain Vic.

"Here's your man," Hugh said. A house hunter Mal had warned about?

"Captain Vic, I'm Jessie? The new cook at Blacktip Haven? They said you had a place to rent?" She looked back to Hugh and her face brightened. "Oh! Hey! From the airplane!" Her smile faded at his bug-bitten legs.

"Hugh. Just leaving."

"Hey, you wouldn't be looking for a roommate, would you? There's a great two-bedroom place…"

"I'm not a roommate person," Hugh said. Rust fell from the scooter as Hugh pushed it around the bright green Blacktip

Haven van blocking the entry path. Jessie was welcome to Southpoint Cottage.

He checked his napkin. Antonio's place was a half-mile farther south. Hugh rode north. Parrett's Nest, past Eagle Ray Cove, had to be in better shape than Southpoint Cottage.

A rumble came from behind him, growing louder. Clattering valves and squeaking sheet metal. Hugh caught a glimpse of a rusty Mercedes convertible as it blew past, shaggy-headed driver waving a beer bottle in greeting. Hugh veered, careening headlong into the ditch. He stood, dusted himself off, pushed the scooter back onto the road. Dust settled over the road, but the car didn't stop. Hugh motored on.

A half-hour later he passed a rough wooden sign for Blacktip Haven at a track leading uphill. Past that the bluff ended so abruptly it could have been chopped off with a giant axe, giving way to the island's flat northern half. The island's east-west road ran across the island at the bluff's base. Where the two roads joined was a wooden sign, painted blue and green, 'Parrett's Nest' scrawled across it in red cursive script. A small cottage, in matching colors, hovered on eight-foot wooden stilts above the inland treetops. The owner introduced herself as Polly, the Club Scuba Doo manager.

"The cottage is lovely, simply lovely. And well back from the sand." She grimaced at Hugh's legs.

Up narrow wooden steps a broad deck surrounded the cottage. The view from above looked west across the turquoise Sound to the deep blue sea beyond. To the north stretched a lake or marsh where seabirds circled. South, the bluff towered over the little house. East, the gumbo-limbo jungle was a riot of tropical green.

Polly opened the cottage door, stepped back and waved Hugh inside. Cool air flowed out of a large central room with a high ceiling. Light streamed in through broad windows. An air conditioner hummed in a far window. Glass doors opened onto the front deck.

"Isn't it lovely?" Polly said.

It was. Hugh walked to the room's center to get the full effect. The flooring bowed slightly with each step. He stopped. The cottage seemed to sway for a moment. His imagination? He glanced at Polly, still standing by the doorway.

"Oh, that's normal." A cheery laugh. "Built to flex with the wind."

"Not damaged this past storm season?"

"Rode it out perfectly." She studied Hugh, reappraising him. "Old Mr. Parrett was an engineer by trade." Like Mal, she pronounced it 'Pah-ray.' "Designed and built the house himself. A lovely man, Mr. Parrett."

Polly motioned for Hugh to look around, then stepped out. Hugh stood still, listening to her footsteps going down the stairs. Was the cottage still moving? He closed his eyes. Yes. The place was swaying in time with Polly's steps. 'Flex with the wind?' Was the woman nuts? The place wasn't safe for him or his cash. Hugh stepped gingerly back to the door, then retreated downstairs.

"Everyone who's lived here says when the wind blows, the house rocks them to sleep." Polly waited at the foot of the stairs. "Like a big hammock."

"I'll bet. It sounds... lovely." Hugh sidled toward the scooter.

"Oh, it is! And the loveliest thing is in the evenings a pair of bobolinks come to the balcony railing, just there, and sing and sing and sing! That very railing!"

For the second time that morning, Hugh sputtered away as calmly as he could, back down the main road until Parrett's Nest was out of sight. This was a joke of Mal's, sending him to two dumps. Southpoint Cottage and Parrett's Nest were probably the places locals sent the all newbies for a laugh. Now he had to at least look at Antonio's. How much worse would it be?

He rounded a curve, swerved to dodge a bright green van racing down the road's center. A brief vision of a startled Jessie mouthing, "Sorry," and then he was in the ditch again. Once more Hugh dusted himself off and muscled the scooter back onto the road.

South of Southpoint Cottage a dirt track led inland, like Mal had said. Hugh turned in. The sun was high now, and he welcomed the shade on the narrow two-rut track. His relief was short-lived. The road sloped up, and the scooter slowed. Trees grew closer, blocking any hint of breeze. The scooter coughed, stalled. Hugh got off, walked it the last thirty yards. Out of breath and drenched in sweat, he finally reached the top.

There, in a broad clearing, sat what had once been a one-story house. To the left, its screen porch had been dry-walled in to form an extra room. On the other side, an ell had been added, connecting the house with what might have once been a large storage shed. A second-floor apartment was cobbled atop the original house. Each section was a different shade of teal, like the place had been painted a piece at a time.

On the stoop outside the shed, a barefoot man in cut-off jeans and a faded concert t-shirt sat whacking conch shells with a hammer, digging out the fist-sized snails with a filleting knife. He squinted at Hugh.

Rusty white SUV A bright green scooter. No Antonio. The squinting man sat motionless now, watching Hugh.

"Excuse me." Hugh stepped toward the man.

The man set down the conch shell, stood, knife still in hand. His chest was even with Hugh's head.

"Hugo! I seen you coming!" Antonio stepped out of the main house's doorway. "Mal said 'first thing,' but I told her, 'no, closer to lunch time.'"

"Hugh." His eyes were on the man with the knife.

"Dermott, this Hugo. The one I told you about."

Dermott put the knife down, stepped toward Hugh. Hugh held out his hand. Dermott's massive fist swallowed Hugh's. Conch slime squished between Hugh's fingers.

"Good to meet you, Dermott." Hugh clenched his jaw, refused to react as slime oozed over his wrist and down his forearm.

"Dermott here does odd jobs around the island," Antonio said. "Anything you need fixing, call him."

Hugh wondered how many people Dermott had fixed. Dermott nodded, hinting he knew what Hugh was thinking, then slowly released his hand. Antonio pulled Hugh toward the house. Hugh wiped slime on his shirttail as they went.

"Used to be one house, but I fixed it up! Made it five houses!" Antonio led Hugh to the converted patio. "This the master suite. Got two rooms, y'know." Antonio slid open a glass door to reveal a large, tiled sitting area with windows on three sides. The walls were a brighter teal. White plastic lawn furniture.

"There's no way to lock the door?" Hugh jiggled the sliding glass door's handle.

"Can latch it on the inside, if you want. No need for locks on Blacktip, though," Antonio said. "In here's the bedroom and kitchen!"

He pushed Hugh through an empty door frame where the original house's side door had been and into a chamber nearly filled by a king-sized bed. Dark faux-wood paneling covered the walls. A step to the right was an alcove with refrigerator, stove, sink and counter, all in a space small enough for Hugh to stand in the center and touch each appliance without moving his feet.

The paneling showed no signs of water damage. Made sense this far inland, this high up. Hugh pushed on a wall. It felt solid. He leaned hard on the paneling. The upper floor didn't budge.

"She sound enough," Antonio laughed.

"I didn't see any wind damage outside from this past storm season." Hugh watched Antonio's reaction.

"Oh, you hear about that hurricane. Yeah, man, blew pretty good. But the trees protect us up here. Reason why old timers live back in the bush."

Hugh stepped back to the outer room. The house itself had the other two places beat. But the door didn't lock. Plus, Antonio was squirrely, no matter what Mal said. And Dermott was scary, no matter what Antonio said.

"Who else lives here?" Mal had said 'interesting neighbors.' Would Dermott or the others paw through his things when Hugh was at work?

"Told 'em all about you. They can't wait to meet you."

Hugh stepped out the sliding door and was engulfed by a frenzy of hair and barking and teeth. Three knee-high dogs jumped head-high, bumped Hugh's chest, barked in his face, shot between his legs, tails wagging and tongues lolling.

"Hey, Cori!" Antonio called. "Cori tends bar at the Sand Spit."

A short woman with bright green hair shuffled from the ell between the main house and Dermott's shed. Pillow wrinkles and a fine speckling of glitter or sand coated one cheek and bare arm.

"Hey, Hugo. Down! DOWN! QUIET!" She managed to grab a scruffy white terrier by its rope collar, extended a hand to Hugh. "Sorry. We were sleeping. They're wired when they first wake up. That's Lettuce..." A shaggy border collie mix. "... Turnip..." A shorthaired island mutt. "And Pea." She pulled the terrier's collar. "My grandmother's joke."

"Hugh. Not Hugo. Hugh." He jumped as a dog licked the back of his leg.

"Oooo! You found the sand fleas!" Cori rubbed her eyes. "Wanna come in?"

A quick glance through the door of her place showed a long, low room with a kitchen and bathroom at one end and a bed at the other. The floor, as well as the rumpled bed, was covered with sand and dog hair. Hugh thanked Cori, backed away.

"Got one more person to meet," Antonio said. "You gonna like him."

Antonio dragged Hugh behind the house. Lettuce and Turnip bounced and barked beside them. A wooden staircase led to a door centered in the second floor. Hugh barely noticed the door at first. The two-story expanse was covered with scraps of wood, old float balls, conch shells, random debris, all painted in brilliant blues and reds and golds, tacked onto the siding in a massive mosaic. A series of mosaics, with the door at the top of the rickety staircase high in the center portion. There was a pattern to it all, though Hugh couldn't make it out.

"Jerrod!" Antonio yelled.

"Hey, 'Tonio," A voice came from above. "This our new lodger?"

Dangling from the roof by a rope and climbing harness was a small, thin man, paint can clipped to the harness and brush in one hand. The white-haired bartender from Eagle Ray Cove the night before. Gold paint dripped across his green shirt. Hugh stepped back, ignoring the man for a moment. A pattern emerged. A pair of twelve-foot figures flanked a third, central figure standing nearly twenty feet high, the second-floor doorway forming its mouth. But figures of what?

"It's a triptych." Jerrod's voice drifted down.

"Triptych?"

"You know, three panels, two-dimensional icons." Jerrod belayed himself to the ground, waved the gold-soaked paintbrush at the house.

"Yeah, I know what a triptych is." Hugh studied two long stalks jutting from the roofline over the door. "I didn't know... which saint had rabbit ears?"

"Close! Nudibranch! Fancy sea slug." Jerrod's voice rose as he stepped closer, eyes fever-bright. "St. Thomas. It's representational, you know? Makes you focus on the connotative, not the denotative."

Hugh didn't dare ask what St. Thomas the Sea Slug connoted. Or point out junk nailed to the side of a house was inherently three-dimensional.

Wind set the treetops rustling. A low moaning filled the clearing, like air moving across the open mouth of a giant soda bottle. Then a rasping undertone, like the island was straining to breathe. Hugh's neck hairs stood on end.

"The south wind has a plaintive voice." Jerrod rocked his head back and forth in time with the sound.

"Oh, duppies're anxious today," Antonio said. "Welcoming Hugo. Lots of 'em, this end of the island, y'know."

"Lots of caves, too," Hugh said.

"All kinds of things on this island." Antonio winked at Hugh.

Hugh nodded, recalled one of his father's sayings, "Argue with a lunatic, he'll drag you to his level and beat you with experience.'" Hugh wouldn't give these lunatics the chance. He backed away from the house. Mal had said Antonio was harmless. She hadn't mentioned the other inmates. Waves crashing through the living room, or a house collapsing around him would be safer than living in this nuthouse.

"You see? Hugo so excited he's already headed back to the master suite!"

"Yeah, I'll get back to you on that, Antonio," Hugh said.

Out front, Dermott raised his fillet knife in what Hugh hoped was a 'goodbye.' The scooter's starter switch wouldn't work. Hugh jumped on the kick-start lever until the machine started, then coughed in the blue exhaust cloud. He rode downhill as fast as he could, making no attempt to look calm. Cori's canine vegetable patch bounded beside him, barking, until he reached the main road.

Anger replaced panic then. This was the punch line to Mal's joke. Only the joke wasn't funny. Especially with her knowing how rattled he was. He would find her, now, tell her what he thought of her prank. Hugh leaned low over the handlebars to get as much speed as he could. At the Eagle Ray Cove sand parking lot, he let the scooter fall and stalked toward the thatched bar.

A few guests sat at the bar with Mickey the manager. Mickey smiled, nodded a greeting at Hugh. Dive staff was on the deck beyond, eating lunch.

"How'd it go?" Mal spoke low. Playing it straight. Lee looked up from his pasta.

"Fun with the new guy?" Hugh said. "Sending me to those crap-hole…"

"Hey! I was nice enough to find the only places available." Mal's eyes blazed. "That's called a 'favor.' The proper response is 'thank you.'"

Every face around the deck focused on Mal and Hugh. Lee whispered to Alison.

"None of those places are livable, and you knew it."

"You act like you have a problem. Hugh. You don't. You have three options. Four if you count going back home."

Hugh sat, chilled by the menace in her final word. The houses weren't jokes? He took a deep breath.

"There has to be someplace else."

"Then find it yourself. Before sundown."

"Oh, snap!" Alison stood beside Hugh now.

"That infection clear up yet, Ali?" Mal said loud enough for everyone to hear.

Alison backed away, eyes wide.

"What infection?" Lee was on his feet, red-faced.

"There's no infection," Alison said.

"No! What *bloody* infection?"

"And *that*," Mal smiled at Hugh, "is how easily rumors start on this little island."

Gage glanced from Mal to Hugh to Hugh's daypack, then looked away.

A greasy feeling spread in Hugh's stomach. He'd made a mess of things. And hurt Mal, too. Given the rumor's new life.

"Sorry." He barely heard his own voice.

"It's good to see you got some fire left." Mal's was voice softer. "If nothing else, we proved that. I thought daddy and girlie'd knocked that out of you."

"We're the talk of the island, huh?"

"You are. There's a pool on what's in your bag. Lee says body parts. Ali says drugs. Gage thinks you're DEA with handcuffs and weapons."

Alison stormed down the boardwalk, Lee on her heels, still shouting. The dive staff went back to their lunches. The guests went back to their drinks.

"So, seriously," Hugh said, "my choices are to die in a flood, die in a house collapse, or die with my throat cut?"

"You met Dermott, then? He's good. Just don't wake him when he's passed out."

"At the Crazy Acres Church of the Sea Gods?"

"And Jerrod, too. Cool! Intense guy. Very smart."

"So we..."

"*You* need to pick a place to live."

Hugh nodded. The longer he spent house hunting, the longer he'd stand out. Across the deck the dive staff were still eying his pack. Should he risk flying to some other island?

"Hugh! Still here!" Ger Latner stomped up to the bar, Casey beside him. Latner slapped Casey on the arm. "Told you he'd stick around!"

Casey's face was expressionless. The earthy reek still clung to him.

Latner dropped a stack of pale blue DIVE STAFF shirts on the bar.

"Find a place to live?"

"I'm, uh, still looking."

"Well, look fast. You and Casey start in the morning."

Casey smirked at Hugh, then glanced at Mal.

Hugh was queasy again. What would Casey do if he found out about Hugh's past?

"These're yours." Latner shoved the shirts at Hugh. "Large, right?"

Dive staff. Yes. Thoughts of crumbling houses, of jail evaporated. After twenty-four hours on Blacktip Island, a pile of shirts was the first thing to make Hugh feel welcome. He was dive staff now. And once he got on the boat, they'd all see he was as good as any of them. So he had met a few crazies. Plenty more people lived on this island. Plenty of friends to be made. He would meet them all, get on so well no one would care about his past.

Hugh slipped on a shirt, did a mock fashion-model turn.

"Does it make me look fat?"

"No. Your arse does," Casey said.

Latner roared. Guests around the bar joined in. Hugh laughed with them.

"Hugh, welcome to Eagle Ray Divers," Latner said. "Hey, 'Tonio! You still got a place open?"

"Dunno, Ger. Depends on Hugo, there." Antonio took a seat.

"There you go. 'Tonio's got a place for you. We start at seven tomorrow." He hammered Hugh on the back and stomped back to the dive shop.

Down the bar Antonio grinned. Hugh's future unfolded in front of him again. He wouldn't have to worry about the cash being washed away or blown away at Antonio's. And maybe the best place to hide on Blacktip Island was in a crowd. His life couldn't get any crazier.

"Antonio, what's that master suite of yours go for?"

Antonio bounced down the bar, pulled Hugh from his chair and hugged him.

"I knew you was coming, shipmate. Didn't I tell you? You a country boy at heart! You'll love it out in the bush!"

5

The next morning, Hugh stood on the pier beside Ger Latner as the crews fetched boats from their moorings. A southeast wind had risen overnight, whipping Eagle Ray Sound into whitecaps.

"Watch and learn," Latner rumbled.

Fifty yards away the *Skipjack* swung at her mooring, a dark figure hunched over the helm. The boat inched forward, and the figure jumped from the helm to the bow, sweatshirt hood flapping in the wind. Casey. He cast off the mooring lines, and the *Skipjack* drifted free.

Casey sprung back to the helm, and the boat straightened toward Hugh and Latner. Hugh stepped back as the boat neared. At the last moment Casey flipped levers, spun the wheel, and the forty-foot boat settled parallel to the pier a foot from the wooden planks.

With two snaps of his wrist, Ger Latner twisted the boat's bow line in a figure eight around a cleat to hold the *Skipjack* in place.

Hugh leaned across the gap between the boat and pier to tie off the stern. Boat, waves, and planking all seemed to move at once. Hugh leaped for the boat, landed on hands and knees on the *Skipjack*'s stern. The metallic grit of blood and chipped teeth filled his mouth. He stood, looped the dock line around the stern cleat, trying to copy Latner's twists. Managed a tangle that held the boat firm against the surge.

Latner gave him a pained look.

"That's a proper pig's ear, that is," Casey said.

"It'll hold." Hugh pulled on the taut stern line. "The rope's tied tight!"

"'Line, Mate," Casey said. "Ropes are for mountain climbing."

Casey jumped from the bridge for a closer look at Hugh's knot.

"I pull forward on *that*, we'll have to cut ourselves from the dock."

Casey undid the line, re-cleated it at half speed for Hugh to see.

"Figure-eight around the horns, then a half-turn to lock it down, yes?"

"Gotcha." Hugh looped his hands mid-air, mimicking Casey's movements.

"Oh dear, oh dear," Casey said. "Don't make us send you back to America your first day. See if you can fetch the ice boxes without hurting yourself." Casey pointed to bright orange coolers outside the dive shop.

Hugh rushed up the pier, imagining Casey hurting himself in multiple ways. Hugh had focused so much on getting to Blacktip, on hiding, it hadn't occurred to him he might get fired. Latner wouldn't axe him this quick, though. Lee was still here, after all. Hugh filled the coolers with ice and water, carted them back to the boat. Latner and Casey fought back smiles.

"Let's walk you through a docking." Casey nodded to Marina bringing in the *Barjack*. "She's docking to windward, yeah? Like I did. Steering with just her engines."

The *Barjack* angled toward the pier. A boat length away, Marina shifted a lever and spun the wheel.

"She reversed her starboard, wheel hard-right. That pulls the stern in."

The *Barjack* settled motionless beside the pier, as the *Skipjack* had done. Lee cleated the boat's lines.

Hugh nodded, trying to remember it all. He knew how to look after divers, but the boating jargon was a foreign language.

"Precious work of art doesn't know everything, eh?" Lee strutted past Hugh. "And where's your little shoulder bag?"

"At the clinic, with your hurt divers," Hugh said.

Lee's face went red, but he said nothing.

The night before Hugh had peeled back the paneling behind his bed, stuffed the cash-filled boating manuals between the exposed beams, then tapped the paneling back in place and re-centered the bed. It was as secure as he could get for now. No one would find the cash without tearing the house down to the studs.

"Well, you don't get on with Lee," Casey said. "That stands in your favor."

Hugh grabbed the roster from Casey, checked off each arriving guest as they stepped aboard, tried to remember their names.

"You're Hugh!" A pasty-faced man slapped Hugh on the back. "Where you from?"

"Um, the States." How did the man know his name?

"Whereabouts?" The man's wife stepped aboard, eyes lingering on Hugh.

"Uh… Out west." Hugh's pulse quickened.

"You sound southern."

"Well, the southwest."

Why were these people so interested in him? Hugh checked in the last of ten divers. Kept an eye on the nosey couple. 'Brian' and 'Karen,' the roster said. If they were cops, they would have already grabbed him. Bounty hunters, making sure they had the right person?

At Casey's okay, Hugh cast off the dock lines, and all his attention was on the boat. Once outside the reef, Casey throttled up and the *Skipjack* sliced through the swells. A school of flying fish exploded from the water ahead, sunlight glinting silver off their wing-like fins. Red-footed boobies swooped on the airborne fish, chased them back into the sea.

"The fish are flying, and the birds are swimming," Hugh said.

"Ever use a VHF?" Casey pointed to the marine radio overhead, as if Hugh hadn't spoken.

Hugh shook his head. He would learn from Casey, no matter how much of an ass the man was. Better a demanding teacher than to not learn properly.

"Most important bit of equipment there is," Casey said. "Someone gets hurt, radio for help. You do nothing else, do that. It's our lifeline. To transmit, push this button on the mike, yeah? Then talk. Then let go."

"Right," Hugh said.

"Now, if *I'm* hurt, you radio, then point the boat toward safety and make it go. Here's how you do that."

They cruised up the coast, Casey explaining, rapid-fire, how to start the engines, how to work the *Skipjack*'s gears and throttles, how to synch the engines. Hugh struggled to store it all, repeated "right" and "gotcha" so often that Casey had to think he was an idiot. It didn't help that Casey peppered his instructions with, "a mistake can get someone killed," and "if someone gets hurt, especially me, what you want to do is…"

They moored in the lee of a rocky spire jutting up a hundred yards offshore from the island's northern tip. Casey gathered the guests on the main deck for a pre-dive briefing.

"Roll up, roll up, ladies and gents!" Casey dropped into a carnival barker's delivery. "Welcome to The Pinnacle and a dive site we call Eye of the Needle! Most beautiful site on the island!"

Conversations stopped. Every guest focused on Casey.

"Beneath us is a shallow reef at forty feet, yes? Light blue water means sand. Dark water means coral. Just off our port side, the dark blue water is where the deep, dark, scary wall drops about six billion feet straight down. We won't go that deep."

Casey shifted pitch, flashed well-rehearsed gestures, holding the guests' attention. Hugh tried to remember it all so he could use it later.

"I'll lead you along the wall at about eighty-five feet, through an archway in The Pinnacle, like camels through a needle's eye, yes? Then back to the shallows under the boat where you'll finish your dive.

"Now, we're out on the edge of things here." Casey's voice went suddenly stern. "If you miss The Pinnacle, your next stop is Cuba, 300 miles that way." A wave toward the empty horizon. "So we stay in a group and watch for current until we're back under the boat, yes?"

The divers nodded, faces as serious as Casey's.

"Back onboard with a 500 psi reserve of air, or one hour, whichever comes first."

Casey and Hugh helped the divers into their scuba gear, steadied them as they stepped into the water. Hugh copied Casey, joked with each diver as he double-checked air gauges. Casey watched Hugh, said nothing. Hugh took that as a good sign.

Casey slipped into a black wetsuit and dive gear as Hugh helped the last couple.

"You're our safety line, Mate, Watch our bubbles. Watch for floaters." Then he was in with a splash.

Hugh climbed to the upper deck where he could see all directions. He imagined bubble trails straying out to sea, panicked divers popping to the surface, injured divers needing saving.

The divers' pale bubbles stood out in the blue water. They merged into a single boil, drifted toward The Pinnacle. The bubbles clustered thick around the spire for twelve, fifteen minutes, like the rock had sprung a leak, and then they drifted back to the shallow reef under the boat.

With the divers in the shallows, Hugh relaxed. He was so worried about doing well he was tripping over his own feet. Blue sky, calm water, beach, and palms a hundred yards away, it was all so beautiful. Tampa seemed a lifetime ago. And Brian and Karen were just over-friendly dive guests.

Bubbles clumped around the boat as the guests finished their dive. Casey surfaced at the stern. Hugh made a show of scanning the water as Casey climbed onboard.

"Good group. Beautiful dive." Casey shook water from his hair. "You see where we went?"

"Along the wall thirty yards, circled back, then went shallow and split up one coral head behind us."

Casey nodded.

Divers popped up at the stern then. Hugh and Casey grabbed fins, helped guests up the ladders, switched gear to fresh cylinders. Brian thanked Hugh. Karen patted him on the arm, making contact longer than necessary. Hugh's paranoia returned, strong as ever.

Divers back onboard, Casey idled the *Skipjack* down the coast for the second dive. Wind fresh in their faces. Hugh, beside Casey, studied Brian from the corner of his eye.

"You're jumpy, Mate."

"That couple." Hugh spoke low so only Casey could hear. "They... They're *too* friendly."

"Divemaster Syndrome." Casey said. "You could look like a rat's arse and smell worse, and it wouldn't matter. As soon as you put on that staff shirt, you're a rock star to them. The better they get on with you, the better their standing with their mates."

"Seriously?"

"They saw your little dust-up yesterday? That's celebrity gossip to them." He grinned at Hugh's look. "Oh, everyone's heard of it by now. The F.N.G. who crossed Mal his second day on island? You're either brave or crazy. My money's on crazy."

Hugh studied Brian and Karen. They did seem genuine. And if they weren't, looking like a divemaster was his best disguise. He'd take a page from Casey's book. He walked back, sat with the guests, told what island stories he had: Antonio's wild jeep ride, the run-ins with Jessie, house-hunting.

"The one place was so bad, the owner used 'being far away from the new airport' as a selling point," Hugh chuckled. "Only there *is* no new airport!"

At the helm, Casey tensed.

"Yeah, folks seem worked up about that." Brian said.

"People here won't stand for it," Casey said.

"For making things better?" Brian gave Casey a disgusted look.

"You realize most people *like* how undeveloped this island is?" An edge crept into Casey's voice.

The guests looked uncomfortable, though several nodded agreement.

A deep drone sounded overhead. The Islander on its final approach, white wings and fuselage so close Hugh could almost see individual rivets.

"That crap plane and dirt strip're the worst things about this place," Brian, when the Islander's engine noise faded. "Real runway'd make it damned easier to get here."

"Stay on Tiperon if you want 'easy'," Casey snapped. "Or Miami." His eyes followed the Islander as it dropped below the tree line. "They start a new runway, someone should blow it up."

The guests' smiles faded. Casey angled the boat toward the nearest mooring ball.

"So, what's this site?" Hugh tried to break the tension.

"Confrontation Reef." Casey's scowl softened. "Seriously."

Casey pulled Hugh aside before the briefing.

"Listen close. You're leading this one." There was a challenge in Casey's voice.

Casey briefed more in-depth this time, his attention split between Hugh and the guests.

"Start at this big coral head below the boat." A glance at Hugh. "Swing in towards shore - 'east' on your compass." A loop of his arm and a nod at Hugh. "Follow the bottom contour at thirty feet." Another nod at Hugh.

"And you lot have the distinct honor of following Divemaster Hugh this time. Please make sure you bring him back in good order."

Hugh studied the reef as he helped divers gear up, rehearsing his course, calculating when he'd need to make each turn to get everyone back to the boat. Scattered coral, with no regular pattern to help navigation. He would stay close, check out the nearest coral formations. He was still studying the water as the last diver stepped off the boat. Ten heads bobbed behind the boat, watching the divemasters.

"Whenever you're ready." Casey shook his head.

Brian and Karen slipped below the surface. Hugh hurried into his dive gear. More divers dropped out of sight. Hugh's knife and light and noisemakers and underwater slates clattered as he shrugged on his buoyancy vest.

"You look like a bloody dive shop exploded on you!" Casey said.

Hugh stepped aft, hurrying to get in the water. A set of plastic fish identification slates, tethered to his gear with a retractable lanyard, caught between the slats on the bench seat.

As Hugh stepped, the lanyard tugged him back. He wobbled, then crashed sideways onto the wet deck.

"Down goes the muppet! And not yet midday!" Casey laughed. Then, his voice went more serious, "Lose the dangly shite. You're not a guest anymore."

Hugh limped past Casey.

"Back on board in thirty minutes," Casey yelled.

Hugh stepped off the stern. Cool water rushed into his wetsuit, cooling his body and his temper. He was in his element now.

Bright coral and sand spread thirty-five feet below, crisp in the air-clear water. Blue clouds of Creole wrasse parted as Hugh dropped. White and yellow flashes of yellowtail snapper flitting past. How could he have questioned if coming back here was the right thing? Bubbles rose from five buddy teams. Swimming five different directions. Hugh kicked hard after the nearest pair.

Ten minutes later he'd gathered everyone together. Hugh motioned them to follow him. He scanned the coral heads. Nothing was familiar. He looked up. No boat. The sand was a uniform thirty-five feet. Hugh sculled in the direction he guessed the boat should be, acting as if nothing were wrong. Hoping for a familiar landmark. He'd chased divers in so many directions, though. Shore was east, yes, but the boat could be anywhere. Hugh zigzagged from coral head to coral head, glancing up for the *Skipjack*. Forcing down a growing panic. He pointed out a stingray, a nurse shark tucked under a ledge, a barracuda hanging motionless mid-water, doing a standard reef tour. His breathing was too fast, burning through his air. A ringing in his ears wouldn't go away. Schools of French grunts parted in a flurry of blue-and-yellow stripes. A spotted eagle ray swam over the group, its bone-white underside wide as Hugh was tall. It circled back, began rooting in the sand. The divers clustered around, watching it feed. Hugh glanced at his watch. Thirty-two minutes in-water. Casey would be fuming.

Hugh raced ahead, looking for anything familiar. He should surface, spot the *Skipjack*, then drop back to fetch the divers. But surfacing meant admitting he was lost. He couldn't do that. Not his first day. Not with Casey.

Behind him, the divers' bubbles were hazy in the distance. Ahead, a long shadow stretched across the sand. A boat. The *Skipjack*. Had to be. Hugh raced back to the guests. The eagle ray had gone, and the group was splitting up again. He circled the group, motioned everyone to follow, led all eight of them toward the boat.

Hugh spun, counted again. Eight divers. He'd started with ten. Cursing through his regulator, he pointed out the boat, then raced back to where the eagle ray had been. From there, Hugh swam a broad, arcing pattern back the way the missing divers had to have gone. This wasn't happening. He wouldn't lose two divers his first dive.

Faint ahead of him, bubbles rose from behind a coral head. His legs ached as he raced to them. Brian and Karen. They signaled 'okay.' Hugh motioned them to follow, led them back to the *Skipjack*.

Casey stood on the swim platform when Hugh climbed from the water. Everyone but Brian and Karen were onboard.

"That thirty American minutes, mate? My watch says fifty-three regular minutes."

"I had to do some chasing." Hugh shot a long look at the just-surfacing Karen.

"You got lost."

"I found the boat, once I got everyone rounded up." Hugh helped Karen slip out of her gear. "Twice."

Casey shook his head, climbed to the bridge, and started the engines.

Hugh cast off the bow line and joined Casey. Casey throttled up. He gave Hugh a cold look.

"Three of your divers came up with less than 300 psi. While you were enjoying your pleasure dive, guests nearly ran out of air."

Hugh went cold. Could he do anything right today? He should have checked everyone's air once he had them together. He had been so concerned about finding the boat, though.

Casey's face was hard behind his sunglasses. The earthy smell was stronger.

Hugh looked away, furious with himself. He wanted to tell Casey he was wrong. But Hugh had screwed up. He was better than this. Except around Casey.

Guests gathered around the helm. Casey morphed back to carnival Casey, joking, swapping dive stories for the ride back. Hugh sat silent, watched the shoreline blur past, half-smiling at Brian's jokes and Karen's compliments.

At the pier he kept quiet, followed Casey's directions to the letter, cleating lines and filling cylinders.

"Look, F.N.G., you're good in the water. I've seen that." Casey closed the valves on the last round of refilled cylinders. "You just have to think like staff. All your focus has to be on the guests."

"They enjoyed the dive."

"You lost them, nearly drowned them, but they still love you." A lighter tone crept into Casey's voice. "Divemaster Syndrome. They don't see you. They see palm trees and beaches and *bam!* They're living on a postcard."

Hugh leaned on the cylinders. He'd done exactly that with Mal. Down to the literal postcard. Was that why she was keeping him at arm's length? He was a cartoon, the island greenhorn. He needed to talk to Mal. Or dig a hole to crawl into.

"You see a ghost, Mate? You're white as one."

Cylinders filled, Hugh headed for the bar. He'd straighten things out with Mal, or see when she was free. Casey trailed behind, flip-flops scuffling on the wooden planking.

Hugh reached the deck, stopped. The bar was packed with guests and locals gathered around a man dressed for a business mixer. Mal's dark hair flew as she slung drinks as fast as she could pour them.

"Got a second?" Hugh caught Mal's eye.

"No. Richie needs a refill." Mal was intent on the group across the way.

"Who?"

"Rich Skerritt. Talking to Elena." Mal nodded toward the well-dressed man. Late forties, salt-and-pepper hair, and button-down shirt. Strangely familiar. The man she'd met at the airstrip. Arguing with an older woman in a Guatemalan sundress and a waist-length ponytail.

Mal centered a beer on a bar tile by the man. He took the drink without looking.

Hugh looked to Casey for a translation.

"Skerritt owns the place." Casey's eyes tracked from Hugh to Mal. "Elena Havens owns Blacktip Haven, up on the Bluff. Beside her's Frank and Helen Maples. They've a place over on Mahogany Row."

Mal frowned at Elena. At the crowd around Skerritt. Ignored the bar top cluttered with empty bottles and plastic cups.

"You people see paradise," Skerritt said. "You move down here and expect it to stay the same. That's not realistic."

"Of course it is, Rich," Frank Maples said. "If we all work with that in mind, we can keep Blacktip pristine."

"Frank, you and Helen moved down here because the island was so... pristine, right?" Skerritt's voice was full of patience. "What was the first thing you did? Cleared some land, dug a cistern and a septic tank, built a big house."

"One house isn't a 200-room resort," Maples said.

"It is to the folks here before you." Skerritt nodded toward Elena Havens.

"Don't use me for your argument," the Blacktip Haven owner said.

"There you have it." Skerritt smiled as if she had agreed with him. He turned back to Frank Maples. "You don't want things to change from how *you* first saw them. But that's exactly what *you* did. Change things. Build things."

"Your plans will damage the island irreversibly," Helen Maples said.

"Helen, Frank's banking career bought your nice house here," Skerritt said. "Elena made a killing in real estate up in Toronto. You're each able to live here because you sold, or financed, exactly the kind of project I'm talking about. Now you move here and tell me I can't do the same thing. With my property. In *my* country." Skerritt's voice tensed.

"You're going to devastate paradise. For a quick buck." Frank Maples jabbed his straw hat at Skerritt's chest.

"You don't have a problem making money, Frank. You have a problem with *me* making money. That's hypocritical."

"That runway will have to be approved, and built, before you can do anything," Maples' voice rose. Beside him Elena's jaw clenched.

"Soon enough. I guarantee." Skerritt settled back in his bar chair, hands behind his head. "Then we'll have more amenities to spoil our guests." He winked at Mal, smiled at the growing crowd. Brian and Karen raised their glasses, tourists enjoying the show.

Frank Maples' shoulders slumped.

Elena Havens shoved past the Maples, threw her arm across the bar, scraped a swath of half-emptied drink cups into Skerritt's lap.

"That's what you're doing to this island! Clear-cutting it! To fatten your bank account!"

Skerritt jumped up, tumbling his chair backwards. Booze and ice and fruit slices cascaded down his shirt and slacks. Elena was on him, finger jabbing up at his face.

"This place'd be empty if your guests knew you were planning to rape the island! Shame on you! You can buy all the land you want! You can buy all the officials you want! But that runway will never go in! I guarantee *that*!"

"Elena, if you were a man, I'd punch you in the face!"

"If I was a man, you wouldn't have the balls! I need to wash your stink off me." She stalked away. Guests shuffled, uncomfortable. The Maples waited a moment then followed. Skerritt smiled at the remaining guests.

"A round on the house, Mal." Skerritt walked toward the resort office. "I'll be back when I've cleaned up."

"And that's Elena." Casey grinned. "Most people come here and say, 'This *is* great!' Some say, 'This *could be* great *if*.' Elena says, '*My* way is great.'"

"Rich just wants what's best for the island." Mal's face was flushed.

A strange look crossed Casey's face. Anger, along with something Hugh couldn't name. Disappointment, maybe. Or pity.

"'Development' doesn't always mean 'progress.'" Hugh said. "Look at south Florida."

"Oh, spare me! There's money to be made. Someone's going to make it. Selling bonds." Mal's eyes locked on Hugh's. "Or just take it."

Casey gave Hugh a long look.

"So you'll stand by and watch?" Hugh didn't give Casey the chance to ask what Mal meant.

"I'll enjoy *this* while it lasts. Then I'll either change with it or leave!" Mal's eyes were the green of a broken beer bottle. "This is Blacktip. What Rich wants, Rich gets."

She went to refill drinks. Hugh watched her glide from guest to guest, slim fingers setting bottles and cups precisely in front of each. Hugh's anger and fear evaporated. He stepped toward the kitchen for lunch, lightheaded.

"You want to be careful with her." A low murmur from Casey. "Play you like a squeeze-box, that one."

Hugh spun, shoulders squared at the insult to Mal.

Casey's black eyes were on Hugh's. A hint of admiration there? That Hugh had braved Mal twice? Why was Casey so down on Mal?

"She's a friend, is all…" Hugh stammered.

"There's no friends on Blacktip, Mate. Only allies."

6

Days later Hugh surfaced from an afternoon dive and found Casey braced against a stanchion on the *Skipjack*'s upper deck, binoculars aimed at a plume of black smoke rising mid-island.

"House fire?" Hugh asked.

"No houses there," Casey said. "Get the punters back, we'll find out."

Guests aboard, Casey raced for Eagle Ray Cove. They refilled cylinders quickly, Casey watching the smoke plume. Then, boat retanked, Casey tied the *Skipjack* to the pier with extra lines and started up the boardwalk.

"She'll be fine overnight," he said over his shoulder. "You might as well come along, F.N.G. Keep you out of trouble."

Hugh followed, surprised by the invitation. And curious about what could be burning that would get Casey so worked up. Hugh had barely climbed in the dive shop's one-ton flatbed when Casey spun the tires and roared from parking area.

They careened north, the boards of the truck's wooden bed rattling. Casey muttered a steady stream of obscenities.

"They can't do this. Whoreson bastard sons of bitches!"

"Do what?"

"Whoreson bastard sons of bitches!"

The Blacktip Haven sign blurred past on their right. Parrett's Nest and the cross-island road passed in a blink, then Club Scuba Doo, bright on its beach to their left. Hugh's teeth clattered in time with the flatbed's wooden slats. The pillar of smoke rose higher, guiding them north.

Just before the airstrip, a rusty Mercedes sat on the road's shoulder. Other vehicles were parked beyond. A fresh-cut lane broke the jungle to their right. Casey stomped the brakes, downshifted, and big truck fishtailed onto the new track.

"Bastards!" Casey hit the brakes, sent Hugh's head bouncing off the dashboard.

The lane ended at a broad swath of land stripped down to pale limestone. To the left, a front-end loader was ripping a tree out by the roots. In front of them, another loader was dragging a tree down the rocky clearing. To the right a bulldozer shoved felled trees into a smoldering mound twenty feet high. Flames shot out around the mound's edges and from its top. Black smoke boiled high.

A dozen onlookers gawked at the cleared land's verge. Mickey Smarr watched the flames as if hypnotized. Frank Maples had his camera out. Elena Havens yelled into her phone. Jessie and a dark-haired woman Hugh didn't recognize stood beside Elena. The shaggy-haired Mercedes driver, in a rumpled button-down shirt and khaki shorts, swayed as he talked to the women, hands on their shoulders for support. Jessie twisted away.

Casey leaped from the truck, shoved through the crowd and onto the cleared land. Hugh followed, excusing himself. Casey stomped across the bare limestone, yelling and waving at the nearest front-end loader. The driver ignored him. Casey jumped in front of the machine, a rock in his hand. The machine stopped. Hugh jogged across the broken ground as fast as his flip-flops allowed.

"… rip things up like this!" Casey yelled as Hugh approached.

The driver climbed down. Dermott.

"You don't get out the way, Casey, you end up in that burn pile." Dermott loomed over them.

"What the bloody hell are you doing?" Casey stepped chest-to-stomach with Dermott.

"My job, Casey. What you doing?"

"Goddamn stopping you, you knob!" Casey looked like he would punch Dermott, thought better of it, jumped onto the front-end loader instead, rock in-hand.

Dermott hit Casey so quick Hugh wasn't sure Dermott had moved. One moment Casey was reaching for the controls, the next he was laying flat on the ground, nose bleeding.

Dermott nodded to Hugh. "Your buddy still there when I get back up, he going in that fire." Dermott slowly climbed to the driver's seat.

Hugh helped Casey stand, walked him away from the loader. Dermott dropped the machine into gear.

"Should've seen that coming," Casey said.

"I'll get you to the clinic."

"No. I'm good." Casey blinked, tried to smile. The side of his face was red and swelling. "Teach me to start rows with a Sasquatch."

"Rich Skerritt finally greased enough palms." Elena Havens still pressed her cell phone to her ear. "You need some ice on that, Casey."

"I have photos if you want to press charges," Frank Maples said.

Casey looked as if Maples had stepped in something foul.

"The place down the road, the Sand Spit? They'll have ice." The dark-haired woman pressed fingertips to Casey's face. "Will you hold still? I'm a nurse."

The Mercedes driver leaned on the woman for a closer look at Casey. Beer fumes washed over them. The woman shoved him away.

Mickey put an arm around Casey, helped him to the dive truck.

"I can drive, if you need," Mickey said.

Casey waved him away, motioned Hugh to drive.

The Sand Spit sat at the end of a rocky peninsula. Cori, tending bar, pressed an ice-packed dishtowel to Casey's face.

"You picked a fight with *Dermott?*"

"More with that bloody runway." Casey swallowed a handful of aspirin, chased them with beer.

"Well, the runway kicked your ass," Cori said.

"Warning shot." Casey tried to smile. "Dermott wanted to hurt me, he would have."

"You made points with the environmentalists." Hugh eyed Casey with a new respect. A 'warning shot?'

"Environ-*mental's* more like it." Casey tapped the side of his head. "Faux-Green wankers. If Elena approves, I was definitely in the wrong."

"Why would Dermott help with that?" Hugh said.

"Dermott making a living, Hugo." Antonio had followed them in. "Nothing wrong with that, man paying his bills."

"But to clear cut that land!" Cori said.

"He don't work there, you pay his rent for him?" Antonio said. "You feed him? Send money to his wife and kids over on Tiperon? Dermott's taking an opportunity. And once that runway's in, construction starts up, he'll have even more opportunity. Me, too."

"But still..."

"You and the tourists. Love the quaint island and the quaint islanders. Well, I'm through with 'quaint,' girl. Time for me to be well off. Maybe me and Dermott'll go to your hometown, watch your family be 'quaint.'"

"How much money's your soul worth?" Casey squinted at Antonio.

"Enough to own a house, rent rooms to your friends."

"Get me out of here." Casey staggered away, ice pressed to his face.

Hugh and Casey walked to the dive truck, the lowering sun stretching their shadows long across the sand parking lot.

"That was the stupidest thing I've ever seen." Elena Havens climbed from the Blacktip Haven van. Jessie and the nurse were still with her. "You deserve a medal."

Casey rolled his good eye. "I'll settle for a pint."

"We came to check on you, but looks like you'll make it."

"Let me have another look at that." The nurse put a hand on Casey's hurt cheek.

"Beth's an old friend," Elena said. "Thought I'd drop her and Jessie here while I make some calls. We'll hit Rich with an injunction so fast his head'll spin."

Jessie smiled quick at Hugh. Red hibiscus flower behind her ear. Casey shook himself free of Beth, climbed into the truck. Hugh slid behind the wheel.

"Oh, how women love scars," Casey said.

Hugh reached for the ignition. Casey swatted his hand away.

"Know what we need? A piss-up. That Beth's not so bad. You take the fat chick?"

"Jessie's not fat." Hugh wanted nothing to do with Jessie.

"Figure of speech. Fly wing." He dropped into an exaggerated American twang. "It's a perk, Mate. We'll make a proper divemaster of you yet. And get your mind off your friend Mal."

Casey hopped from the truck.

"Ladies! If you'd care to join us, the Last Ballyhoo has the finest sunsets on the island!" The carnival barker delivery. A low bow.

Beth and Jessie glanced at Elena.

"Casey's an ass, but he's all right. No matter what he might think." Elena waved, already thumbing numbers into her phone.

They all four piled into the cab, Jessie pressed against Hugh, the stick shift jutting up between her knees.

"Sorry." Hugh finger tipped the stick back into reverse.

"How about I shift and you clutch?" Jessie laughed.

Gray eyes. Skin freckling, trying to tan. She tugged at her necklace. Why couldn't this be Mal beside him?

Casey waved Hugh south, and they bounced down the sandy road, sardines in a rattling can.

Past Antonio's turnoff the sea crowded close. The central bluff's face steepened to a jagged wall, black stone pocked and broken, the petrified teeth of some enormous sea creature. Gumbo-limbo trees lined the cliff's top, their paper-thin red bark peeling, dropping in shreds among the black teeth along the road.

"Ironshore." Casey pointed to the wall. "Eroded limestone. Razor sharp."

"Pretty," Beth said.

"Tear you up, you're not careful."

"Hmm. I'd like to see my ex on that."

The road swung left, angled up the cliff face. Caves riddled the limestone, some the size of downspouts, some big enough to crawl into. Soon they were atop the bluff. The road ran along the cliff, turned east with the coast. Then, at the island's southernmost point, a long, low building with peeling teal paint clung to the bluff's edge. 'THE LAST BALLYHOO' had been freehanded in neon orange above the door. Below the sign hung a carved wooden fish with a long, pointed lower jaw. Casey led them around back to a wide patio hemmed with rusty iron railings at the cliff's edge. A bar and kitchen opened from the rear. A small, tree-fringed bay spread a hundred feet below, orange with the setting sun.

"Welcome to the Ballyhoo," Casey said. "Far away as we can get from bulldozers and burning."

The four of them sat facing the sea, feet propped on the railings. Casey and Beth with beer, plus tequila shots, Jessie with a vodka and orange juice. Hugh sipped at a soda. Breakers hissed on the reef below. A thick, sweet scent flowed up the cliff face.

"What *is* that stink?" Beth asked.

"Mangoes." Casey said. "You're looking down at Mango Sound."

"Mango stench's more like it."

Casey tried to grin, managed a grimace. The side of his face was purpling now. Beth leaned close, stroked Casey's cheek. Handed him a shot and some pills.

"Aren't you hot in that sweatshirt?"

"I like it hot, Love. It can never be too warm."

"I am *so* sorry I ran you off the road the other day," Jessie said to Hugh.

"Happens all the time," Hugh said.

"Really?"

"That day, yeah."

"You ended up at Antonio's, didn't you? It's way more secure than the others."

"Secure?"

"Sturdy, I mean. During storms." Jessie fingered her necklace again. "I'm in Parrett's. It's wobbly, but it has the view. I didn't move to paradise to look at moldy walls, you know?"

"What's with the bird cross?"

"Oh!" Jessie dropped her hand. "Nervous habit. My grandma's cross. Not religious, just good luck. And I found a garage sale ring to match it." She wiggled her fingers to show Hugh a silver ring with a spread-winged bird and cross on it. "The cross was hers, but the ring's all mine. Family's once upon a time from Brittany. She's the one hooked me on Medieval lit."

Hugh watched the breaking waves. The more Jessie talked, the less sense she made. If she couldn't be Mal, at least she could be silent. He sipped his soda, wished it were scotch. Across Mango Sound waves broke white across the fringing reef. Inside, a pair of sailboats sat moored for the night.

"The practice was exhausting, you know?" Jessie drained her drink. On to another topic without Hugh noticing. "It was Dad's firm, so that was a gimme. But there's things I *want* to do, you know? Blew them all away when I just up and left."

Hugh stared. There was no way her background was so similar to his. She was fishing. He would volunteer nothing.

"To cook at a resort?" he said.

"Like see the world beyond Sarasota," Jessie said. "Cooking lets me do that. Paid for college. And it's fun. Funny how we keep running into each other, isn't it?"

"Small island."

"So where's home?"

"Here." Hugh was learning to hate the question.

"Wow. So you'd been to Blacktip before."

"Only online." Hugh said. An attorney, from west Florida, grilling him about his past? This couldn't be coincidence. Or was he being paranoid again? She could be just trying too hard to make friends.

"It freak people out when you bolted, out of the blue?" Jessie said.

"Who says I bolted?"

"Oo! More people!" Jessie spun toward the sound of feet shuffling behind them.

A group of tanned locals in assorted dive staff shirts wandered onto the patio. Four men in construction clothes came behind them. No sign of Dermott. A minute later Kitty Smarr strolled out, arm-in-arm with a man with spiky blond hair and a Club Scuba Doo dive staff tank top.

The sky darkened. Forty-watt bulbs, strung from a high lattice, snapped on, threw pools of yellow light on the rickety tables. Music crackled from a cheap stereo. Casey and Beth sang along to a scratchy reggae song blasting through salt-riddled speakers.

"It was so cool, what you and your friend did today." Jessie sipped a fresh vodka and orange. "We all wanted to charge out there, but y'all were the ones who actually did it!"

"I'm not sure he'd do it again."

"Oh, he's doing all right."

Casey had pulled Beth to an open patch of patio, was swaying in time with the music. Others pulled partners onto the floor. Soon a half-dozen couples were dancing in the gloom. Stars, boat lights glimmered beyond the railing.

Jessie grabbed Hugh's hand, tilted her head toward the dancers.

"Care to dance?"

"I'm, uh, not much at dancing." Tess had made him dance once, howled laughing, then never asked him again.

"Everybody can dance." Jessie gulped her drink, pulled Hugh from his chair.

Hugh shuffled his feet, trying to get them moving in the same three-beat rhythm as Jessie's.

"It's a rumba, silly," Jessie said.

"Oh, sure." Hugh kept shuffling, no idea what a 'rumba' was.

"Boom, chick-chick. Boom, chick-chick." Jessie put her hands on his waist, twisted his hips with each word. "See? You *can* dance!"

Hugh relaxed, followed Jessie's feet. He would do this all night if it kept her from asking more questions. Jessie smiled as if he were Fred Astaire.

Two songs later, Casey and Beth were on the bar top, other partiers cheering and clapping. Kitty and her friend joined them. Jessie pulled Hugh onto the bar, too.

"What'd I tell you?" Casey yelled, voice as distorted as his face. "What the doctor called for!"

Jessie pressed against Hugh, moving to the beat. Hugh pressed back. Having fun in spite of himself. Someone bumped against him. Dark hair, light eyes. Beth. Hugh blinked. In the dim light her face could have been Mal's. He shouldn't be here, like this. He pulled free from Jessie.

"I need to go." Hugh jangled the truck keys at Casey.

"Brilliant!" Casey hopped off the bar, helped Beth down. "Drop us at the Cove."

Jessie looked confused, downed a fresh drink, and followed them out.

Casey and Beth sat with their backs against the creaky flatbed's cab. Their laughter drifted through the open windows. Hugh drove slow, trying not to bounce them. Jessie sat close to him, her honeysuckle scent drowning out the stale booze-and-smoke smell from the bar. Hugh felt her watching him, waiting for him to speak. He had nothing to say to this strange woman.

"Sorry," he said. "Long day caught up with me."

"Divemastering's hard work, especially if you're not used to it," she said. "And then you played knight in armor."

Hugh watched the road. Dashboard lights the green of Mal's eyes.

"Ever seen the stars from a boat, love?" Casey's voice drifted into the cab.

"You have a boat?" Beth's voice, eager.

"Have one? It's home sweet home. Left me by a dying uncle. You have to come see the *Bident*."

"She's getting over an ugly divorce." Jessie's voice went serious. "Elena asked me to look after her."

"Casey's okay," Hugh said. "He's only an ass to me."

"And what are you?"

"Poison."

At Eagle Ray Cove, Casey steadied Beth as she climbed down. She wobbled on her first step in the soft sand. Casey slapped the truck door.

"Thanks, Mate. See you in the morning."

Beth whispered to Jessie a moment, nodded reassurance, followed Casey through the breezeway by the resort office.

"Like a drink?" Jessie said.

"I… need to go." Mal would be at the bar. And he wanted to be rid of Jessie as soon as possible. "Rain check?"

Hugh drove north for Parrett's Nest. Dashboard lights and pale roadway in his headlights the only visual references. Awkward silence. He hadn't meant to be rude, but at least Jessie had shut up.

"So what'd you do? Before?" Jessie's words slurred at the edges. "For a living, I mean?"

"Boring office stuff." The woman couldn't help herself.

"You must've been good at it, to be able to just quit. Divemaster pay doesn't even cover the bills."

"Can we stop playing *Twenty Questions*?" Hugh took a deep breath. "I made some mistakes, and I'm here to fix them. If it's the last thing I do. Now can we just talk like human beings?"

Silence again, more awkward than before. Trees flashed past in the headlights. The truck bounced over half-exposed rocks. Jessie sat across the cab now. The Blacktip Haven sign appeared. Parrett's Nest wasn't much farther.

"Turn here." Jessie waved at the Blacktip Haven sign. "Leave me at work."

The track to Blacktip Haven, barely wide enough for the truck, climbed steeply to high on the bluff. There the trees thinned, revealing cottages scattered among the untrimmed sea grapes, pathways between them lit by footlights snaking through the underbrush. To the left the island's flat northern half stretched below, stars reflected in the brackish pond. The northern horizon glowed yellow from Club Scuba Doo, and closer, orange from the runway burn pile. Hugh stopped the truck, killed the headlights. He searched for words. He had spoken harsher than he'd meant to. He was here to make friends, not piss off strangers.

"Look, I didn't mean to snap. I'm just stressed settling in and all."

"Sorry I was so nosey." Jessie slipped out the door and was gone.

Hugh watched the darkness where she'd disappeared. He was a jerk. Jessie was annoying, but she didn't deserve this. He'd find her tomorrow, apologize properly.

He parked the truck at Eagle Ray Cove and walked to his scooter, Jessie's honeysuckle scent still clinging to him.

"Late night for you." Mal's voice came from the shadows. She stepped into the sliver of light spilling from the lobby's glass door.

"Dropping off a guest." His heart jumped at seeing Mal. At hearing her.

"Nice of you." Mal's nose twitched. "Out of the way place, the Ballyhoo." Eyes searching. Gauging his reaction.

"Nice enough." Did Mal know *everything* on this island? She'd worked here tonight. Casey had talked, on the way to his boat. Had to be.

"The new girl at The Haven seems sweet." Her voice was inviting. Too inviting.

"Should have been you."

"I wouldn't have gone." There was an edge to her voice. "We're not together, remember? And Casey wouldn't have asked."

"I..." He was still an idiot. A postcard-charmed idiot. "Look, I'm sorry I crowded you. Am crowding you. Coming back like I did. You've got to have guests crushing on you left and right. Last thing you need is a… me."

"You do have to be careful with that sort of thing." Her hint of a smile. "But you're on Casey's good side. That's… unexpected."

"That's temporary. Captain Potting Soil'll be back."

"Potting soil…? Oh, he caving again?"

"Caving?"

"We're in the heart of the Spanish Main, boy-o. Casey spent years hunting pirate treasure in Blacktip's caves," Mal lowered her voice, stepped close. "He have a new lead?"

"I wouldn't know," Hugh hoped he looked uncaring. His mind raced, though, at the word 'treasure.' "I'll… see you when I see you."

"Soon. We still need to talk money. And you can help me find my pawn."

Hugh barely felt the scooter bouncing over rocks on his ride home. The fireflies in the underbrush flashed like a hundred gold coins. If he could find hidden treasure, even a little, his money problems would be over. Could he find something Casey had missed? Someplace Casey hadn't looked yet? Or would Casey maybe let Hugh throw in with him, double the effort and split the take? He'd have to sound Casey out. Carefully.

At Antonio's, Hugh turned on the shower to wash off the bar stink before he fell into bed. Cold water rained from the showerhead. He let it run. Still cold. Then he remembered: one water heater, five lodgers. All the hot water was gone. Hugh stopped the shower, ran his fingers across Mal's pawn on his nightstand, then lay back on the mattress and slept. He dreamed of gold doubloons and jeweled necklaces. Of green eyes and honeysuckle scent.

7

L ight filtered through yellowed miniblinds. A bird chirped a high, reedy '*quit-quit-quit*' somewhere outside. Mal's pawn stood guard on the nightstand, smooth and shiny. Stale cigarette stink. The house was silent.

Hugh scrambled from bed. He *would* get a shower this morning. He opened the hot water tap, let it run, then stepped to the kitchen and started coffee.

Water steamed from the showerhead by the time coffee was ready. Hugh carried his mug to the shower, let the hot water cascade over him. He scrubbed his scalp, face and arms until his skin smarted.

The water slowed. Stopped. Someone shouting. Banging on the wall. Hugh wiped soap from his face, wrapped a towel around his waist and stepped from the shower.

The stench of melted plastic and scorched wiring caught in his throat. Hugh slid across the glazed floor tiles and into the outer room. The burned smell was stronger there, set him coughing. His eyes stung from soap and fumes. The sliding glass door boomed. Antonio's face was pressed to the glass, his fist back for another blow.

"Hugo! Can't be using water like that!"

"I can't take a shower?"

"Not so long! Pump burned out!"

Hugh slid the door open. Maybe Antonio would make more sense without the glass between them.

"Water pump burned." Antonio waved his hands, wafting more burned wire smell inside. "Can't run that long."

"What pump?" Hugh envisioned an Old West hand-pump in a black-and-white cowboy movie.

"This an old place Hugo. Used to be one place. That means it does have *one* electric pump to pull water out of *one* cistern. That cistern goes dry, the pump burns and no water for the whole place."

An angry Cori stuck her head in the door. Muffled cursing came from Jerrod's upstairs.

"You didn't tell me." Soap burned Hugh's eyes.

"Everyone on island's careful with water," Antonio said.

Dermott loomed behind Antonio, unreadable. More unsaintly oaths drifted down from Jerrod's.

"I didn't know." Hugh stepped toward the bedroom, slipped, grabbed the doorframe to hold himself up. "I'll get dressed, go get another pump."

"No other pump," Antonio said.

"No pump?"

"Not on island."

"Then where?"

"Tiperon. Maybe. 'Course, we have to wait for businesses to open. I'll call, see if I can maybe find something, have it shipped over."

"And in the meantime…"

"In the meantime, we don't have water!" Cori snapped. "For who knows how long."

"I'll pay for the new pump," Hugh pawed at his burning eyes.

"Oh, yeah," Antonio said.

"I'll help put it in, too."

Dermott snorted.

"You don't look like a plumber, Hugo," Antonio said.

"I'll do what I can."

"You'll haul water up here for us?" Cori said. "We have toilets to flush, dishes to wash, dogs to water. Oh, yeah, and showers to take. You haul up that much water?"

"I… sure… I'll borrow the dive truck. Get water bins."

"We sort it out," Antonio said. "Should've seen this. Looking so far into the future, I didn't see today." He paused, eyes unfocused. "I do recall Sandy Bottoms may have an old pump spare. Small, but maybe work 'til we get a new one. Long as no one uses too much water." A hard look at Hugh.

"Understood."

Hugh closed the glass door, nervous having so many people looking into his place. He toweled off, dressed for work. Dried soap crackled across his shoulders as he shrugged into his shirt.

Visions of hidden gold pushed aside water pump worries when Hugh, on his scooter, sputtered past the bluff. The cliff face along the road was pocked with caves big enough for him to get into. But caves that obvious would have been scoped out years ago. Where to start searching that no one else had searched? If he were a pirate, he would have hidden stolen goods inland. High enough to be safe from flooding. Someplace screened by underbrush. Underbrush that had grown into a jungle in the 400 years since. He needed to pick a thickly-wooded spot and work out from there. This stretch was as good a place as any. He'd need a rope and a light. Long pants and real shoes, too.

At Eagle Ray Cove, Hugh's treasure hunting plans evaporated. Lee was waiting out front when Hugh arrived.

"Well, if it's not Ger's favorite pet. Making friends with the locals last night , were we?"

"The ones worth making friends with." Hugh pushed past Lee.

"Oh, you want to be friendly with me, us knowing each other like we do."

"Except we don't."

"Oh, but I reckon there may be them who'd care to know about 'Hugh,' who used to be 'Blake,' working as a divemaster after quitting his posh job of a sudden."

"Nice try." Hugh kept walking. Lee was guessing. But that guessing could ruin Hugh's new life in a flash.

"Might be money for me, them knowing." Lee trailed Hugh. "Or maybe more money for them not to know, if you take my meaning."

"Fun story." Hugh headed for the dive shop, hoping he looked uncaring. "But you're delusional."

"Ah, we'll chat. Later. We know how to find each other, eh?"

No one at Eagle Ray Divers noticed Hugh or Lee. The staff was watching Ger Latner and Casey talking with a policeman on the dive shop porch. Latner and the policeman were red-faced. Casey gave Hugh a lopsided grin, waved him toward the *Skipjack*. What would Casey find funny that Latner and the policeman didn't? If something had happened with Beth… Hugh spun, anger building. Casey was just catching up to him.

"Divide and conquer, eh, Mate? The cook get your mind off Mal?"

"What the hell did you do?" It was all Hugh could do not to punch Casey's bruised face.

Casey paused, puzzled. Then he laughed.

"No! That, just now, had nothing to do with last night!" Casey held out a sheet of paper. "A.S.B.O. Police Constable Marquette says I'm to stay 200 meters from the work site. And will cart me away if I don't."

Hugh took the paper. A restraining order.

On the pier, Hugh ignored Lee, helped divers board the *Skipjack* on the pier's leeward side. Casey motioned Hugh to the bridge.

"Climb up, F.N.G. Time you learned to drive."

Hugh, surprised, joined Casey at the helm.

"Start with your wheel amidships," Casey said. "Always know where that is. Now, the levers with the red knobs are your throttles; the levers with the black knobs are your gears." Casey pointed to pairs of chromed handles on either side of the wheel, colored balls at their tips.

"Gotcha."

"So start the engines, Knobby." Casey nodded for Lee to cast off the *Skipjack*'s lines. "Now, as the wind catches our bow, put us in gear and make us go."

Hugh raised the red-handled levers, like he'd seen Casey do. The engines revved, but the boat went nowhere. Lee and the other staff on the pier laughed.

"We usually put the engines in gear before we apply power." Casey pulled the throttles down, pushed the black-knobbed levers forward. The *Skipjack* idled toward the channel markers. "Don't break my boat, F.N.G."

Hugh's pulse quickened as they neared the cut. Waves rolled across the channel in sets: small rollers, then a flat spot, then rollers again. Casey sat silent beside him, gauging Hugh's response. At a flat spot, Hugh raised the throttles and powered past the reef. Once they were through the surf, he turned north, brought the engines up to cruising speed.

"Open sea now," Casey said. "Can't do too much damage. Just don't crash into the island."

The chrome steering wheel slid slick through Hugh's sweating hands as he wracked his brain to remember all the driving instructions Casey had barked at him. The twin diesels pulsed through the deck, through Hugh's feet. Pleasing and terrifying all at once.

"One way to tell if you're steering a straight course is to look back at your wake," Casey said without turning his head.

Hugh looked over his shoulder. Their wake snaked behind them like they were on a slalom course. Hugh clamped his hands on the wheel, aimed the *Skipjack* at a cloud on the horizon, steered straight at it. The *Skipjack* edged closer to shore as the cloud drifted east. Hugh corrected his course, watched the compass, steered due north before Casey could say anything.

At the first dive site, Casey talked Hugh through the mooring approach.

"Bow into the wind, engines in neutral - the black knobs, Knobby - and let the boat glide to a stop."

Casey nodded approval when the *Skipjack* stopped at the yellow mooring line. He jumped to the bow, grabbed the line from the water with the boathook, and tied off the boat.

At the second dive site, Casey let Hugh pull up to the mooring with no coaching. Hugh's approach was off, and the breeze pushed the bow away from the line's spliced eye as they glided in. Casey stretched as far as he could, hooked the line, and tied them off.

"Not perfect, but fair progress." Casey sounded disappointed. "We may not send you back after all."

Hugh couldn't tell if Casey was serious.

As they neared the cut at noon, Hugh studied the waves again, looking for a pattern to the sets. There were flat spots, sure. But when to turn?

"Line the range markers on shore," Casey said, as if he had read Hugh's mind. "The big white square and triangle."

Casey pointed to the beach where a six-foot-wide square balanced on a tall white post, an equally-large triangle on a shorter post in front of it.

"Start your turn early so they're in line when you straighten out. I'll handle the throttles this time."

Hugh steered toward the break in the reef. Casey backed the throttles slightly so the boat settled on the back of a wave.

"You match the speed of the sea here, yeah? Pick a small-ish swell and ride it in."

Hugh nodded, fighting to keep the boat pointed at the range markers as the wave tried to push him sideways. Once inside the reef, Casey backed the throttles to idle.

"Make a silk purse of you yet," he said.

At lunch Hugh avoided the dining room, and Lee. He had no appetite anyway after Lee's threat. And he needed to call Jessie. He ducked into the lobby and shut himself in the courtesy phone closet. A list by the phone gave the number for Blacktip Haven, and in moments he was listening to someone at the bluff top resort yelling for Jessie.

"I need to apologize," Hugh said when Jessie picked up. "Again. For last night. I didn't mean to be rude, but I…"

"Nope," Jessie said. "I got tipsy, got nosey, and got what I deserved."

"No, it wasn't…" Hugh couldn't lie. "Can I make it up to you?"

"No. Look, I've gotta run. We're double clutching with all these guests *and* Elena's crusade in overdrive."

"Oh. Sure." She was blowing him off. He deserved that.

Silence in the receiver. Then shouting in the background. Elena Havens' voice thundering.

"I don't care about our fertilizer! Get the Pelagic Society! The Earth Federation, too! If Rich Skerritt ignores this injunction, he'll have a hundred protestors with cameras to deal with!"

"Gotta go." Jessie hung up.

Hugh went down to the pier. Most staffers were there, though there was no sign of Lee. Good. Hugh hurried toward the *Skipjack*. He was nearly there when Lee stepped from the air fill station's shadow.

"Had time to think over our arrangement?"

Hugh wanted to punch the grin from Lee's face. He could take the little divemaster. But that would only make Lee angrier, hungrier for revenge.

"What is it you think you have on me?"

"That's the beauty," Lee said. "I don't need to know. I just need to *know*, eh?"

"You're an idiot."

"Easiest way, for both of us, I reckon, is weekly installments." Lee's grin widened. "Saves me the trouble of research. Saves you the trouble of P.C. Marquette dragging you off. Of course, if others turn up as wants to pay a lump sum up front, we'd need to…"

"You need to get to work." Ger Latner's voice rumbled behind them. "Both of you." He spun Hugh and Lee toward their respective boats. "Play grab ass on your own time."

Hugh couldn't concentrate that afternoon. There wasn't a good option with Lee. If Hugh didn't pay, Lee would drop the dime on Hugh in a heartbeat. If Hugh paid, there was no guarantee Lee wouldn't take Hugh's money and turn him in anyway. Hugh had to keep the little bastard at bay, though, buy time to treasure hunt. He needed to get on Casey's good side, too, for advice on where to start hunting.

"A 'course,' by definition, is a straight line, F.N.G." Casey said from behind him. "Try to steer a straight line to that big, white mooring ball up ahead."

Hugh focused on driving.

After work Hugh left before Lee could corner him. He cut behind the dive shop and the bar to get to his scooter. As he passed, the storeroom door behind the bar swung open. Mal stepped out, a case of wine in her arms. Their unfinished talk from the night before came back to Hugh.

"Hey, can we…"

"Busy," Mal snapped. "Barge just came in."

"I wanted to clear things up. About last night."

"Not *now*," she whispered.

"When's good? We can talk money, too."

"No. We can't."

"Some evening…"

The storeroom door swung open again. Rich Skerritt stepped out.

"There a problem?" He glared at Hugh.

"Rich, this is Hugh," Mal said. "He just started with Ger. He's quite the day trader, if rumors are true."

"Hugh. Right." Skerritt's eyes bored into him. "Hugh, if you want to work here, you need to keep your schemes to yourself. And mind your own business." A glance at Mal, then back at Hugh. "You understand me?"

Skerritt stepped back into the storeroom. Mal gave Hugh a tight-lipped glare, then followed Skerritt and closed the door.

Hugh backed away. Whatever was going on inside, Mal wanted Hugh far away from it. Was Rich Skerritt up to something illegal, hiding something in the storeroom? Or was he that demanding of a boss? Either way, Skerritt's threat had been clear.

Riding home Hugh's mind crept back to caves and his own safety. Worst case, if he couldn't find hidden gold, maybe he could find a better place to hide his cash. If investigators tracked him down and searched his place, they'd find the hollowed-out manuals in no time. If the money was stashed in a cave, he'd have a bargaining chip.

Hugh stopped just past Captain Vic's where the bluff face was shot through with caves. No one on the road in either direction. He shoved the scooter into the bushes and climbed to the lowest opening. The ironshore bit into his hands and knees, but inside the cave was smoother, as if it had been carved by flowing water. If all the island's caves were like this, exploring would be easier.

Inside, the cave opened up big enough for Hugh to stand. Light filtered from narrow shafts in the roof. Three steps in were ashes of a small fire and some empty beer bottles, red labels still bright. Beyond the fire pit, the cave wound another thirty feet then narrowed and ended in a rough wall.

Hugh climbed back out, scraping his hands and knees again. Other caves pocked the cliff higher up. He'd have to get at them from above, rappel down. Or see if any shafts on top were big enough to climb into. He could bushwhack back from Antonio's, follow the cliff, and use this spot as square one. The search would take a while, though. In the meantime, he'd have to finesse Lee, tease him along with little bits of money and hints of bigger payoffs to come if he'd only hold off on turning Hugh in. Hugh would gather what climbing supplies he could and get started the next day.

The scooter stalled again on the track up to Antonio's clearing, and Hugh pushed it to the top. Hugh froze at the clearing's edge. A figure was hunched over something outside of Hugh's place. Police? The figure raised a hammer, slammed it down on an oversized pipe wrench.

"Tighten it good! I seen this place floating away in a dream." Antonio's voice drifted from inside the house.

"That's got it!" The hunched figure yelled back. It stood straight. Jerrod. Standing over the rusty water pump.

"Stand back and I throw the switch." Antonio's voice echoed out.

Hugh walked the scooter to the house.

The pump clattered to life, shaking on its base. Water hissed through pipes. The pump shuddered off a moment later once the system was primed.

"Let me run the spigot, see how it does." Jerrod opened a faucet beside the house, ran water into a bucket. The pump chattered, shook, but kept running as the water flowed.

Antonio stepped from behind the house. Jerrod closed the faucet, and the pump shut off again.

"It's not a thing of beauty, but, praise be, it works," Jerrod said.

"Got water again, Hugo." Antonio waved at the rusty pump. "Old pump, but it does need to be paid for."

"Oh, sure. How much?"

Antonio was looking at Hugh's scraped knees, though.

"You been exploring, Hugo?"

"No, no. I was… I saw something red… like the fireflies, but different… I thought, back by the bluff and wanted a closer look…" The story formed as Hugh spoke, his brain racing to come up with a reason for him to have been crawling over ironshore.

"No fireflies on Blacktip, Hugo." Antonio went still, his face stern.

"And there was nothing but beer labels when I got there, either. Got scraped up for nothing." Hugh kept his voice light, hoping the two men hadn't guessed why he had been in the cave. "Working too hard. Imagining things."

"This by Captain Vic's?"

"Somewhere along there, I guess." Was his treasure hunting so obvious? Another cliché for the island newbie?

Antonio shook his head, face down.

"Wives' tales, 'Tonio," Jerrod said. "He saw sunlight on a broken bottle or something."

"Bad stretch of road." Antonio searched Hugh's face. "What fireflies you been seeing, Hugo?"

"At night. In the underbrush." The conversation had taken a confusing turn.

"Along that bit of road?"

"All over."

Antonio gave Jerrod a worried look.

"Don't go chasing lights, Hugo. Don't know what the duppies want with you, but they surely taken an interest." Antonio walked away.

Hugh looked to Jerrod.

"The road along there's supposed to be haunted," Jerrod said. "Lights, shadows luring people off the road, that sort of thing."

"You believe that?"

"Not so much." Jerrod shrugged. "Good idea to stay on the road, though. It's easy to get lost in that jungle. And there's places the limestone's hollow underneath. It looks solid, but it'll crumble when you step on it, cut you up way worse than that." He pointed at Hugh's knees. "Fall in too far from the road, no one'll find you."

The water pump clattered, shaking so hard rust flecks flew from it.

"Toilet flush just fine!" Antonio yelled from his bathroom window. "I'm fetching the bill, Hugo!"

"I'll get money." Hugh stepped toward his place.

"Hold off on that." Jerrod put a hand on Hugh's chest to stop him. "Dermott's passed out in there. It's best not to wake him."

"What the hell's he doing in my house?" Fear shot through Hugh. How often had people been inside his place when he wasn't home?

"Sleeping one off," Jerrod said. "He does that. No telling where you'll find him. He crashed in Cori's last week. Not a big deal. Unless you spook him."

"Then what?"

"He goes kinda berserk. Put Jay Valve up at Scuba Doo in the hospital last month when Jay tried to roust him out of the resort lobby. If you absolutely have to go in, make lots of noise outside so he wakes up on his own. C'mon, I'll get you a beer. I want your thoughts on these sea fan seraphim I'm working on."

8

In the predawn silence, Hugh pulled the blinds tight and pried the paneling back far enough to dig out a half-dozen $100 bills from his wall stash. He set aside two for Antonio and kept the others for Lee. He would break the $100s into smaller, Tiperon currency, pay the rat a little at a time, put him off as long as he could. Hugh didn't want to dip into the cash, but he hadn't expected a broken water pump. Or a blackmailer. He checked the blinds again, then pressed the siding back into place.

At Eagle Ray Cove, Hugh talked boat handling with Marina in the dive shop until Lee went out to get the *Barjack*. On the pier Lee's dry bag lay beside the stacked scuba cylinders, a white 'England' cap carabinered to the strap. Band yellowed by sweat. Salt crust on the brim. No other dive staff in sight. The embroidered crest with its three lions was rough under Hugh's fingers. The carabiner opened with a touch, and the cap slid smoothly to the bottom of Hugh's daypack. The sun seemed warmer, the day brighter as Hugh stepped to the pier's end where the *Skipjack* would dock.

Casey grinned when he saw Hugh.

"Make any headway with your bit?" Casey asked.

"My bit?"

"The cook."

"Definitely not 'my bit.'" Casey was still trying to divert Hugh from Mal.

"Suspected as much. A sad excuse, you are."

"Why do you care…" Hugh stopped himself. Casey wanted a reaction. Anything Hugh said would be gasoline on a fire.

Across the pier Lee was docking the *Barjack*. Alison caught his bow line.

"Grab her quick," Casey said. "She won't last long on this island. If you can't be the only one, be the first one."

Hugh tied off the *Skipjack*'s stern.

"Where the bloody hell is my cap?" Lee yelled at Alison.

"How should I know?" Alison shrugged. "Put it on your head, you'll know where it is."

"It was clipped to my knapsack."

"Maybe it blew in the water."

"Do you understand the word 'clipped?'" Lee shook the empty carabiner at her. "If it was clipped on, it couldn't blow off!"

Hugh walked past them up to the dive shop and filled the coolers. When he came back, Alison was gone and Lee was venting at Gage.

"… someone's nicked it!"

"Why in the world'd anybody want to steal your crusty cap?" Gage said.

On the *Blackjack* Marina rolled her eyes as she filled the water tanks.

"One of you lot's messing with me, and I'll find out who!"

Hugh jumped on the *Skipjack*, shoved his pack in the forward hatch, and made a show of checking the names on the roster.

"What's Lee on about?" Casey said.

"Dunno," Hugh said. "Lost his hat, sounds like."

"Punter can't keep track of his hat, and they let him drive a boat," Casey said. "At least it wasn't a diver."

Calm seas and light wind made for an easy drive up the coast and an uneventful first dive. For their second dive, Casey had Hugh drive to a site he called Jawfish Reef, offshore from Sandy Bottoms Reef Resort: three stories of teal and pink sprawled along the beach. Hugh jumped in with the divers and signaled to descend.

Here, instead of bright coral, was a broad plain of coral rubble, the few limestone skeletons still standing coated in green algae. Even the few parrotfish looked drained of color. Sad-eyed jawfish popped from their burrows like yellow-headed ghosts. There was little for Hugh to show the guests. Why would Casey bring them here? To test Hugh? Hugh kept the group together, made sure no one wandered off, checked everyone's air.

A stingray swam past, wings flapping fast, crossing the barrens as quickly as possible. A moray eel swam across the rubble, an olive-colored ribbon five feet long. Hugh banged on his cylinder to get the guests' attention, then chased after it. The divers followed. The eel wove through the algae-coated coral then dropped over the wall. Hugh followed it down. When the eel swam into a crevice, Hugh grabbed its tail, eased it out for the guests to photograph. The divers would love this dive despite the lifeless reef.

The eel swam deeper. Hugh brought the group back to the shallows, looped around to the boat, and was back on board in half an hour, leaving the guests among the jawfish.

"Show them a good time?" Casey smirked from the upper deck. It had been a test, then, seeing how Hugh would handle a bad dive site.

"Sahara Desert." Hugh dried off, refused to rise to Casey's bait. "But I found them an eel, a stingray, all kinds of cool stuff."

When the divers surfaced, though, none of them looked happy.

"We may take some flak on this one," Hugh said.

"We're tour guides in a dying world, Mate." Casey said it loud enough for the surfacing guests to hear. "This used to be an absolute garden. Six, seven years ago even. Run-off from the new resort killed it. "

"We came here just so you could make that point?" a woman said.

"People need to see this. Especially new dive staff."

Hugh joked with the rest of divers as they climbed aboard, trying to take their minds off the dead reef.

"You know this was a fifty-foot dive?" Casey held a diver's gauge console.

"Oh, sure," the man said.

"What were you doing at sixty-three feet?" Casey waved the depth gauge in man's face.

"I followed Divemaster Hugh." The man gave Hugh a thumbs up. "Thanks for that eel, bud! I'd a never seen it if you hadn't pulled it out for us!"

Casey's neck reddened.

"Keep to your profile," Casey said.

"Oh, it was just for a second." The man beamed. "Best dive of the week, Hugh!"

Hugh couldn't hide his smile as he helped the remaining guests. He'd outmaneuvered Casey, salvaged a lousy dive, then smoothed the guests' feathers after Casey's rant.

Divers up, Casey climbed to the helm. When Hugh cast off, Casey shoved the throttles in gear. The *Skipjack* leaped forward. Casey was in a hurry to get back? Or angry Hugh had shown him up? Hugh climbed to the helm, plopped onto the seat beside Casey.

"My driving lessons done?"

"Hugh, why is it you broke a fifty-foot profile by thirteen feet?"

"I… what?"

"Why is it, *exactly*, you violated marine park rules by not just chasing, not just touching, but physically pulling an eel from the coral?" Casey's voice shook.

"They loved it! You heard the guy: 'The best dive of the week!'"

"Never, *ever* break profile. Not by a *centimeter*. Not by a *second*."

"You're the one talking about silk purses. I made that pig's ear into pure gold."

"No! One of our guests gets hurt because you led them beyond a safety profile, a judge or jury won't give a damn about an eel! We won't have a leg to stand on. The company will be out of business. We'll be out of jobs. You'll never work as a divemaster again."

"No one got hurt," Hugh said. Technically, Casey was right, but he was overreacting.

"Second," Casey's voice was harsher now. "'Marine Park' means no one touches anything underwater. Not a fish, not a bit of coral, *nothing*. That's a $5,000 fine. We lose our business license. You go to jail."

"It was all dead." Hugh flinched at the mention of jail. "And everyone touches stuff."

"Not on this boat. Grab another eel, you'll be back in the U.S. so fast your head will spin. 'Selling bonds,' did Mal say?"

A chill shot through Hugh. How much did Casey know? How much had he guessed? And was he serious about Hugh being fired, or just bullying him?

"You sound more pissed about the eel than the blown the profile," Hugh said.

"Guests have brains to protect them. We're the only protection that reef has."

This couldn't be about an eel. Casey had had it in for Hugh from the start.

"Why do you have so little respect for me?"

"Why should I? You don't respect the reef. You don't respect the people you work with. You don't respect your job. You're a guest on vacation, playing-acting at being a divemaster."

Hugh wanted to hit Casey. But that would land him on the next flight to Tampa. He climbed to the bow, forced his jaw to relax, his hand to unclench.

He was a good divemaster. He'd led a hundred dives in the Gulf and in lakes, murky dives that challenged a dive leader way more than any tropical dive ever could. Casey was a burnout who thought he knew everything because he'd been on the island forever. If Casey was so great, why wasn't he running the place? Or at a big operation on Tiperon? Hugh couldn't work with... this. He'd talk to Latner. Train with someone else.

At the pier Hugh unloaded cylinders, filled them without speaking. Ignored Casey. The other divemasters watched them, but didn't interfere. Even Lee kept his distance.

"Get as brassed as you like. It won't change a thing," Casey said. "Anyone else you train with will tell you the same."

Hugh said nothing. If Latner wouldn't reassign him, he'd talk to Polly at Scuba Doo. Elena at Blacktip Haven. Whoever at Sandy Bottoms.

Cylinders filled, Casey climbed into the skiff and motored out to his catamaran. Hugh went looking for Ger Latner.

No Latner in the dive shop. Hugh checked the front desk, then the bar deck. Jerrod was behind the bar. Mal's day off, then. Mickey and the dive staff sat across the deck eating lunch. Mickey waved Hugh over.

"Two weeks on the boat with Casey and this is your first blow up? You're doing all right!" Mickey pushed a chair toward Hugh.

"He's Eagle Ray Divers' test of fire," Marina said. "Everybody goes through it."

"Took you on a Ballyhoo run, too," Alison said. "You're in."

Lee glared at Hugh.

Hugh looked from one divemaster to another, not sure he had heard them right.

"I'm doing *well* with Casey?"

The others nodded.

"You'll be fine," Gage said.

"Before, I thought he hated me," Hugh said. "Then today after I grabbed that eel, I was sure he hated me."

The smiles faded.

"Don't touch anything," Alison said. "Casey's mental about that."

"Volunteer Marine Parks officer, too," Marina said. "Badge and arrest powers."

"No one told me this?"

"We did now," Gage laughed.

What else could Hugh have screwed up? Sink the boat? Kill a diver? No. The only person who thought he was doing poorly was Casey. Gage and the others said Hugh was doing well. And aside from Lee, they were great. Hugh was one of them now, taking his lumps.

Hugh finished lunch and walked back down the pier. Sound of feet on the planks behind him. Hugh spun, ready for Lee.

"Hugh," Ger Latner said. "How you doing?"

"Ger, you got a minute?" Anger surged up again.

"So. Casey hit the fan, did he?"

"My 'test of fire?'" It came out sharper than Hugh intended.

"There's my soldier!" Latner threw an arm around Hugh's shoulders. "Look, Hugh, you're green as owl shit. But you grit your teeth and listen to Casey, you'll come out damn good."

"I think it'd be better…"

"Nope. You're with Casey. And before you embarrass yourself asking Polly or Sandy about a job, they can't hire you even if they wanted to. You're on an Eagle Ray Divers work permit, for a year's contract. Condition of an expat working in the Tiperons. Work anywhere but here, Immigration'll ship you home. You don't want that, do you?"

The boardwalk tilted. Hugh couldn't be trapped with Casey. And how did Latner always know Hugh had been thinking about going to another resort?

"Small island." Latner grinned at Hugh. "Not a lot of dance steps. And I've seen 'em all. I'm not blind, either. Or stupid. Blake."

The boardwalk tilted again.

"You think my memory's that bad?" Latner said. "Or I don't have sense enough to look at a week-old dive waiver?"

"You never said…"

"I don't know why you're here. I don't *care* why you're here. I care about you doing your job. Period. And you are. But you hack off the guests, or don't play well with the other kids, you're gone. You hear me? Told your pal Lee the same thing this morning."

Hugh stared at Latner, numb. Ger knew about Lee's extortion threat? And had shut it down?

"Now, Casey can teach you." Latner's rumble softened. "You listen and learn. Stick to the profiles. And no more eel pulling. If he's riding you extra hard, it's 'cause you and Mallory got his shorts in a wad." Latner's hand pounded down on Hugh's back. "Your mouth's still open."

"Mal and Casey…?"

"Casey, anyway. Wasn't pretty. Learn from him."

Latner stomped away.

Casey had been interested in Mal? Still was? That explained their tension. And Casey trying to set Hugh up with Jessie. And Mal keeping Hugh at arm's length.

Hugh kept quiet that afternoon, mentally sorting through his options. If he and Mal were going to be together, working with Casey would be miserable. And picking Casey's brain about treasure hunting was shot to hell. He still needed information about caves, about pirates, though.

The pier was more pleasant at day's end. Casey's temper had cooled and Lee ignored Hugh except for random scowls. Hugh slipped a docking line in his backpack when Casey wasn't looking and rode home quick as the scooter would go. He would start exploring that afternoon. Latner had warned Lee off, but if the reward for Blake Calloway was big enough, Lee could still claim it and not need a job.

At Antonio's Hugh slipped on jeans and sneakers, tossed a dive light in his pack with the rope, made sure no one was in the clearing, and stepped back outside. A creaking sound came faint through the clearing, like branches rubbing together in the wind. But there was no wind. Hugh waited. The creaking stopped. Hugh pushed his way north through the jungle.

Half an hour later, he judged he was even with the road-side cave he had explored the day before. He hung Lee's cap on a bush to mark his starting point, then worked his way inland from the cliff, pushing aside branches and underbrush until he found a tire-sized opening that dropped down through the limestone. His light's beam disappeared in the blackness. He tossed in a rock, waited several seconds before it hit bottom. Deep, but not too deep. Hugh tied his rope around a tree trunk and lowered himself down.

The shaft's sides bit into his hands, but they provided plenty of handholds. Cool, moist air wafted up, as if the island were exhaling around him. There was the whisper of wind, or water, somewhere below. Above, the opening could have been jaws rimmed with dark teeth. Seven, eight body lengths down the rough wall turned smooth. Hugh's feet touched bottom. His light revealed a smooth stone floor. Remembering Jerrod's warning about crumbling limestone, Hugh tapped the floor with one foot before he put his full weight on it.

He shined his light in a circle. Dark stone arched over him, streaked by centuries of seeping water, a rough chamber twice his height, equally wide and maybe twice as long. A few shafts led off horizontally. None were large enough for him to get into. They were big enough to hide a small chest or a bag, though. Hugh shined his light into each one. Nothing but dirt, dried leaves, a rat's skeleton. He lay on his stomach, slipped his arm into one as far as he could, swept his hand across the bottom, feeling for coins, anything. Something palm-sized scuttled across his hand. Hugh yanked his arm back, scraping his hand, and rolled sideways across the cave floor. Other, smaller somethings crawled over his bare arm. Hugh dropped the flashlight and scraped his free hand down his arm. A dozen pale, quarter-sized spiders ran from the flashlight's beam.

Hugh took a deep breath, tried to stop shaking. Two more breaths and his hands steadied. Of course spiders, or worse, lived down here. That was part of what made this such a good hiding place for pirate gold. Or for his own ill-gotten cash.

A draft swept through the cave, set the dark air trembling with a low hum. The hair on Hugh's arms stood on end. The hum rose and fell, almost forming words. A word. His name? Lights flickered in the corners of his eyes, but when he looked toward them they were gone. Antonio's ghost stories were getting to him. Hugh shuddered, suddenly eager to be back in the sunlight. He scrambled back to his line and shinnied up from the darkness, scraping his hands and arms in his rush. Outside the treetops quivered with a light wind. That explained the sudden draft in the cave. Hugh laughed at himself for getting spooked. He'd have to get used to cave creatures and cave noises if he was going to strike it rich.

Hugh poked through the surrounding underbrush for more caves, found several openings, but none large enough to get into. The sun was setting when he made his way back to Antonio's. He checked the clearing for watching neighbors, then slipped inside his apartment. After a quick bowl of noodles, Hugh fell back on his bed, exhausted from the morning's work and the afternoon's caving.

Wind grew outside, sounding full of voices, as if Antonio's duppies were circling the house. A weather front must be coming through. Hugh closed his eyes, imagined Mal in the cave with him, saw her morph into piles of coins, jeweled necklaces, and gold crowns.

A shriek woke him. Hugh jumped from bed, heart pounding. Part of his dream? More wind? Another yell of sheer terror. Upstairs. Jerrod.

Hugh ran outside. It was pitch dark now. Another shout. Hugh stumbled around the back of Antonio's, hands on the wall to guide him in the utter blackness. He stubbed his toe on the uneven pavers, howled as loud as Jerrod, then crawled on hands and knees up to the second-floor apartment. Pounded on the door.

"Jerrod!"

"Yo." Jerrod's shaky, muffled voice came through the door. "I'm fine."

The door opened a crack, spilling light over the landing. Jerrod's face was pasty with sweat. Eyes red. Pale hair splayed out in a white halo.

"Sorry. Bad dream." Jerrod's voice was steadier. "I'm good. It happens. With the wind. Sometimes. Thanks." He shut the door.

Hugh felt his way back down the steps, hands locked on the rough handrail, retinas glowing from the sudden light of Jerrod's doorway. At the steps' foot, he fumbled for the house wall. His hands touched fur. Barking exploded around him. Wet tongues slopped over his face and arms.

"Jerrod does that." A flashlight snapped on. Cori, in sleep pants and t-shirt. "Used to scare the crap out of me."

"You warn people about that kind of thing." Hugh shivered.

"You get no warnings here."

"So I'm learning. What's his story?"

"Ask him. And good luck." She swung the light to guide Hugh around the building. Lettuce, Turnip, and Pea bounded beside him. "You should get a flashlight or something."

"I'll do that."

Hugh stepped back into his place and dropped onto the bed. His heart still raced. He stared at the ceiling, wondering what could terrify Jerrod like that. Was it whatever had driven Jerrod to the island? Hugh had no clue why Jerrod, Casey, Mal, anyone was here. For all he knew, they might have pasts worse than his. Except Mal. She couldn't have done anything too terrible. He thought of Mal that first night. Mal on his first night back. Mal acting jumpy yesterday with Rich Skerritt. They needed to sort things out. And with his heart pounding like this, he wasn't about to sleep anytime soon. Hugh grabbed his flashlight and kick-started his scooter.

Wind gusted around him, calming him as he rode. Lightning flashed offshore. North of Captain Vic's, orange lights flashed in the bushes by the bluff. Hugh stopped. He was *not* imagining it this time. The light flickered more as Hugh moved. The warm orange of firelight. Figures moved in front of it. People. Enjoying a fire and probably a beer. So much for Antonio's duppies. Hugh rode on.

At Mal's place Hugh hid his scooter behind the hedge and walked to the cottage. He cut past the front window, headed for the kitchen door around back, away from prying eyes.

Faint music came from inside. Laughter? Hugh glanced through the gap in the curtains. Froze.

Mal knelt on the couch, her back to the window. Head back and black hair flowing over her bare shoulders, she straddled a man's pale legs. Chubby hands on her waist held her down as she rocked forward and back. The man's fingers dug into her tanned skin. Mal shifted sideways as the man raised his head, eyes closed and mouth open. Rich Skerritt.

Hugh couldn't look away. He forced his feet to move, stumbled back from the window. It all made sense now: Mal and Skerritt at the airport, Mal and Skerritt at the bar, Mal shooing Hugh away yesterday, Skerritt's hostility. She had strung Hugh along, enjoying the attention, but had had Rich Skerritt on the hook all the while.

Hugh squatted beside the road, breathing heavy, willing his pulse to slow. Trying not to vomit. Still seeing Mal riding Skerritt, his sausage fingers clawing at her smooth back.

Had she ever cared for Hugh? Or was she keeping him on hold in case things didn't work out with Skerritt? Coming back here, everything he had done on Blacktip Island had been based on Mal. On him and Mal. On a lie. He was an idiot. Anger at Mal flared, eddied, swirled back on himself.

Something splatted on his head. Then on his arm. Rain. Hugh didn't move. Maybe the rain would wash his idiocy from him.

A pulsing of tires and the syncopated *bwop-bwop-bwop* of a misfiring engine. Headlights rounded the curve. Hugh bowed his head, closed his eyes, waited for the car to pass. Instead, it slowed, stopped.

"Hugo! What you sitting in the road for?" The screech of rusty hinges, then Antonio knelt beside him. "Drunk? Get hit?"

Hugh waved him away without raising his head.

"Can't leave a shipmate here, not knowing if you okay." Antonio's hand was firm on Hugh's shoulder. "It's raining, y'know."

"I'm fine. Just thinking."

"Bad place to think, Hugo. Get run over thinking in the road." Antonio gave Mal's cottage a long look. "How 'bout I run you home."

Hugh stared at the shuddering S.U.V. He had promised himself he'd never again set foot in Antonio's deathtrap. But promises were fleeting on Blacktip Island. Dying in a fiery crash sounded great just then.

Antonio ground the car into gear, and they lurched down the road. Antonio kept uncharacteristically quiet, drove uncharacteristically straight. Hugh sat silent, barely registering the branches slapping past the open window.

"People on this island can be two-faced." Antonio broke the silence as they reached the turnoff to the house.

"You have no idea."

"See more than you think, Hugo. Selfish people, doing for themselves anyway they can. Can't let them keep you from trusting, though. Let that happen, 'selfish' wins."

Great. The craziest person on the island was talking sense to him. And was making sense. Hugh stepped inside his apartment, left the lights off. He wanted to go back to Mal's, kick the door in, tell her what he thought of her. And Skerritt. The vision of Mal straddling Skerritt returned. His stomach tightened. No, he couldn't go back.

9

After a sleepless night, Hugh stepped out the next morning into air thick from rain. His scooter was missing from outside his door. Someone had stolen the piece of junk? No. He had left it at Mal's. Antonio had given him a lift. Visions of Mal and Rich Skerritt tore through his head again. Hugh pushed them aside. He was late for work. Again. He would have to grab the scooter that afternoon. Or sooner, if Latner fired him for being late. Whenever he retrieved it, he'd give Mal hell when he did.

Hugh jogged down the muddy road as fast as he could in flop flops. Soon he was soaked with sweat and coated in pale limestone mud from the knees down. A buzzing, like a giant insect, sounded behind him, grew louder. Tires splashed through puddles, and a bright green scooter pulled even with him, Jerrod driving.

"Exercise's good for the soul, but this's a bit extreme," Jerrod said.

"I... lost track of my ride." Hugh leaned on his knees, tried to catch his breath.

"Ah. Penance run after a rough night?" Jerrod glanced at Hugh's scraped arms. "You crawl home?"

"Something like that. You gimme a lift?"

Hugh climbed behind Jerrod. The scooter wobbled as they started down the road, engine screaming with two people riding. Hugh's feet barely cleared the ground. The heels of his flip-flops scraped muddy gravel every time Jerrod hit a pothole. A group of people in tie-dyed Earth Federation t-shirts walking north stopped, stared, then laughed as the scooter buzzed past. When Jerrod finally stopped at Eagle Ray Cove, the other dive staff were arriving.

"The circus in town?" Casey laughed.

"I seen clown cars," Gage said, "But I never seen a clown scooter."

"Whatever gets me to work on time," Hugh said.

"The Lord does provide, brother." Jerrod gunned the scooter and buzzed away.

Hugh rinsed his legs and hurried after the other divemasters. With luck, he could get his scooter at lunch and have it out with Mal before she came to work.

At noon, though, Ger Latner stopped Hugh on the pier.

"You got something from the real world." Latner handed him a postal pick-up notice, a bright blue Tiperon government seal stamped across the name "Hugh Calloway."

"What is it?" Hugh felt cold, despite the sun. No one off-island knew Hugh Calloway.

"I look like a psychic?" Latner stomped back to the dive shop.

"You've the face of a scared rabbit, F.N.G.," Casey said from the *Skipjack*'s bridge. "It's just the post. Or is that reason for fright?"

"Hey, you can ride with me," Gage said. "I gotta pick up bags at the airstrip. The P.O.'s right behind the terminal."

Hugh followed Gage to the dive truck, Casey's words in his ears. Had Casey been digging into Hugh's background? Did he have anything to do with this mysterious package?

It was a slower trip north with Gage than with Casey. Steam rose from the muddy roadway now baking in the midday sun. A smoky haze hung above the tree line as they neared the construction site. At the site entrance, the people in tie-dyed shirts Hugh had seen that morning blocked the gravel track, Elena Havens at their center.

"Runway?" Elena yelled into a megaphone.

"*No way!*" The Earth Federation people chorused back.

"Runway?"

"*No way!*"

"What the hell?" Gage slowed to keep from splattering mud on the group. "Picketers on Blacktip?"

"They were hiking in this morning," Hugh said. "I think Elena's flying them down."

"Damn, boy, you just got here and you're already in the know!"

The airstrip was deserted except for the rusty Mercedes, top down. Gage walked to the terminal to ask about the bags. Hugh stepped around back to the post office, a six foot-square room with a chest-high wooden counter and a 'Dervil Conlee, Postmaster' nameplate to one side. A tall, graying man stood behind the counter.

"You have a package for me?" Hugh slid the notice across the counter.

"You Hugh Calloway?" The postmaster studied him.

"I... yeah." Hugh's heart raced. Was this a setup? He glanced at the door, half-expecting police to burst in.

"Good to know you!" Dervil gave Hugh a gap-toothed smile. "Welcome to Blacktip! Dermott and 'Tonio told me about you. You from Florida!"

"Why do you say that?" Hugh's pulse beat faster.

"Package from Tampa, Florida." Dervil set a shoebox-sized parcel on the counter and pointed to the address label, then to a blue Customs sticker. "Customs due on it, too. Be $2.65."

Hugh put a $5 bill on the counter with a shaking hand. Dervil looked as if Hugh had dropped a rattlesnake in front of him.

"Don't have change?" Dervil said.

"I have a one and…" Hugh dug for coins, "… forty-six cents."

"Goddom change!" Dervil snatched the $5 and ducked below the counter top.

Paper rustled. Coins jangled.

"Sonofabitching sixty-five cents." A gnarled hand rose, slapped two $1 bills on the counter. More cursing and coin rattling. The hand slapped a stack of coins next to the dollar bills. Dervil's head popped up, glaring at Hugh. "Two dollars and… sixty-five cents!"

He shoved the money at Hugh.

"That's what I owed you," Hugh said.

Dervil snatched the two dollars back.

"This is…" Hugh sorted through the pile of coins, "… seventy-eight cents."

"Sonofabitch!" Dervil snatched the parcel off the counter. "You come with the right goddom change, or don't come at all!"

"You bet." Hugh stepped back, glad the high counter was between him and the postmaster. "So the duty's $4.22?"

"Duty's $2.65! You take your goddom change and go!"

"But I need my package." Hugh pointed to the box under Dervil's arm. He had to see who the box was from and what was inside.

"Can't have it."

"You can't do that!"

"Do any goddom thing I want, sonofabitch come here haggling over duty! This is government fees, you know! You trying to cheat the government!"

The door creaked open behind Hugh.

Hugh spun. Behind him was the Mercedes driver. Faded khaki shorts and a frayed button-down shirt open at the collar.

"Hey, Dervil. What's up?" the man said.

"Sonofabitch arguing the price of duty!"

"Ah." The man winked at Hugh. Held out his hand. "Payne Hanover. Like 'hangover,' but without the 'g.' He's new, Dervil. What say we give him a break?"

Dervil looked skeptical, but set Hugh's parcel on the counter.

"You'll be at the fête, Dervil?" Payne set a letter on the counter, held out a handful of assorted coins.

"Oh, this fine weather does call for celebration."

Dervil picked out some coins, paused. Put two back. Plucked one more. Stamped the letter and dropped it in the 'Local' bin. He studied Hugh a moment more, then slid the box over to him.

Payne laughed.

"Comes a day born of the gentle south, and clears away from sick heavens all unseemly stains!" Payne waved a hand dramatically, quoting something. "Pick up the whole island." He faced Hugh. "You'll be there? Yes? You know Toad Hall?"

"I... *The Wind in the Willows*?" Was everyone on this island nuts?

"That's it! East coast, beach cottage up from Blacktip Haven. The beer's chilling, the pig's in the pit, the bonfire's set."

"What's the occasion?"

"Founding of the House of Hanover!"

"The... George III, Queen Victoria Hanovers?" If this scruffy beach bum was related to royalty, it didn't show.

"No, no. *My* house!" Payne eyed Hugh like he was reappraising a dusty find in an antique shop. "The whole island'll be there. Right, Jess?"

Jessie was squeezing through the doorway, coins rattling in her hand.

"I dunno." She looked away from Hugh. "If I am, I'll be a little late."

"Oh, we'll be going all night!" Payne squeezed past Hugh and Jessie and out the door.

"I see Elena got her protestors," Hugh said.

"And more on the way." Jessie eyed Hugh's parcel. "It's all over the internet."

Hugh squeezed past Jessie and stepped outside. The package labels were in Adam's handwriting. "Hugh" in quotation marks. Great. How had Adam found him? How did Adam know about "Hugh?" And what would he be sending? 'Sundries,' the Customs label read. The packing tape had been cut, resealed with white Customs tape. Great. The government knew what was inside. Hugh fought down panic.

"Hey, y'all give me a lift?" Jessie had followed Hugh out. "I'm supposed to go to the Sand Spit, but Elena's got the van out deploying her troops."

Gage lifted her bike onto the truck's bed, and Jessie climbed in the cab between Gage and Hugh.

"So what'd you get?" Jessie craned her head sideways to read the package labels. Gage peered across Jessie.

"Dunno." Hugh slid his hand to cover the return address. "I'll save it for later."

"You're not gonna open it *now?*"

Hugh didn't dare open it in front of them. There could be anything in the box. But not opening it would make them suspicious. Hugh said a silent prayer to any deity that might be listening and yanked the Customs tape off, making sure he tore off the address labels with it.

Inside, rumpled sheets of newspaper served as packing. *Tampa Tribune. St. Petersburg Times.* A plastic bag full of chocolate chip cookies. A bottle of aspirin. A box of condoms. Smart-ass Adam.

"Ooo! Cookies!" Gage grabbed the bag, took a cookie, passed the bag to Jessie.

Hugh barely noticed. The packing was the business section of both papers. He skimmed the headlines. 'Local Firm Investigated,' read one. 'SEC Probes Tampa Brokerage,' read another. Hugh stuffed the papers back in the box. His pulse boomed so loud he was amazed Gage and Jessie couldn't hear it. He wanted to pull the articles out, read them now, but he couldn't until he was safe at home.

Gage handed the cookies back to Hugh and dropped the truck into gear.

"They're all yours." Hugh waved the bag away. The last time Adam had given him chocolate chip cookies, the chocolate had been a laxative.

Jessie and Gage watched him, eyes questioning.

"What's with the crazy postmaster?" Hugh hoped they'd fall for the misdirection.

"What'd you do," Gage said, "ask him to make change?"

"All I had was a five…"

"Dervil hates math," Jessie said. "Give him a pile of coins and let him take what he wants."

"You piss off Dervil, your mail gets lost," Gage said. "A lot."

"But how's he figure postage?"

"It's whatever he says it is," Gage said. "Once he stamps your letter, you're good."

Gage slowed again as he passed the protestors, steered wide of multiple mud puddles.

"And Payne with the Mercedes?"

"Mr. Happy Hands?" Jessie rolled her eyes.

"Steady stream of drop-dead gorgeous model-types cycle through his place." There was admiration in Gage's voice. "Not a brain cell among 'em."

"So his party's for real?" Hugh said.

"Oh, yeah," Gage said. "Definitely go. Payne never stints. Great way to meet the island."

Hugh tried to smile, not sure he wanted to meet the island.

At the Sand Spit, Hugh helped Jessie lift her bike from the truck. Kitty Smarr sat at the outdoor bar. Next to her was her spiked-blond friend from the Ballyhoo in his pale blue Scuba Doo staff top. Kitty winked, waved at Hugh, then whispered to her friend. They both laughed.

Hugh climbed back in the cab. Gage, box open beside him, munched on a fresh cookie. Hugh snatched the box back, stuffed it in his pack.

"Kitty's giving you the big eye, Dude," Gage said.

"Yeah, I've met that part of the island," Hugh said. "You get us out of here?"

At the Eagle Ray dive shop, Ger Latner and Casey were grinning so big Hugh thought their faces would crack.

"How'd it go with Dervil?" Casey asked.

"That was the joke? Sending me to Mr. No-Change?"

"No more post for you, then?"

Feet shuffled behind them. Mickey Smarr stumbled onto the porch, eyes bloodshot. His polo shirt was untucked on one side.

"Seen Kitty?" Mickey's words slurred. He scanned the porch. Hugh and Casey shook their heads.

"She was headed for Elena's a bit ago," Latner said.

Mickey's eyes snapped into focus on Latner. "Good! Thanks, Ger!" He wove back toward the resort entrance.

"She was at Scuba Doo just now," Hugh said when Mickey had gone. "At the bar with her guy from the Ballyhoo."

Latner looked to Casey.

"Finn," Casey said. "You can't keep a thing like that to yourself, Mate. Could have been brilliant to see, Mickey bursting in on them. Again."

"She wasn't keeping it a secret," Hugh said.

"She never does." Casey walked down to the boats.

Then, end of the day, diving finished and *Skipjack* moored, Hugh was eager to head home and read Adam's articles. His scooter was still at Mal's, though. Angry as he was at her, he wasn't up for an argument. He had the energy to deal with one crisis at a time, and the box from Adam was more important than Mal sleeping with her boss. He swung past the bar to see if Mal was working. Jerrod was there, white hair wild, but otherwise showing no signs of his night terrors. Mal was working the night shift, then, and still at her place.

Hugh didn't have the time, the patience to walk home. Or to wait for Mal to arrive. He would snag the scooter, hope it started, and chance he didn't run into her.

He headed up the road, ready to step aside if he saw Mal coming. He reached her cottage. No signs of life in the place. She should be at work by now. Maybe she'd walked to the resort along the beach, was already at the bar with Jerrod. The scooter's rear wheel stuck out from behind the roadside hedge. Even if Mal was home, Hugh could grab it and be gone before she knew it. He stepped to the scooter, pulled the handlebars free and headed toward the road. Click of a door handle behind him.

"I was wondering when you were gonna get that." Mal smiled from the doorstep. "When'd you leave it there, anyway?"

"Last night. In the rain." Hugh kept walking, anger rising at the sound of her voice.

"You have time to get together the next day or so?" Mal followed Hugh to the road.

"No." Hugh gritted his teeth. If he hadn't seen her with Rich Skerritt, he'd still be falling for this cheery-voiced act of hers.

"We need to." Mal's voice dropped to the purr that had drawn Hugh in his first night with her. Her eyes were bright, as inviting as ever. She was working him, as sure as she had been working him that night. Mal put a hand on his scratched arm. "We need to reconnect."

Hugh snatched his arm away.

"Last time I saw you, you were connected to Rich Skerritt!"

It was the first time Hugh had seen Mal look surprised. Then her mouth tightened.

"So you're Peeping Hugh now?"

"No. I'm the cheap banjo you've been playing. I'm entertainment when your boss's off island?"

"You know *nothing* about me. What I do when you're not here is none of your business."

"You lied to my face. I came back because of you. And you let me."

"I *knew* it!" Mal's face took on a sly look. "No, Hugh, I don't like you the way you like me. But I do like you. And the only lying I've done is *for* you. I'm your only friend on this rock. And you need friends."

"Casey says there's no friends here, just allies."

"He your friend? Your ally? Uh huh, that's what I thought. Name one friend you have here besides me."

"Friends don't stab you in the back."

"On Blacktip, friends stab you in the back, the front, and anywhere else they see an opening. And I haven't stabbed you." Mal's sly look returned. "You have any idea how many calls for 'Blake Calloway' I've put off? How many times I've said there's no 'Blake' here?"

"Who?" Hugh steadied himself on the scooter. Who besides Adam had tracked him to Blacktip Island?

"I'm supposed to say, 'No one here by that name, but who's calling?' Really?"

"Same person each time?"

"Oh, so we *are* friends?"

"Not like you and Skerritt." Anger surged back, hotter than ever.

"How dare you, you spoiled little rich boy! You've always had Daddy and Daddy's money, haven't you? Or someone's money. This is the real world, Hugh. I'll take whatever opportunity I can to get to happily ever after."

"Then why not turn me in?"

"You know what entertains me? Watching you scramble to survive without your safety net."

"We're done."

Hugh stomped on the scooter's kick-start lever two, three times. The engine hacked, spewed blue smoke, and clattered to life. He rode away without looking back, hands aching from clenching the handlebars so tight. How could he not have seen what Mal was? Because he hadn't wanted to. And she had given him every reason to believe her. But why? She could have separated him from the cash, then turned him in any time. To watch him struggle? No, she wasn't so heartless as that. Mal wasn't a threat, but she wasn't completely on his side, either. And still he wanted her to be more than that.

Maybe it had been Adam calling for him. No one could know he was here. But no one should be mailing him packages, either. He had to see what was in this damn box, figure out his next move.

A clatter of sheet metal and engine valves sounded behind him. Hugh stopped, waved as Payne rattled past, splattering mud across Hugh's feet. Hugh rode on. Near the place where firelight had been the night before, the group of tie-dyed protestors walked back south along the road. There was no lodging this far south. Had it been their campfire he'd seen? He had assumed Elena's protestors would stay at Blacktip Haven. Maybe she couldn't afford to give away free rooms.

Once home, Hugh smoothed out the newspaper pages on the floor. Calloway, Olivetti, and Nieves was being investigated, yes. Both papers mentioned a rogue trader, but no names. No mention of charges being filed, though both said the authorities were looking for the person responsible. It was a warning from Adam, then.

But how had Adam found him? And so quickly? Hugh had chucked his credit cards, left his phone on the New Guinea-bound airliner, and hadn't used "Blake" on Blacktip Island since he'd come back. His passport, maybe, when he entered the Tiperons. No. There was no way Adam had access to the Tiperon Immigration computers.

Was Adam helping the investigators? Sending packages to every place Hugh had contacted those days before he ran, hoping Hugh would give himself away? Throwing in cookies and condoms as a joke, while secretly tipping Hugh off by adding the newspapers? That had to be it. If Adam knew Hugh was here, the Feds would, too, and they would have already hauled him back to the U.S. Hugh took a deep breath, then another. The knot inside him loosened. He was safe, so long as he didn't do anything stupid.

His best bet was to hide in plain sight. Payne's party would be perfect for that. Hugh would blend in, another divemaster on a backwater tropical island. Opportunities, Mal had said? Hugh would make the most of this one, meet more than the few nut cases he had seen so far. Maybe find someone who knew a pirate legend or two. Make some real friends, too. Or as real as he could without giving himself away. It would be good to relax, get his mind off this paranoia that everyone who talked to him was plotting against him.

10

Toad Hall was a pleasant twilight ride from Antonio's: up the west coast past Eagle Ray Cove, over the cross-island road that skirted the bluff's northern face, then up the island's east side. Campfires flickered in the underbrush north of Captain Vic's cottage. At the crossroad, Parrett's Nest perched lightless above the trees. Jessie was already at the party or still at work. As Hugh crossed the island, the first stars merged with Blacktip Haven's lights on bluff's top to his right. To the left the island's central pond spread, red-footed boobies circling above. Beyond the pond, the sky glowed from the burn pile, stretching sunset to the northern horizon.

Once across the island, Hugh turned north and found himself at a brigh-lit wooden compound tucked behind dense sea grapes. Rusty cars lined the road's sides. Music pulsed from inside the compound. Hugh took a deep breath to calm himself and stepped through the main breezeway into a terra cotta courtyard.

Toad Hall was a low, rambling cluster of a half dozen stand-alone rooms connected by covered breezeways to form a semi-circle facing the ocean. Five steps led down from the courtyard to a broad beach. A bonfire roared near the water's edge, lighting dozens of partygoers in flickering yellows and reds. A pit nearby held a halved fifty-five gallon drum filled with ice and drinks. Heat lightning flashed silent on the horizon.

"Hugh! Welcome!" Payne Hanover separated from the crowd. "You need a libation!" He handed Hugh a beer, dripping and cold from the ice, before Hugh could ask for a soda. "The pig's nestled snug in the next pit over." Payne waved his beer toward a pile of green palm fronds and a table tucked close against the brush higher up the beach. Smoke curled from under the fronds. A shift in the breeze brought the scent of roasting meat. Payne steered Hugh toward the nearest partiers.

"You know Alison and Lee." Alison smiled. Lee scowled. "And your neighbor, the good Cori."

"What makes me so good?"

"Oh, now. Every saint has a past and every sinner has a future. Right, Reverend Jerrod?"

"Reverend?" Hugh said.

"Former. Thanks, Payne."

"What are you now?" Hugh wasn't sure if they were joking.

"A drunk." Jerrod raised a plastic wine cup.

Hugh pushed aside his nervousness. He was here to mingle. Make friends. He excused himself, worked through the crowd, introducing himself as he went. Nods from Dervil and Captain Vic. Waves from Marina and Polly. Welcomes from dive staff, whose names he couldn't keep straight, from other resorts. Antonio and Dermott talked by the bonfire.

Frank and Helen Maples stood among a knot of neatly dressed people at the firelight's edge.

"I'm Hugh." He joined the group, hand extended.

"Of course." Frank Maples gave Hugh's hand a half shake.

"Ah. Casey's compatriot." Helen Maples gave him a thin smile.

The others nodded greetings, didn't introduce themselves. The Maples turned back to their little group.

Hugh looked from the Maples to the others. Who had he offended, and how?

"The island gentry can be a bit standoffish with newcomers." Payne pulled Hugh back into the growing crowd of locals. "They'll warm up to you in a year or three."

"No resort guests here?"

"Not unless you brought one. You don't have to smile and make nice unless you want to. Ah! Here's Finn! Runs dive ops at Scuba Doo."

"The eel-puller! All right! " Kitty Smarr's friend bobbed his head in greeting. "Welcome to Blacktip Island! *Bam!* Yank an eel in front of the island's biggest reef Nazi!"

Lee choked, shot beer out his nose.

Hugh forced a smile. Great. People thought he was a reef trasher. And how did everyone on this island know everything?

"Hey, it happens." Finn was still grinning. "The key's how you followed up. Went back out the next day, head high? There you go!" He tapped his beer bottle against Hugh's. "Getting out, mixing, this's good, too. Blacktip only makes you crazy if you let it."

"He's right." Jessie was suddenly beside Hugh, out of breath, face flushed and sweaty, as if she had been running. "Scary as it is, this is our support group."

Lee looked like he'd been insulted, but wasn't sure how. Finn and Payne laughed.

"Ah, the lovely Jessica, come down from the mountaintop to thunderclap us in the face!" Payne said. "Delighted you could make it."

"We crazies have to stick together." Jessie sipped at a cup of orange juice. "Besides, Elena gave us all the night off. I had to go somewhere."

Payne laughed again, put his arm around her waist.

Jessie twisted away, smiled at Hugh. She walked to the water's edge, leaving Payne open mouthed. Hugh followed her.

She wanted an escort to keep Payne at bay? Jessie stopped when the foam rolled over her bare feet.

"I'm glad you came," she said.

"I never miss a therapy session," Hugh said. "What'd you do, run all the way here?"

"Oh! No. It's just the humidity, is all." She sipped her drink, avoided Hugh's eyes.

"If you don't like Payne, why come?" It had been humid dancing at the Ballyhoo, too, but Jessie hadn't looked this flushed.

"Payne? Oh, he's… well, a pain, but a pussycat."

"Especially when you've got someone else for cover?"

"When I…? No! That's not what this is." Jessie paused. "That's genius, though. We can have a do over, and it'll save me from having to dodge him."

"No Twenty Questions?"

"Promis juré." She crossed her heart with her index finger.

"I have no clue what that means."

"It means no questions unless you ask them."

"So… how's Parrett's Nest?"

"It definitely dances in the wind. More of a waltz than a rumba." Jessie flashed a quick smile. "Dry as a bone inside, though."

"And all the French?"

"Family, remember?" She tugged at her necklace again. "And the undergrad in Medieval lit. I'm a nerd."

"And that led to law school?"

"No, my folks did that."

"So what'd you *want* to do?"

"Research. I was all set to parse the whole *Roman de la Rose.*"

"I… a Roman rose?" Did everyone here speak in riddles?

"Medieval French poem." Jessie laughed. "It defined a way of life for centuries. Gave us chivalry and questing knights and troubadours."

Hugh imagined jesters in pointed shoes and belled caps.

"The *Romance of the Rose* was *the* quest song," Jessie said. "The first time I read it, I just fell in love. I mean, what girl doesn't dream of a knight? Or want to be one? Eleanor of Aquitaine encouraged the troubadours…"

Firelight danced across her face, flashed in her eyes as she talked. Hugh understood little of it, but was caught up by her enthusiasm. She could have been one of the singers she talked about, her voice rising and falling in a sort of melody, her hands flying like she was playing an invisible instrument. Hugh nodded, trying to keep up.

"Oh my God! I'm boring you to tears!" Jessie said.

"No. It's cool. It's just… unexpected."

"History's not your thing."

"More modern history," Hugh said. Would Jessie know anything about pirate lore? "I'm still trying to get a handle on Blacktip Island's story."

"Like all the locals with the same four last names?"

"Like the first settlers and where they lived and how they managed to fight off raiders, that sort of thing."

"You watched too many B movies growing up."

"No, Blacktip was a big buccaneer hangout. Blackbeard or Bluebeard or Redbeard or someone could've buried treasure on this beach."

Jessie rolled her eyes.

"To hear Elena tell it, locals've scoured this island for ages. Any treasure that might have been here is long gone." Jessie gave Hugh a sly smile. "What would you do if you found buried treasure?"

"Undo some mistakes. Make things right."

"You're on a quest." She gave him a measured look.

"I'm making small talk. Playing what-if." So much for getting Jessie off her Middle Ages jag.

"No, you've got a good heart." Jessie's face reddened. She looked down.

Was Jessie flirting? Had all her questions at the Ballyhoo been flirting, too?

"Kitty Alert!" Marina's voice sounded behind them.

Kitty Smarr strolled across the Toad Hall courtyard, leopard-print skirt swaying. She greeted partygoers without breaking stride as she stepped to the beach. She nodded to the people ringing the fire, then threw her arms around Finn's neck and kissed him long and hard. Finn picked her up by the waist, spun her around. Kitty scanned the crowd again, daring a reproach.

"She's in rare form tonight," Marina said.

Kitty and Finn kissed again.

"Who's ready for charred pig flesh?"

Payne flung smoking palm fronds aside, sending a cloud of smoke and the scent of roast pork rolling over the beach. The crowd around the fire swarmed to the table, where Payne chopped the meat, mounded it onto trays. Kitty and Finn walked down the beach, away from the firelight.

A distant boom, then a faint rumble, as if thunder had caught up with the heat lightning. Partygoers went silent, looked up for clouds, held hands out for raindrops. Stars winked in a clear sky.

"I ordered a storm-free night, and by God that's what we'll have!" Payne shouted at the sky.

Guests laughed. Conversations resumed.

Hugh and Jessie grabbed plates and settled on the bottom courtyard step, Hugh with a fresh beer and Jessie with a vodka and orange. Jessie ate in silence, finally talked out. Hugh relaxed, though he wasn't sure what to make of Jessie.

"So why Blacktip, if you don't like pirates?" Hugh kept his tone casual.

"Oh, I never said I didn't like pirates." The sly smile again. "And I'm on a bit of a quest myself…"

A shout came from above and behind them. Mickey Smarr, Hawaiian shirt half-buttoned, staggered down the steps, kicking Hugh and Jessie as he passed.

"Where's m'slut wife?" Mickey tripped, caught himself, stumbled on. The crowd parted.

"Lit like a bloody torch, he is." Casey stood behind Hugh and Jessie, grinning. A blonde guest from the dive boat was with him. His usual earthy smell was mixed with a hint of diesel.

"You just get off work?" Hugh sniffed at Casey.

"What? Oh. Fueling the truck. Pump didn't shut off. Ran into Mickey on the way. Right Cecilia?"

"Cassandra." Casey's date giggled.

"You brought him here?" Hugh glanced around for Kitty.

"It was that or let him drink-drive the resort van into the booby pond."

"Kitty and Finn just left," Hugh said.

Down the beach Mickey wobbled to the fire. Casey leaned closer to Hugh, eyes on Jessie.

"You finally working this, Mate?" He gave Hugh a knowing wink.

"We're talking."

"Uh huh." Casey slipped an arm around Cassandra's shoulders. "Care for a drink, love?"

By the fire pit, Payne pulled Mickey back from the flames.

"You don't see her here, right?" Payne's voice drifted up to them. "So what say we get some food in you, relax, and enjoy a beautiful evening?"

"Doan see that son-a-bitch Finn here, either!" Mickey spoke slowly, enunciating each syllable. "Scuba Doo truck out front, though. Kitty's shoes in th'seat!"

Payne led Mickey away from the fire.

"C'mon, Mick. We'll go up to the house and sort this out."

Mickey's rum reek washed over Hugh as the two walked back past. Mickey's eyes were unfocused. Payne grinned like a circus ringmaster.

"See? Master Payne has him well in-hand," Casey said. "How are you tonight, Jess?"

"Good." Hugh said. He was enjoying the evening and didn't need Casey, or Casey's sarcasm, ruining it. And Hugh knew just the thing to chase him away. "We've been discussing medieval poetry."

"Silver-tongued charmer, you are," Casey said. "Know just what a woman wants to hear, eh?"

"I find it fascinating." There were swords in Jessie's voice.

"Then F.N.G. here is your man. If you can stay awake." He winked at Cassandra.

Another boom, then a crackling overhead. Blue and yellow light washed over the beach.

"Ooo! Fireworks!" Jessie said. "Of course Payne has fireworks."

Partiers watched the starbursts brightening the sky. Red-footed boobies, startled by the light and noise, launched from the trees by the pond and wheeled above Toad Hall, silhouetted by the rockets.

"That's got to be what coral looks like, right?" Jessie said.

"Without the light and the fire and the noise, sure," Hugh said. "You've never seen coral?"

"On TV." Jessie's eyes never left the exploding fireworks. Her upturned face was tinted blue and white with the skyrockets. "I can't even swim."

"What are you doing on a middle of nowhere sand bar?"

"I told you. I'm on a quest."

"You should learn to swim, or to float, at least," Hugh said. "That might come in handy."

Shouts echoed from Toad Hall. Kitty Smarr exploded from a small room, hair wild, tugging on a Scuba Doo DIVE STAFF tank top. Mickey was on her heels.

"You whore!"

"That's it! Say it in front of everyone!" Kitty spun mid-step.

Mickey grabbed at her wrist. Missed. A skyrocket burst green and yellow above them.

"Flirting in public 'sbad enough!" Mickey yelled. "But a sneak over here, to actually *do* that with… with… *that!*"

"I did not sneak."

"Hey, beast, everybody knows you don't care." Finn strolled from the room, shirtless.

A boom sounded behind the house. A silvery brocade crackled low over the rooftops.

Mickey stepped toward Finn, then rounded on Kitty.

"You have any r'spect at all for me?"

"No." Kitty's voice was flat, her face emotionless.

Mickey swayed toward her, hand raised. Payne appeared, caught Mickey's arm, pulled him away from Kitty and Finn.

"What a show!" Casey laughed.

"You brought him here knowing this would happen!" Jessie looked shocked.

"A kindness, really," Casey said. "Keeps things self-contained."

"What if you need someone to look after you someday?"

"They will. Or they won't. Either way, I'm good."

"A tough guy for a tough island, is that it?"

"That's it exactly, Love." Casey made a half bow, palms out.

"You two lose a fight with a cat?" Jessie glanced from Casey's hands to Hugh's.

Casey's arms had the same scratch marks as Hugh's. Hugh stuffed his free hand in his pocket. Casey put his hands behind his back, studied Hugh.

"Been exploring, have we?" Casey said.

"I fell. Out back of Antonio's..."

A shout came from above. Mickey teetered at the top of the steps, arms windmilling as he tried to regain his balance. He tripped, stumbled down the steps in a semi-controlled fall. Hugh started to duck aside, too late. Mickey slammed gut-first into Hugh's lowered shoulder. They balanced against each other for a moment, Mickey bent double over Hugh's back. Then Mickey hiccupped, gurgled, spewed rum and pork over Hugh. Hugh shoved him away. Payne appeared again, caught Mickey before he hit the ground. Jessie and Cassandra jumped clear, noses wrinkled. Casey bent double laughing.

"I am so sorry." Payne grimaced at Hugh's back. "Thank you for catching him, but... here, help me wrangle him back inside and we'll get you cleaned up."

Hugh and Payne half-dragged Mickey up the steps.

"Love you, man," Mickey mumbled.

"Great, Mick. You vomited on my friend." Payne walked them to the courtyard's far end, away from lights and guests.

"Too good t'me. Both you. Not like m'whore wife." His voice caught. Hugh pushed him away, expecting more vomit. But Mickey was crying.

They lowered him into a chaise lounge, rolled him on his side.

"There's a shower in there." Payne pointed to the nearest building. "Towels on the wall. I'll find some fresh clothes. God, I'm sorry."

Hugh waved him away, stepped into a small bedroom with an attached bath. He took his time showering, scrubbing his back until his skin hurt, not caring if he burned out a hundred water pumps. When the water finally ran cold, Hugh stepped from the shower. His clothes were gone, replaced by a fresh t-shirt and cargo shorts.

On the patio he found Payne spraying an unconscious Mickey with a garden hose. Mal stood beside him, a stack of towels in her arms and a smile playing across her face. Mal gave Hugh a long look, then set the towels on the terrace, squared them with the tiles. She took a photo of Mickey with her phone. Then another.

"Rinsing the worst from him," Payne said. "He'll sleep it off here just fine."

"Anything else you need, just let me know, Payne." Mal's voice took on the sugary tone Hugh knew too well.

Payne gave her a quick bow, then looked to Hugh.

"I'll make this up to you…"

"Keep him away from me." Hugh wanted away from Mickey. Away from Mal, too, and the flutter in his stomach when he saw her.

Mal fell into step with Hugh.

"If Mickey was a wildebeest, the lions would've had him ages ago," she said.

"I feel sorry for him," Hugh said.

"Oh, please," Mal's voice was full of disgust.

"Was he a friend or an ally?"

"He's a pawn who left himself exposed." Mal's eyes bored into Hugh. "Don't leave yourself exposed."

"A warning from the queen?"

"We are friends, you know."

They were back at the steps then. The crowd below had grown since Hugh left. The bonfire crackled higher, whirling sparks into the dark sky. Near the steps Jessie, Casey, and Cassandra were still talking. Hugh rejoined them, ignored Mal frowning down from the courtyard.

"You certain you're completely cleaned?" Casey made a show of sniffing at Hugh.

Cassandra giggled.

"How's Mickey?" There was concern in Jessie's eyes.

"Out cold. Payne's looking after him."

"Was." Casey nodded toward the courtyard above. Next to Mal, Payne was looking down on the party, hands on his hips, nodding approval.

"We'll talk about your explorations tomorrow, Mate," Casey whispered in Hugh's ear. "We'll leave you alone, then," Casey said louder. He guided Cassandra down the beach.

"Another drink?" Jessie asked. She raised her near-empty cup.

"No. I've had all the fun I can stand for one evening." Hugh shuddered thinking of Mickey barfing down his back. Of Casey knowing he was exploring caves. "I'm headed home."

"Good luck... on your quest." Her gray eyes searched his. Anxious.

Flirting or no, she was an odd one. Hugh climbed the steps and crossed the Toad Hall courtyard. At the road he pulled his scooter from a tangle of island bikes. The glow from the runway site seemed brighter now in the full dark.

Hugh was glad for the slow ride home. He had been vomited on and threatened, but the night had gone well. He had patched things up with Jessie, and anyone from off-island looking for a fugitive wouldn't give Hugh a second glance.

He understood Mal better now, too. She wanted Mickey's job. That was why she had hooked up with Rich Skerritt. Why she had taken pictures of Mickey passed out. And she wanted Hugh on her side. He was an idiot not to have seen it. He would avoid her, as much as he could. Yet still something jumped inside of him at the thought of her.

At Antonio's all the lights were off except one in his apartment. Strange, since he never left lights on. Hugh stepped inside and froze. Things were out of place. A clothes drawer was partly open, with a t-shirt sticking out. Mal's chess piece was overturned on the nightstand. The bed sheet was untucked from one corner. Someone had been here. Had searched the place.

Hugh started for the bed. Stopped himself. Whoever had done this might be outside watching, waiting for him to check on the money, give away its hiding place. But he had to look, make sure it was still here. Hugh drew the blinds, clicked off all but the bathroom light, then, quietly as he could, pulled the bed from the wall and peeled back enough paneling to slip his arm in. His fingers slid across the books' rough covers. He felt inside them. The wrapped money was still there. Hugh didn't dare take it out to count it. He didn't need to. If someone had found it, they would have taken it. Hugh pressed the paneling back in place and slid the bed against it.

Whoever had been here had waited until Hugh left for Payne's party, then ransacked the place. Someone who knew, or suspected, he had something valuable hidden. Someone in a hurry. Or someone out to spook Hugh, get him panicked enough to move the stash. But who? Someone not at the party. Or who had come late.

Mal knew about the money, but she would have taken her pawn back. If she had seen it. Antonio, Jerrod, Dermott, and Cori had been at Payne's when Hugh got there. So had Lee. Or had Lee come late? Casey had arrived late, too. But Casey didn't know Hugh had anything valuable. Or had it been a thief rummaging through the new guy's stuff to see if there was anything worth stealing? The thought felt hollow, like wishful thinking.

Whoever it was, moving the cash to a cave was off the table now, if someone was watching his place. And he couldn't go to the police. Or ask any questions that might get the island gossiping about why his place had been ransacked.

A scraping sound came from outside the kitchen window. A branch on the tin roof, maybe. Or a footstep. Hugh fumbled for a weapon. The butcher knife was too much - he wanted to defend himself, not kill someone. He grabbed a frying pan and his flashlight and charged outside, pan back and ready to strike. There was no one there, and no obvious footprints in the dirt. Hugh played the light beam through the underbrush. Nothing. He stepped back inside.

He had to secure the place as best he could, try to get some sleep. Hugh changed into fresh shorts and shirts, then folded Payne's clothes and stashed them at the bottom of his clothes drawer. Who would have thought there would be thieves on such a small island? He latched the sliding glass door, pulled all the pots and pans from the cupboard, then doused the light so anyone outside couldn't see him. He stacked the pans ankle high against the door. If someone jimmied the latch and came in, they'd stumble over the pans in the dark, give Hugh plenty of warning. He squatted by the door in the darkness, back to the wall and weapons in hand. If someone came in, he'd snap on the flashlight, blind them, whack them with the pan.

It might be a blessing in disguise, really, the break-in. If the thief was satisfied there was no money here, then leaving it here was the best way to keep it hidden. As for the thief, he'd see who acted suspicious the next day. Track down his mystery burglar and get some answers.

11

Antonio was pounding the new water pump with a pipe wrench when Hugh stepped out for work in the morning. Hugh wanted to ask for a lock for his sliding door, but couldn't. If he asked for a lock, Antonio would ask why, and word of the break in would spread. Hugh didn't want his mystery vandal to think anyone was onto him. Or her.

"You set for your visitors, Hugo?" Antonio's eyes went vacant, like he was seeing through Hugh.

"Visitors?" Antonio knew Hugh's place had been tossed? And who had done it?

"They be here soon, y'know. Seen it just now. Waking dream."

"Day after a big party, Antonio?" Hugh relaxed. "Sure it's not the rum?"

"No, no. This's the Sight. Guests from off island."

"I'll keep an eye out." Hugh kicked the scooter started, trying not to laugh. Antonio truly thought he was psychic, but he couldn't even get Hugh's name right.

Hugh rode up the coast road thinking of ways to question Lee without making him suspicious. It had to be Lee. Or Hugh wanted it to be, anyway. Casey would be a tougher nut to crack. And Mal even harder. Hugh turned into the Eagle Ray Cove parking lot hoping Lee would be waiting again. Instead, the island police car was parked at the resort entrance. The lobby, usually bustling in the morning, was deserted. Hugh walked on toward the pier, looking for other staff.

Outside the dive shop, a crowd of resort staff had gathered, Police Constable Marquette's head and blue cap at its center. Had there been other break-ins? Or was the constable looking for Hugh? He kept his head down. If the constable was here for him, he wanted to find out before Marquette saw him. At the crowd's edge, Alison stood on tiptoes, straining to see. Hugh slid beside her.

"What's going on?" he whispered.

"Dude! Shh! Something about the new runway!" Alison whispered. "I think Marquette's busting Casey, but I can't see. Or hear."

"That's all?" Hugh stood tall, scanned the crowd.

"The cop's grilling your buddy and you say, 'That's all?' Seriously?"

"He's not my buddy."

"Whatever. Here, lift me up!"

Alison climbed on Hugh's back, straining to see over the crowd. Hugh pushed his way closer.

"Lean left." Alison wiggled to see around Hugh's head.

The constable had Casey aside on the dive shop porch.

"… and where were you yesterday evening, Mr. Piper?" Police Constable Marquette flipped to a fresh sheet in his notebook.

"Toad Hall. Home."

"Witnesses can vouch for that?" The constable studied Casey's scraped hands and legs.

"Only half the island."

The staff around him nodded.

"I came with Mickey, had a laugh with my mate Hugh," Casey pointed to Hugh, stifled laugh at Alison perched on Hugh's back. "Then I left with Cassandra, here. We spent the night on my boat. Right, Love?"

Casey slid an arm around Cassandra's waist, nodded toward the catamaran cross the Sound.

"Oh, yes!" Cassandra giggled.

The constable's eyes went from Cassandra to Hugh and Alison, then back to Casey.

"Did you and… your guest… visit the construction site?"

"We had other things to do. Look, tell me what you think I did. I'll do all I can to help you."

"You were nowhere near the construction site last night?"

"After a black eye and your A.S.B.O.? You must be joking!"

"This is no joke," Marquette said. "And no time for games, looking for stolen fertilizer and drug fields." He gave Casey a long, measured stare. "I have my eye on you, Mr. Piper."

P.C. Marquette flipped to the front of his notebook.

"Now, where would I find Mr. Mickey Katz."

"In his office. If you can wake the dead."

Casey walked down the pier. The dive staff trailed behind him.

"Got a monkey on your back, Boy," Gage laughed. "That high as you could climb, Ali?"

"Only way to see what was happening." Alison slid from Hugh's back. "Only I still couldn't hear."

"Big-ass explosion," Gage said. "Blew a crater smack in the middle of the track. Marquette thinks someone set it off."

"Who'd blow up empty land?" Marina joined them.

"Drunk workers, on accident, duh," Alison said. "Or tie-dyed hankie-heads on purpose."

"Those hippies couldn't blow their own noses without help," Gage said. "Some smoker flicked a butt too close to a gas can, is all."

"Elena put them up to it, then, you reckon?" Alison ignored Gage.

"She's not that crazy," Marina said.

"Oh, she's a nutter," Casey said. "And loves stirring hornets' nests."

Hugh hopped onto the *Skipjack*'s bow. Across the pier Lee was aboard the *Barjack,* eyeing the *Skipjack.* He looked away when he saw Hugh watching him.

"Been searching for pieces of eight, have you, young Jim Hawkins?" Casey smirked at Hugh from the helm.

"You find what you were looking for?" Hugh had wanted to tackle Lee first, but Casey had given him an opening. If Casey had been in Hugh's apartment, it would show on the man's face.

"The red herring won't do, F.N.G. Don't dodge the question." Casey's expression didn't waver.

"That dive truck gets you all over the island, doesn't it?"

"You young Sherlock now? Helping the nice policeman?" Casey hopped down, stood nose-to-nose with Hugh, his decaying smell overpowering. "Where I go, with or without a truck, is none of your concern."

"It is when there's big tire tracks outside my place." A bluff, and it gave away too much, but Hugh needed Casey rattled. "And when my door's pried open."

"Why in hell would I go to your grotty house?" Casey's scorn shifted to anger. "Show Cassandra the slums? Think I'm shadowing you, eh? I'll do you a favor, save you years of wasted time. There's no treasure to find. Not buried on any beach, not stashed in any caves, not anywhere but in every F.N.G.'s sperm-and-stupidity stoked imagination."

If Casey was acting, he was doing a great job. He hadn't been in Hugh's house. But lying about island treasure hunting being a waste of time, judging by his scraped hands and his earthy smell.

"That's just what you'd say if you wanted me to stop looking."

"You'll want antibiotic cream for the cuts." Casey's face went guarded. "Buy a case. Nasty stuff down underground."

Hugh went below to greet the guests. Lee it was. In spite of Latner's warning. Lee had to have thought he would find something important enough. It wouldn't matter if he were fired. Hugh could use that against him.

Casey was in a foul mood after the constable's questions and Hugh's talk. He cut off anyone who asked about the runway or about the island police.

"It's crap, talk of a bomb," he snapped at one guest. "It's a construction site, with a bonfire burning day and night. They're surprised something exploded?"

"But the policeman…" the man started.

"Is useless," Casey said. "Except perhaps to sober Mickey up."

At midday, with boats re-tanked, Hugh and the other dive staff headed up for lunch. At the resort entrance, Mickey and Kitty stood side-by-side facing the road, neatly dressed and sunglasses in place. Kitty wore a leopard-print scarf over her hair, knotted under her chin, and a matching mini skirt. She and Mickey stared straight ahead at the dirt roadway. Pink polka dot luggage stood stacked between them.

"Anyone *else*?" Mickey's voice came faint.

Casey edged closer. Marina, Alison, and Lee followed. Hugh hesitated, sick at the pain in Mickey's voice. Then, drawn by a morbid curiosity, he stepped closer, too.

"Any *place* I should know about? On the bar? My desk?"

"Our bed." Kitty's voice hissed like escaping steam. "Bunch of times. You weren't using it."

Mickey groped for Kitty's hand without looking. She pulled away at his touch.

The resort van pulled into the parking area, dust roiling. Antonio climbed out.

"If you leave…" Mickey's voice cracked.

"If?"

"… don't come back."

"You wish!"

At a nod from Kitty, Antonio slung the bags into the van. Kitty straightened her sunglasses, climbed in the van, and slammed the door without looking back. Antonio slid behind the wheel and drove away.

"Mickey? You okay?" Casey put a hand on the manager's shoulder.

"No… I… sure. Whatever." Voice flat.

A familiar numbness seeped through Hugh, bringing back all the misery of his last days with Tess. Mickey was teetering at the edge of a bottomless void. Hugh wanted to reach out, ease Mickey's hurt, but he was still too off-balance. If he was close when Mickey fell, Mickey would take Hugh down with him.

Marina put her arm around Mickey's shoulders and walked him into the resort office. Hugh grabbed food with the others and retreated to the bar deck. He sat opposite Lee, studying the little divemaster. Lee wouldn't make eye contact, but that wasn't unusual.

At the bar, staff and locals shouted theories about what had happened at the runway.

"Rich Skerritt probly did it himself," Dermott grumbled. "For insurance. Rafe Marquette asked me about that, y'know."

"That's near slander." Mal glared at Dermott. "Besides, once they round up all those protestors, one'll crack."

"Uh uh," Antonio said. "Duppies angry with us tearing things up. Striking back."

A shout came from behind Mal. Mickey pushed through the crowd, then past Mal. He grabbed a bottle of rum and staggered back to the manager's office, oblivious to the surprised guests.

Mal smiled, took a tab from beneath the register, scribbled something and slid it back.

Hugh's gut tightened. How could anyone so beautiful be so treacherous? Mal circled the deck, gliding from guest to guest. A headshake sent her dark hair rippling across her shoulders. Hugh stood to go back to the boat, watching Mal move.

Mal looked at him, smiled, her eyes inviting and cautioning at the same time. Hugh missed a step, recovered, retreated down the boardwalk.

"Fancy Mal, do you?" Lee dropped into step beside Hugh.

"No," Hugh said. "She's got it in for Mickey, is all."

"Ah, Blake the Hero saved Mickey at Payne's eh?"

Hugh tensed at his first name. Lee knew more than he had let on.

"Now you're carrying on looking out for him?" Lee kept on. "That's precious. And now you'll scamper home to hide? Like last night?"

"You following me?"

"It's as if you don't like talking to pretty girls," Lee said. "Or are hiding more than your name."

Hugh's face burned, but he kept his features frozen. Lee knew Hugh's name, that Hugh was running from something, but that was all. Lee probably had no idea what he had been looking for at Hugh's. But Hugh needed proof Lee had been there before he could rat the man out.

"Find anything interesting?" Hugh kept his voice even.

"Oh, I find interesting things all the time," Lee lowered his voice as they neared the dive shop.

Latner stepped from the shop, hands on his hips, scowled at Lee. Lee gave Hugh a wink and jogged ahead down the pier.

Hugh spent the afternoon wracking his brain for what to do about Lee. He could corner him at the day's end. But if he hit Lee, it would confirm Lee's suspicions and land Hugh in jail. But there was nothing to stop Lee from searching Hugh's place again, more thoroughly, some day Hugh was working and Lee wasn't.

Hugh had to hide the cash someplace Lee would never look. A cave. Moving the money was risky, but it was riskier leaving it where it was for Lee to find.

At day's end Hugh raced home quick as the scooter would take him, hunched low over the handlebars more speed. He would stuff his pack with all the rope he had, grab his headlamp, and slip into the brush before any of his neighbors knew he was there. If he could find a well-hidden cave, he could stash the money there early next morning before work.

When he turned off at Antonio's, Lettuce, Turnip, and Pea erupted from the roadside bushes, bounded beside him, barking, as he sputtered uphill. At the house, Cori stood out front talking to Jessie. Hugh stopped the scooter, and Cori's dogs swarmed over him. Cori yelled until the dogs quieted and she could grab their collars.

"We'll leave you two alone." Cori grinned at Hugh and dragged the dogs inside her place.

"I am so sorry," Jessie said before Hugh could speak.

"About...?" The dogs? That she was here?

"Everything. I mean..." She scanned his face. "Last night. I crossed a line..."

"Oh, I couldn't follow most of it, but that Roman Rose business is nothing to apologize for." Hugh stepped around her. She needed to go so he could pack his caving gear.

Jessie looked puzzled, followed him.

"I heard you were questioned," she said. "This morning. By the police."

"Casey was. No reason to question me. How'd you know?"

"People exaggerate so much on this island," Jessie said. "The constable's been at Elena's all afternoon. It sounded like you were *grilled*. I'm glad you didn't have to go through that."

"Sure. Thanks." At the sliding glass door, Hugh turned to keep Jessie from coming any farther. "Was there something else you wanted?"

"No, I just… to clear the air." She peered past him, through the glass door. "I've never seen this place. 'Tonio told me it was gone before you even took it. What's it like inside?"

"Like Parrett's, just sturdier." Hugh stepped sideways to block her view. Why would she not take the hint?

"Who's your decorator, the junk man?" Jessie laughed.

"I need to go. You mind?"

"Oh! I'm sorry."

Jessie's face reddened. She half-ran back to a bike leaning against a tree and rode away.

Hugh watched the drive for several minutes, making sure she was really gone before he stepped inside. He walked out a few minutes later in jeans and sneakers, with his overflowing pack on his back. The creaking sound came from above again, but the treetops weren't moving. The old house was settling, maybe. Or Antonio's duppies really did exist. There was no sign of Cori or the other lodgers. No sign of Jessie or Lee watching at the clearing's edge, either. Hugh slipped into the jungle behind the house as quickly as he could.

He would work his way farther north today, farther back in the brush from where he'd already explored. Hugh stopped every few minutes, crouched down, scanned behind him, listening for anyone following. Nothing. He came to Lee's cap, still marking his starting point, and cut inland. The ironshore underfoot became sharper, more broken as he went. It crunched under Hugh's sneakers, bit into the soles, like he was hiking across shark teeth. This had to be one of the places Jerrod had warned about, where the rock was so porous it could crumble under the slightest weight. Hugh slowed, grabbed tree limbs to steady himself, tested each step. A misstep here would be painful. A fall could be fatal. If the new runway site was like this, he was surprised it would support the heavy equipment there.

Ahead and to his right, the underbrush grew in a dense thicket. That meant water, maybe a hole leading down to the water table. Hugh pulled a swath of branches aside. Sure enough, at the bushes' center was a four-foot-wide hole dropping straight down. This could be perfect. There was no sign of anyone being here in years, and no one would pick their way across this ragged ironshore on a whim. Hugh tied one end of his rope around a tree trunk and tossed the rest down the hole. He clicked on his headlamp and shinnied in.

The headlamp cast a faint oval on rough stone fifteen, twenty feet below. The floor was covered in limestone. Rubble from the ground above had crumbled to form the shaft. Hugh's feet touched bottom. He spun in a slow circle, playing his light around him.

He was in a cavern larger than the others he'd found. Rubble covered the floor, fallen from the eroding ceiling. Knee-high tunnels opened ahead of him. Jerrod's warning about crumbling rock foremost in his mind, Hugh shuffled forward. With the rock so crumbly, the shaft he had dropped down had probably opened in the last few decades, far too late for 18th century buccaneers to have lowered treasure down it. But this could still be a great place to hide his cash. He would find a good nook, climb out, then bring the cash back later. Rubble crunched under his sneakers, giving the sensation the floor itself was cracking.

Hugh played the headlamp's beam across the nearest tunnel eight feet ahead, its opening a rough limestone arch choked with cobwebs. The beam bounced as he picked his way across the uneven floor. More rock crackled underfoot. The limestone trembled beneath him. Hugh shifted his weight backwards. Too late. The floor crumbled. Hugh clutched at jagged rock, missed, fell in a cascade of stone that sent his headlamp flying. He landed pack-first on a mound of broken rock, breath knocked out of him and teeth jarred. More rubble cascaded around him. The headlamp landed beside him, throwing its beam through a veil of dust. Hugh wiggled his hands, then his feet. Good. His back wasn't broken. He picked up the light, checked himself for injuries. Torn pants, scraped legs, a cut on his left arm, the grit of chipped teeth and the metallic taste of blood, but nothing worse.

Hugh panned the light around him. He was in a smaller cavern. The hole he had fallen through arched ten feet above him, and the curved walls made climbing to it impossible. He had done it this time, all right. He was who-knew-how-deep underground in a cave no one knew about. And no one knew to look for him. The headlamp flickered, went out. Great. Hugh smacked it and it came back on. There had to be another way out. He shined the light around the cavern's edges. The only option was a low opening to his left, just big enough to crawl into, its edges water-carved smooth.

Hugh strapped the headlamp on his forehead, brushed spiders and webs away, and peered inside. The tunnel ran straight and level as far as the beam reached. He couldn't go back. He had to go forward and hope for the best. Hugh crawled into the tunnel, headlamp casting a bright oval on the floor in front of him.

The way ran straight for what seemed like forever, with no side passages big enough to fit into. Then it turned, narrowed. The light went off again. Hugh whacked it three, four times, and it flickered back on. There was a faint vibration now, a low sound on the verge of forming words. Flowing water? No, the island had no streams. Wind outside? That was good. There might be an exit big enough for him to get out. Hugh crawled on through more turns. The tunnel roof lowered, and soon Hugh was on his stomach, wiggling forward.

The headlamp died again. Hugh smacked it. Nothing. He pulled the light from his head, whacked it with both hands. Still nothing. Great. His heart raced. His mouth felt dry as the cave floor.

"Calm the hell down, idiot. Calm the hell down."

The words, spoken aloud, slowed Hugh's pulse, focused his mind. He was trapped underground in total darkness. He could trust this narrowing tunnel led to an exit, or he could wiggle back the way he had come. Back in the cavern, he could maybe pile rubble high enough to climb back to his rope… if he could see well enough without a light. No. Hugh gritted his teeth and wiggled forward.

Soon he thought he saw a faint blur. Hugh blinked. Had his eyes adjusted to the darkness, or was he hallucinating? He rubbed his eyes, looked again. The gray smear was still there, faint vertical light on the rock. On another turn in the tunnel. Light was coming from the other side. An opening. Hugh wormed his way to the bend. The light grew as he went. He rounded the curve and stopped.

The tunnel narrowed to a slit barely wider than Hugh's head. Beyond was what seemed to be a cavern lit with faint sunlight. The jungle's musty scent washed over him. A light breeze sounded more full of voices than ever. Could he get past the slit, though? Hugh shoved his pack through, then slid his arms after it. So far, so good. He turned his head and pulled himself forward. Rock scraped his ears, then his head was through. The light in the next cavern, though dim, made Hugh's eyes water. He turned his shoulders, pulled again. His chest jammed in the slot. Hugh pulled hard as he could, pushed his feet against the tunnel wall, but he didn't budge. Ahead was a hint of late-afternoon sunlight shining green through sea grape leaves at the cave's mouth. There was a fire ring inside, too. And a pile of bright-colored backpacks. A new bunch of protestors? He couldn't have crawled as far north as their camp. He tried to breathe, but the rock walls pressed too tight on his chest. Freedom was in sight, and here he was stuck like a cork in a bottle. The wind voices solidified into human ones talking low outside the cave. All thought of secrecy gone, Hugh tried to call for help, managed a faint croak, then gasped for breath. His lips tingled. His head felt light. The cave dimmed. At least the campers would find his body.

Then something big and spike-footed crawled across his leg back in the tunnel. Hugh kicked it away. The thing, or another thing, crawled up his other foot and onto his ankle. Hugh kicked hard to keep whatever it was from crawling up inside his jeans. The thing kept coming. Hugh tried to yell, flailed his legs like he was swimming, tried to pull his hands back to swat at the thing. Pain seared through his chest and he popped onto the cave floor, swatting at his legs. A land crab big as both Hugh's fists scuttled sideways out the cave mouth.

Hugh sat up, stared at the sunlight filtering into the cave. He was out! His shirt was torn, and blood oozed from scrapes down his chest, but he was out. He took a deep breath, then another. The cave stopped spinning.

"It wasn't any of us." The voices outside were clear now. "We agreed."

"Don't know some of the new folks, though," a second voice said.

"Meantime, we got that cop ready to bust us all," said a third voice.

Other voices murmured agreement.

They were talking about the construction site. They wouldn't be happy to know a stranger was listening, but Hugh wasn't about to hide in the cave until they all fell asleep. There was nothing to do but brave it out. He slung on his pack and walked from the cave.

"Evening, guys." Hugh smiled as he stepped through a semicircle of a dozen seated, scruffy campers. "Beautiful night for a walk."

The men and women gaped, too surprised to move. Hugh ducked under a clothesline draped with wet tie-dyed shirts and down a path toward the setting sun, expecting footsteps or shouts from behind him. None came. After ten paces he reached a lime rock road. The setting sun flashed over the sea and dark ironshore. He was north of Captain Vic's cottage, then. This *was* the same camp he'd seen the last week. The bluff, the entire island, had to be shot through with holes like a giant block of Swiss cheese.

He couldn't hide his cash in this cave, not with the protestors knowing there was a way in. But it was good to know if he needed an escape route or a place to hide.

He would have to leave the cash in his wall one more day, hope Lee wasn't bold enough to break in again. Or he could confront Lee, let the little rat know Hugh was onto him. In the meantime, he had to keep searching caves. And on the boat, he would have to change into his wetsuit quick as he could so Casey wouldn't notice all his new cuts.

12

The next morning Hugh slipped Mal's pawn in his pocket and stepped outside. He sprinkled flour over the tiles inside his door, then slid the door closed and pressed a strip of clear tape high across the door and frame. If anyone went inside, the tape would be broken and there would be footprints on the floor. It was the best he could do on short notice.

He kept his head low when he spluttered past the protestors' campsite. A few of them were already walking north. They stopped, stared at the passing scooter belching its blue smoke. One man started to yell something but was cut off by the rumble of a vehicle behind Hugh. A red Skerritt Construction gravel truck thundered past filled with construction workers. Dermott stood at the back. He nodded a greeting at Hugh. The man next to Dermott lofted a beer bottle at the protestors. The glass shattered on the roadway, sent the men and women scooting for cover.

At Eagle Ray Cove Hugh cut through the lobby, was surprised to see Mal sitting behind Mickey's desk.

"Give yourself the promotion?" It was out before he realized it.

"Someone has to keep the place running," Mal said, as if Hugh had asked politely.

Her eyes locked on his. Hugh stopped mid-stride, unable to break her gaze.

"This was last night." Mal held out her phone, showed a photo of Mickey splayed face down beside the pool, an inflatable yellow duck pool ring around his neck.

"I just sent that to Rich. Here's more."

She flicked through more photos. Mickey, shirt rumpled and glasses crooked, draped over a woman at the bar. The woman pushing him away. Mickey, red-eyed, trying to kiss an elderly guest.

"He put on quite the show." Mal put the phone away.

Pity for Mickey welled up in Hugh. Mal's hold on him evaporated. More than anything, he wanted the smug smile wiped from her face.

"Done everything you need to bury him, huh?"

"Ritchie's only decision is how much of a raise I get." Mal smiled. "You hear anything from the States?"

"What's that got to do with anything?"

"I do have your best interests at heart. Remember that."

"Ten steps behind your own."

"Not everyone has jobs handed to them." Mal's voice went hard.

"Mickey may still surprise you."

Shouting came from outside. Guests quick-stepped through the doors, running from something. Hugh and Mal ran outside to see what. Mickey was clinging to the office railing, coated in brown slime and reeking of swamp muck. His broken glasses hung from one ear. Car keys dangled from his hand.

"Mickey? Good God, what happened to you?" Rich Skerritt came from behind the office, then stepped back, arm across his nose and mouth.

"Los' th' van." Mickey tried to focus on Skerritt. Waved the keys.

"Don't remember where you put it?" Skeritt's jaw muscles bunched and rebunched.

"No. Put it in th' pond." Mickey waved back up the road. "Big truck. Had to dodge 'im. Big red truck."

"Mick, go get yourself cleaned up. Now." Skerritt's face reddened.

Mickey stepped toward Skerritt, arms wide to hug him. Skerritt stepped back, fists clenched, and Mickey veered toward the manager's quarters.

Skerritt pulled out his phone.

"'Tonio? Van's in the booby pond. Mickey. I hope to hell he's hurt, damn fool wrecked my van! You get it out before Marquette gets involved? All right then."

Mal raised an eyebrow at Hugh, then stepped back in the office.

Hugh retreated to the pier and joined Casey prepping the *Skipjack*. The wind had picked up overnight, and the waves bounced the boats against the pier. Once the *Skipjack* guests were loaded, Casey motioned Hugh to take the helm.

"Time to test your skills, F.N.G."

Casey was punishing Hugh for their argument the day before? Fine. Hugh would prove he could handle the boat as well as anyone He pivoted the *Skipjack* from the pier and headed for the cut.

Beyond the reef the seas were bigger than any in which Hugh had driven, with waves crashing white across the cut. Hugh put the engines in neutral and studied the breakers for a pattern in their sets. Casey climbed to the bridge.

"Not have the stones for this, Mate?"

Hugh put the engines in gear, picked a gap in the white water, and bounced the *Skipjack* out the cut. Once past the breaking waves, he headed north, fought to steer a steady course as the boat slewed in the following seas.

A half-dozen guests climbed to the upper deck and dropped onto the bench seats, their hands white from gripping the stanchions. Several stared toward shore, wishing they had stayed behind. Hugh sympathized, but there was no turning back. The boat would wallow until it reached the island's sheltered east side. Casey grinned but said nothing. He was setting Hugh up to fail so he could berate him with guests watching. Hugh smiled back. He wouldn't fail. Or back down.

They rounded The Pinnacle, turned east, and the seas flattened in the island's lee.

"Try a site out from the old Civil Defense pier." Casey pointed to a cement slab on shore inside the reef ahead of them, tree branches marking what might have been a break in the reef. "Old World War Two job. Pray you never have to offload anyone there."

They tied off at a mooring Casey called Battleship Reef.

"I need off this boat," a green-faced woman said.

Behind her, the other divers nodded, looking just as queasy.

"You'll feel better once you're under water," Casey said. "Though if you vomit on deck, Hugh will be happy to clean it up."

Casey briefed the dive while Hugh hustled the sickest guests off the boat. Hugh pulled his wetsuit on quick, wincing as he forced it over his scraped chest. He jumped in to lead the dive, bit hard on his regulator mouthpiece when the salt water seeped, stinging, across his torso.

The rough seas had churned up the bottom, cutting the visibility to barely twenty feet. Hugh kept the divers close, with no thought of pointing out fish in the murk. He could have been back in the cave the day before, feeling his way and praying for daylight. He herded the divers back to the boat and let Casey lead the next dive. Then, guests aboard after the second dive, Casey called the divers together.

"Right. It's going to be rough once we round the point. You all need to sit down and hold onto something. Fail to do both those things, you *will* get hurt."

Casey cast off and climbed beside Hugh, grinning again. Waiting for Hugh to screw up, or admit he wasn't good enough. Hugh throttled up and turned the *Skipjack* for home.

They neared The Pinnacle. The wind had freshened, building the seas into eight-foot rollers beyond the rocky spire. The first wave slammed the *Skipjack*'s bow, sending cold spray arcing across the bridge. Hugh eased the throttles back.

"Wind like this, cut'll be ugly." Casey was a barely-heard voice.

Hugh clutched the wheel, not caring about anything beyond the next wave. The bow plunged through each swell, sent spray flying over the open helm, drenching Hugh despite his rain gear.

Hugh bumped the throttles down again, angled into the waves, trying to lessen their impact. Small mistakes he'd been able to get away with before were being punished now. He played with steering, with engine speed, searching for the best combination. His hands ached from gripping the wheel so tight. He wiped his stinging eyes with a wet hand, which made them sting more. A helm-high wave rushed at them. Hugh throttled back yet again. The boat still shuddered at the impact.

"You okay driving?" Casey leaned close to be heard. There was no mockery in his voice.

Hugh nodded. He would throttle back to idle if he had to, but he wouldn't quit. He stood to see the oncoming seas better, ignored the spray pouring over him.

They neared the cut. Waves bunched outside, breaking well out from the reef, then thundering white across the coral. Salt haze blurred the shore.

Hugh scanned the approaching waves for a small set. Around him watery hills rose as high as the *Skipjack*'s bridge. He glanced at the cut, then back out to sea.

"Okay taking her in?" Casey's voice again.

Hugh nodded once, not wasting energy on speech. It was like any other day going through the cut, just bigger. That was all. They were even with the cut. The smallest oncoming waves were eight feet high.

Then, ahead and to port, spread two boat lengths of flat water. Hugh pushed the throttles forward, turned hard toward the cut. Good or lucky, it didn't matter. He had found a flat spot. They'd get in safe.

Casey faced aft, watching for overtaking waves.

"Good back here, Mate."

The range markers on shore were dead ahead.

"Good. Still good."

The engines pulsed through the throttles and into Hugh's hands.

"Oh, bloody hell!"

Their starboard quarter lifted as Casey yelled. The *Skipjack* slowed, her bow slewed to starboard as a wave surged up beneath their stern. Hugh slammed the throttles forward to outrun it, but the wave had them.

The *Skipjack* rose eight feet, turned sideways and tilted forty-five degrees to port. Hugh was tossed from the helm, clung to the wheel and braced his feet on the port rail. Something, someone thudded to the deck below. A metallic shriek that had to be the starboard prop out of the water. Hugh stared past his toes, down the wave's face. Green. Translucent. Flecks of foam scudded up it, defying gravity.

The wave rose higher, tilted the *Skipjack* to near sixty degrees, rushed it broadside toward the green channel marker and the reef's white boil beyond. Hugh's eyes locked on the steel marker. Even if they somehow missed the post, the boat would still hit the coral, barrel roll.

Time slowed, bringing a silence and a strange calm. And the thought: 'So this is how I'll die.'

Then a vision of ten guests onboard. Of Casey clutching a stanchion. They were all in his care. He would *not* give up. The prop's scream returned. Time resumed, though the calm remained.

Hugh couldn't straighten the boat. But maybe he could spin on the wave, drop down its back, go out and try again. A glance behind him. Another wave was coming. A smaller one. No, the same size as the others, but smaller than the beast he was on.

Hugh pulled at the wheel, trying to turn it to the right, nudge the boat to starboard. The wheel barely budged. The prop still shrieked, drowning out all other sound. Hugh pushed off with both feet, getting as much leverage as he could.

The boat yawed right, as if Hugh's steering was working. Then it swung back to the left. The green wave whitened with foam, began to break in the shallower water. *Skipjack*'s bow now pointed slightly down the wave face. Hugh pulled down on the wheel as hard as he could, steering back left. Then again. The *Skipjack* angled to port, gained speed and surfed bow-first down the wave. The green channel marker blurred past barely a foot from their port rail, and the wave crumbled white behind them.

Then flat water. They were in the Sound.

Hugh throttled back with shaking hands, barely able to hold the levers. Cheering, clapping came from below.

Hugh braced for Casey's eruption. Just when he thought he might gain the man's respect, he'd screwed up. And had nearly paid for it with their lives.

"Good job," Casey said. "Got yourself in a crap situation, but you recovered."

"I don't understand…"

"Your flat spot was two waves cancelling each other out, yeah?" Casey's voice was matter-of-fact. "Then in the shallows

166

the one in front slowed and the one behind caught up. Combined to make your monster."

Casey slipped below to check on the guests.

Was Casey setting Hugh up? Waiting until they docked to rip into him in front of everyone?

At the pier's end, Ger Latner stood with his hands on his hips, watching the *Skipjack* approach. That explained why Casey had gone easy on Hugh. He had saved Hugh for Latner. Hugh was done on Blacktip Island, but he would finish proud. He visualized setting the boat parallel to the pier, settling it soft against the wooden planks despite the crosswind.

"Don't screw up," he whispered to himself. "Don't screw up."

The wind pushed the *Skipjack* hard toward the pier. Hugh spun the wheel, jockeyed the gears, set the boat against it with barely a bump. He helped the divers off, checked each for injuries. One man nursed a cut arm. Several had bruises already forming, but nothing more serious.

"Hey, Hugh! Thanks for the E-ticket ride!" the cut man yelled.

"Yeah, man! Let's do it again!" the man's bruised friend bellowed.

"You do realize when you're below yelling, 'yeah, man,' we're up top thinking, 'bloody hell'?" There was no humor in Casey's voice.

"Oh, come on. What's the worst that would've happened?"

"We hit the reef, roll, and everyone would be crushed," Casey said.

Hugh shivered, hearing it so bluntly.

"Yeah, but these boats are self-righting." The men were still grinning.

"No."

Their grins faded.

Latner stepped aboard. Hugh waited for his boss' roar.

"Hugh, welcome to the club," Latner said. "You're not a boat captain 'til you've spun one in the cut or put one on the reef."

"I almost killed us all." Hugh shook now that the guests were gone.

"Yep. Know what you did wrong?"

Hugh nodded, not trusting himself to say anything.

"You gonna do it again?"

Hugh stared at the manager. Casey *and* Latner were being forgiving?

"That was the best lesson you could get," Latner said. "Look, P.M. dives are scrubbed with these seas. Go relax. Tomorrow, you're getting back on the horse. No, shut up. You are."

Across the dock Marina flashed Hugh an 'okay' sign. Gage gave him a double thumbs-up. That helped, though Hugh still shuddered at what could have happened. He washed the boat by himself while Casey filled cylinders with the others.

Lee came down the pier, bouncing with excitement. Hugh readied himself for whatever insult the little divemaster threw at him.

"You hear?" Lee stopped mid-pier, yelled to all the staff, "Mickey's been sacked! They just stuffed him on the last flight to Tiperon!"

"No great loss." Gage said from the *Barjack*. "Guy never knew whether to scratch his watch or wind his butt."

"Who's the new Mickey's the question," Marina said.

"Mal. Duh." Alison rolled her eyes. "Girl's already running the place."

"Let the reign of terror begin," Gage said.

"Skerritt *has* been in with her all day," Lee said.

Hugh's gut tightened at that. Could the day get any worse?

"You rather your friend not be the boss, F.N.G.?" Casey was watching Hugh.

"She has the inside track." Hugh kept his voice neutral.

"It won't be Mal." Latner's low rumble came from behind them.

"When's the last time Mal didn't get something she wanted?" Alison said.

"It won't be Mal." Latner stomped up the pier.

* * *

After the boat was moored, Hugh put Mal from his mind, used the slow ride home to mentally replay everything he had done wrong in the cut. He hadn't known waves could combine like that. What else did he not know that might get him killed?

At his apartment the tape over the doorframe was intact. He stepped around the sprinkled flour and shouldered his pack. He had to get back to the cave, retrieve his rope, look for another, safer cave. A tapping came from his sliding door. Hugh dropped the pack, stepped to the outer room, and froze.

Outside the glass stood his brother, Adam, smiling. Behind Adam was Antonio, chest puffed out.

"Told you company was coming, Hugo. Even if he don't know your name."

"Surprise, Bro," Adam said.

Hugh pulled Adam inside, ignored Antonio.

"What in hell are you doing here?" Hugh snapped.

"I can't visit family?"

"How'd you find me?" Hugh scanned the clearing outside for the island police truck, for off-island police. Antonio was still watching, but no one else was in sight. "Who'd you bring?"

"Whoa. Slow down." Adam glanced into the other room. "Anything to drink in here?"

"*How did you find me?*" Hugh shoved Adam into the inner room where Antonio couldn't see them.

"You're a numb-nuts bonds salesman, Bubba, not some secret agent. You left a trail a mile wide. Took me three phone calls."

Hugh sat on the bed, heart racing.

"Tell me you didn't bring the cops. That they're not waiting to grab me when I step outside."

"Seriously?" Adam looked puzzled. Then he laughed. "Here I thought you did one intelligent thing, and it was blind luck? You didn't know there's no extradition treaty between the U.S. and the Tiperons?

"No one's after me?" Hugh breathed more slowly.

"Oh, folks're after you, all right. They just can't get you. Not legally, anyway. Kinda why I'm here."

"You're *with* the cops?"

"Officially, I'm a family member here to tell you to turn yourself in." Adam held up a hand to silence Hugh. "Unofficially, I'm telling you they can't extradite you, but there's nothing to stop a bounty hunter with a go-fast boat from doing a snatch-and-grab."

"That in the works?" Hugh gripped the mattress edge.

"Don't know, but maybe. I do know there's someone here, on island, keeping tabs on you. No idea who, but you definitely got a bird dog on your trail."

Lee. Why else would he have broken into Hugh's place? Or was it someone less obvious? Someone who had managed to ferret out most of Hugh's secrets under the guise of friendship?

"It a female?" Hugh said. "Who works at a bar?"

"Mal?" Adam laughed again. "No. She's been keeping *me* updated, but no one else."

"You and Mal… for how long?"

"Since call number three. She's the one who answered."

"And she knew you were coming today?"

"She asked me to keep it quiet, but…"

"I bet she did!" This was why Mal had asked Hugh about the U.S. that morning.

"She cares about you."

"Mal cares about Mal." She had been giving Adam a play-by-play while keeping Hugh on ice to use later, when it suited her. Why else would she not mention Adam to Hugh? "The cops had to have listened to every call."

"Me coming was their idea, remember?" Adam shrugged.

"I'm gonna pay all the money back."

"You know things don't happen that way, Bubba."

"No chance of a deal?"

"Not one that doesn't put you in jail."

"So... give myself up, or they send in the Special Forces."

"In a nutshell."

"You supposed to bring me back?"

"No one expects that. And I leave in the morning, charming as your place is."

"You came just to tell me this?"

"They call it 'cooperating with the authorities.' And it was the only way I could warn you properly without anybody knowing. Newspaper clippings could only do so much." Adam grinned. "Kinda cool being related to an international fugitive."

"Yeah. Great. How's Dad with all this?"

Adam's face went serious.

"The feds grabbed every computer he had. Come back, or stay. Your choice. But don't expect support from Dad. You sure you got nothing to drink?"

The next morning Antonio drove Adam and Hugh to the airstrip, swerving across the roadway as he talked.

"Good to get the old crew together again, eh, Hugo? Eh, Aaron?"

"What the hell are you on about?" Adam said from the back seat. "Who the hell's Aaron?"

"Oh, Hugo knows." Antonio winked in the rearview mirror. "We been across the Pacific together, old times."

"I bet you've been all kinds of places no one's seen," Adam said. "Alonso."

Antonio laughed, waggled a finger at Adam.

The Islander was taxiing in when Antonio pulled up at the airstrip. Next to them was Constable Marquette in the police truck. The airplane's hatch opened, and a uniformed police officer climbed out, followed by two men wearing sport coats and badges on their belts. Hugh slid down in the seat.

"Easy, Bro," Adam said.

"No worries, Aaron," Antonio said. "They not after you two. Now, they would be if they knew you was the ones tossed Captain Bligh overboard, but they don't. They looking into that runway business."

The police piled into the police truck and raced away. The Islander pilot waved for passengers to board.

"Thanks. For the warning." Hugh hugged Adam. "Tell them I'm thinking about it."

"Watch your back, Bro."

After the plane left, Antonio dropped Hugh at Eagle Ray Cove.

Hugh tried to push thoughts of Adam, of bounty hunters, from his mind, but his brain could barely focus on driving as he steered the boat out the cut. Thankfully, the seas had calmed, and oddly enough, thoughts of jail kept him from overthinking his driving. All went well that morning, with Casey nodding his grudging approval.

Hugh sat by himself at lunch, thinking through all the implications of Adam's warning. Confronting Mal could wait. It was more important than ever to hide his cash away from Antonio's. He wouldn't surrender. If bounty hunters grabbed him, and only he knew where the money was, the feds would be willing to deal. He would search for caves closer to Eagle

Ray Sound after work, caves that didn't have campers and didn't need climbing rope to get into.

Going home that afternoon, Hugh pulled off the road well north of the protestors' camp. Here the bluff was pocked with small cave openings, and the underbrush was sparse enough for him to push through almost to the outcropping rock. He stashed his scooter in a cleared spot behind the sea grapes and followed what might once have been a trail up to the bluff's base. There, behind a cluster of palmettos, was a hole big enough to wiggle into. Hugh clicked on his dive light. Inside was a small cavern, rough-walled, with smaller openings farther in. Any of them could lead to more caves and a convenient hiding hole.

The cavern's floor was free of debris found in other caves. So close to the sea, the wind probably kept the place scoured. No campfires or garbage or other signs of recent use, either.

Hugh shined his flashlight into one chamber after another. Most were dead ends, rough alcoves rather than the tunnels he had hoped for. In one, a breeze blew on his face. He followed it back to a rough chimney, easily climbable, leading up to the bluff. A nice back door into the cave, but it offered no good hiding spots.

Back in the main cave, Hugh peered into the last opening, big enough for him to walk into. Hugh played his light inside and stopped. Against the grotto's far wall were stacked fifty-pound bags, labeled as chemical fertilizer. Were landscapers using the cave for storage? That made no sense, so far from any resort. Or was this the stolen fertilizer P.C. Marquette was looking for? That someone was using to grow a secret crop? On the bluff's top?

Hugh backed from the alcove. He was in enough of a mess without getting mixed up in drug fields. He didn't even dare tell the constable and draw more attention to himself. Hugh glanced outside the cave mouth. He saw no one, heard no one.

Good. He crawled out and half-ran back to the road, brushing the ground behind him with a palmetto frond to cover his tracks. In the grass by his scooter were faint impressions of truck tires. Idiot! He had been so focused on the cave, he had missed the obvious. Hugh scanned the road in both directions, then walked his scooter onto the road. He cursed the machine when it wouldn't start. Then on the fourth kick, it coughed to life, belching burned oil. His future caving would be far away from here.

Near the protestors' cave, their campfires blended with the odd lights in the underbrush. Hugh passed without slowing. At home, his door tape was still in place. Good. He was putting his pack away inside when he saw Jessie biking up the drive. Had she followed him? No. That was paranoia.

"I don't want to be rude, but why do you keep stopping by unannounced?" Hugh blocked Jessie's way, angry at her coming uninvited, and in no mood for her squirrelly attempts at flirting.

"I needed a friendly face." Jessie's face was flushed. Her hands shook. "They're absolutely tearing The Haven apart. The kitchen, the storerooms, the sheds, everything. Marquette's convinced the runway was sabotaged and Elena's the one behind it."

"Is she?" Hugh remembered Casey's comment.

"Of course not!"

"If there's nothing to find, they should be out of there pretty quick," Hugh said.

"They tore apart the staff's housing, too. My place's shredded. I got sick just looking at it." Jessie gave Hugh a nervous smile. "I can't sleep there."

"Uh uh," Hugh said. "Don't even think of staying here."

"You're the closest thing to a knight this island has, and I'm definitely in distress. I could camp in the outer room. Just one night. It's… they pawed though everything."

"And have the cops shred my place, too, when they find out you're here?"

"Well, I have to sleep somewhere."

"Throw a sheet on your couch and call it good. I sympathize, but here's not gonna happen."

Hugh walked Jessie to the drive, watched until she reached the main road and turned north in the dusk. The last thing he needed was a lawyer, practicing or otherwise, poking around his place.

An odd thought struck Hugh at that. Maybe a friendly lawyer was exactly what he needed. U.S. authorities knew where he was. It was a matter of time before they sent someone to bring him back. And if he ran with no idea what Caribbean countries had extradition treaties with the U.S., he could be arrested as soon as he landed somewhere else. Hiding his cash, then getting an attorney to bargain with the feds might be his only chance. If he could trust Jessie. And if he could get the cash properly hidden.

13

The next afternoon Hugh rushed through cylinder filling, eager to talk to Jessie about being his go-between. He moored the *Skipjack* quick and rushed back to shore. If he left now, he could catch Jessie before she got off work. At the pier, though, Ger Latner had the dive staff gathered around the cylinder fill shack.

"Staff meeting on the deck," Latner boomed. "We're meeting the new managers."

"Plural?" Gage asked.

Latner walked away without responding.

"It's Mal, you twit." Marina fell into step beside Gage.

"We've already met Mal. She's singular."

"She's that, all right," Casey said.

Lee and Alison exchanged worried looks.

At the bar deck, Rich Skerritt joked with a tourist couple, fresh from the plane judging by their pale skin and bright clothes. Beside Skerritt, Mal glared at the approaching dive staff. Hugh glared back, still furious she had spied on him.

"Say it ain't so," Gage muttered.

Dive, maintenance, and housekeeping staff murmured agreement. Rich Skerritt's voice crackled through the sound system, silencing them.

"Eagle Ray Cove's always been the premier dive destination on Blacktip Island!" he said. "It's only fitting our management be top shelf as well. I'd like you all to welcome

Barb and Brandon Schaft, our new guides to continued greatness!"

He gestured to the couple, handed the microphone to the man.

Mal stared straight ahead, face glacial.

Brandon took the mike, belly straining the seams of a still-creased yellow Eagle Ray Cove polo shirt.

"Thanks, Rich! Barb and I are excited to be here! Excited, I tell you!" Brandon pumped both fists over his head for emphasis, setting his potbelly jiggling. "Excited by the opportunity to work with each of you!"

Hugh stifled a laugh. Was this a joke? The other staff looked equally amused.

"Running a business this size is really very simple." Brandon's hint of a moustache quivered. "Barb and I owned a frame shop in Houston, and the principle's the same. You treat people well, watch costs, and laugh all the way to the bank!"

"Frame shop?" Gage whispered.

Barb snatched the mike from Brandon.

"We'll redefine customer service." Her black eyes were nearly lost in her plump cheeks. "It's our top priority. *Your* top priority. We'll have weekly wine-and-cheese parties. Staff-hosted video shows every week's end. A planned activity every night so we can entertain the guests the way *we'd* like to be entertained."

Muttering from the staff.

"Like I'm coming back in after work for some jackass video," Gage whispered as the other voices died. His voice carried around the deck.

Barb's face went purple.

"You!" She jabbed a stiffened index finger at Gage. "Will attend because that is your job!"

"So we'll be on the clock for this?" Gage said. "Like for night dives?"

"Your payment will be happy guests coming back, keeping this resort in business so we can continue to employ you."

"After a ten-hour day, you want me to come back and monkey dance for guests? For free?"

"You can entertain our guests, or you can work elsewhere." Barb's eyes glinted in fat cheeks.

Behind Skerritt, Ger Latner stood statue-still, except for his clenching jaw muscles. The crowd on the deck was silent, with all eyes on plum-faced Barb. On Brandon behind her, nodding.

Mal smiled faint, like a child watching an unexpected show.

Barb blinked. Scanned the crowd.

"Well. Now that we have that settled, you all need to get back to work. We have some exciting changes planned, starting with tomorrow's video show. Fly, little bees, fly!" Barb made shooing motions with her hands.

Staff drifted away in twos and threes. Behind the bar, Mal was still smiling.

"Where'd Rich dig up these two?" Gage kept his voice low, eyes on Barb Schaft talking with Skerritt.

"It won't last," Casey said. "Every new manager breathes fire, make changes. Then everything settles, and we go back to business as usual."

"So you'll be at the video shows?"

"The first few times. Make certain Queenie sees my face, then nip out when the lights go down. There's ways to manage her sort."

Riding home, Hugh passed protestors walking back from the construction site, placards in hand and blue Pelagic Society shirts bright in the dying light. At their camp multiple fires flickered in the underbrush. More people had joined the group.

For the Schaft's wine and cheese gathering the next evening, a king-sized sheet was strung between two palm trees as a makeshift video screen. The setting sun tinted the sky behind a deep purple. Bamboo torches guttered around the deck. Three dozen resort guests babbled, intent on free drinks, ignored the video and Marina's narration.

"Here's the little juvenile queen angelfish we found at Halyard Wall," Marina shouted above the crowd babble.

The thumbnail-sized blue-and-yellow fish, magnified 100 times, darted across the cotton screen.

"We are so very, very happy you all could come!" Barb Schaft plowed through the crowd, wine glass in-hand, blue and green muumuu brighter than the magnified angelfish. "Welcome to our little tropical chapeau!"

In her wake came Brandon, bamboo tray of toothpick-impaled cheese cubes in one hand, bottle of chardonnay in the other. He had dressed in a red Hawaiian shirt and leather boat shoes so new they squeaked with each step. Resort staff fought back smiles. No one had told the new managers only aging tourists dressed like that.

Hugh, talking with a couple from the *Skipjack,* caught a fleeting glance of Casey greeting Barb mid-crowd. Then Brandon barreled into Hugh and the couple.

"Care for some cheese?" Brandon thrust the tray at them.

The woman reached for a toothpick.

"I feel like a walking mousetrap." Brandon grinned. "SNAP! And I have you!"

The woman pulled back her hand.

"No. Thank you."

"Oh, not that you're a mouse. Or any rodent." Brandon grinned bigger. "You're much too large for that."

"Who are you?" The woman's husband looked unsure whether to laugh or demand an apology.

"Brandon Schaft! I manage the place! With my wife." Brandon raised his right hand, seemed surprised to see the chardonnay bottle. "Well! I can't shake your hand, but I can top off your glass!"

"No." The man pulled his beer away. His wife did the same with her margarita.

"Okay, then. Enjoy the show!" Brandon squeaked to the next group of guests.

"He on his meds or off them?" the man asked.

"We're not sure yet," Hugh said.

Across the crowd Casey handed Barb off to a guest and edged toward the steps behind the deck. Hugh started after him, eager to be gone, too. He was stopped by Rich Skerritt's booming voice.

"Now this is what I call a party!"

Skerritt strode to Barb Schaft, slipped an arm around her waist. Barb wiggled free, shot a glance toward Brandon. Across the deck Brandon shoved his cheese tray at a group of puzzled divers, oblivious. Mal watched Barb and Skerritt with a look that sent chills down Hugh's spine.

Hugh edged toward the steps, keeping Barb between him and Skerritt. Barb spun, bumped into Hugh.

"Oh!" Barb smoothed the front of her muumuu, noticed Hugh's staff shirt. "Now, which one are you?"

"I'm Hugh."

"Hugh." A crinkling around the eyes and tightening of her lips might have been a smile. "So many of the staff seem so hostile to Brandon and I, it's good to meet a friendly face."

"Sure." Hugh wondered what made his face friendly.

"I know we weren't the popular choice for manager, but we were the wise choice." Barb leaned close, lowered her voice. "And we do reward loyalty."

"Oh, I'm as loyal as the next guy."

"Maybe a little more, hmm?"

Mal brushed past, tucked her hair behind her ear. Barb scowled at her.

"Our door's always open if you have any concerns. Or problems with other staff. Hugh." Another crinkly smile and Barb trailed Mal through the crowd.

Hugh reached the steps, traced Casey's route off the deck, then circled around to his scooter. There was a boom, like distant thunder. The northern horizon glowed. He walked the scooter down the road so no one would hear when it started. The clatter of bicycle chains made him stop.

"Go! Just go!" a woman shouted.

A half dozen men and women in green Earth Federation shirts streaked south on pink Eagle Ray Cove one-speed bikes.

"We didn't do anything!" a man yelled.

"Cops won't care! Pedal faster!"

The last rider glanced back over her shoulder. A siren wailed somewhere to the north. Hugh stepped off the road, waited until the police truck sped past, lights flashing and siren screaming, before he started the scooter. He wasn't about to get mistaken for a protestor fleeing who-knew-what.

Hugh took his time riding home, giving the police plenty of time to round up the campers. He didn't want any protestors spotting him, telling a constable Hugh had popped out of a cave behind their campsite, getting the police curious as to why Hugh had been in the cave.

He needn't have worried. At the campsite the police truck sat on the roadside, lights still flashing. No protestors were visible. No fires showed in the underbrush, though several flashlight beams dancing near the bluff showed where the police were searching. Good. P.C. Marquette deporting them all would make his life easier. Hugh bore the protestors no ill will, but as long as they were here, he couldn't search the caves along this coast. He had the next day off. He would explore the island's deserted east coast, maybe find some undiscovered cave off the beaten path there.

Early the next morning Hugh retrieved his rope, stuffed it in his pack, and biked south, mask and fins sticking out of the top of his pack. If anyone saw him, they would think he was out snorkeling. To his left loomed the ironshore bluff, pocked with caves too high to reach easily or secretly. The breeze moaned through them. The scooter coughed, slowed, belched blue smoke thicker than ever when the road angled up the cliff face. Hugh climbed off, pushed it to the top, then rode on. Soon the Last Ballyhoo appeared on his right. In the dirt turnout sat Payne Hanover's rusting Mercedes, a beat-up pickup, and a military surplus jeep. Payne and his buddies had started drinking early. Hugh kept on, hoping no one inside had seen him biking past.

Beyond the Ballyhoo the road turned north, narrowed to a two-rut track. Sea grapes pressed close on either side. An occasional break in the bushes on his right showed hints of sea. The air clotted thick here where the brush blocked the breeze. The road twisted up the coast, and soon Hugh's shirt was sweat-soaked, his pack glued to his back.

A low grumble sounded behind him. The rattle of loose metal, clatter of valves. Hugh stopped, pulled the scooter as far off the roadway as he could. Seconds later Payne's rattletrap Mercedes rounded the curve, dust swirling around it. Payne was singing, beer in-hand. Beside him sat a tanned woman with wide sunglasses and dark hair streaming, right hand out, air foiling in the car's slipstream. They shot bored glances at Hugh as they thundered past. Behind Payne came another vehicle, obscured by the dust.

Payne stomped the Mercedes to a stop. The car skidded sideways, brakes screaming. The truck behind slid half into the sea grapes to keep from rear-ending him. Brakes from a third and fourth vehicle squealed farther behind. Dogs barked.

"Hugh!" Payne yelled. "Going primitive on us?"

"Snorkeling." Hugh swatted at the gear on his back. The dust settled on his sweaty skin, turned to mud.

"Yeah, well, toss that piece of crap in Marina's truck. You're with us now!"

"No. But thanks."

The truck's horn honked. Marina and Alison laughed. Dogs still barked beyond that. Cori was in the mix, then.

"We're Spider Bight-bound!" Payne said. "Perfect for snorkeling! Then we'll sit in the warm water, drink beer, and make up stories about people."

Payne jumped from the car, hauled the scooter into the truck, and motioned Hugh into the convertible's back seat. Hugh sat sideways, clutching his over-full pack to his chest.

"Hugh, Anya. Anya, Hugh." Payne slid back into the driver's seat.

The woman rolled her head back, extended an amber-braceleted hand in Hugh's general direction.

"I am pleased to meet you," she said in an eastern European accent.

"You'll recognize Anya from magazine covers." Payne grinned. "Only here for a few days, so I'm giving her the king's tour!"

Payne popped the clutch and Hugh's head snapped sideways. They careened along the overgrown road faster than Hugh would have dared. The speed sent a cooling wash of air over him, though. Hugh climbed to the Mercedes' trunk with his legs in the back seat, ducked whenever low branches slapped past.

The road turned left, and the brush fell away. Tall palms in neat lines bordered a broad beach to the right. A half-dozen houses of dark wood, built on stilts, storm shutters closed, were spread among the trees.

"Mahogany Row," Payne yelled. "Used to be a coconut plantation, back in the day. Third and fourth homes for most owners. None of 'em under $2 million. They come here for seclusion. Electricity from generators. Only sat-phones work out here."

"The Clew place." Payne waved as they roared past the first shuttered home. "The Garboards. The Battens. The Fairleads. The Damsils."

The last house was unshuttered. Out front, a man stood from planting a palm sapling and waved his straw hat at them.

"The Maples live here?"

"Oh, sure. About the only year-round residents down this way."

A mile past the stilt houses Payne pulled off the road under a stand of palms. Beyond stretched a broad beach and wide cove. A jutting of ironshore a half-mile east, stretching a mile or more to the north, shielded the cove from the open sea. An offshore sport-fishing boat swung at anchor in the calm water. The other vehicles pulled in behind Payne.

"Voila! Spider Bight!" Payne stood in the seat, raising his arms to the sea. "Roll on, thou deep and dark blue ocean - roll!"

"Payne! It is doing it!" Anya clutched Payne's leg.

Payne raised his eyebrows at Hugh.

"Most beautiful spot on the island! Let's forget about the world for a while." Payne studied the anchored boat. "Never seen that one before. Frank and Helen must've bought a new toy. Or it's visitors who like their privacy."

Gage, Marina, and Alison hauled an ice chest and beach chairs from the truck. Lettuce, Turnip, and Pea bounded up, followed by Cori and Jessie lugging another ice chest and a barbeque grill. The dogs tore down to the beach. Cori dropped her end and chased after them.

Hugh pulled out his snorkeling gear and crammed his pack in the floor behind the Mercedes' driver's seat, hoping no one would ask what else he had in the pack.

"Drop that stuff, Jack Cousteau." Gage shoved an open beer at Hugh. "We're here to forget about island B.S. for a while."

The beer was cool, soothing after the dusty ride. Soon Payne had the grill going. Marina was in the water with a mask and snorkel. The others were plopped in beach chairs, drinks in hand. Music blared from the jeep's speakers. Hugh went to the water to rinse the sweat and dust from himself. Payne handed him a second beer when Hugh rejoined the group.

Soon Marina waded from the lagoon, four conchs in her arms. With a crack to each shell and a quick slit of her knife, she scooped out the meat, chopped it, mixed it in lime juice, onions and mango for ceviche. She passed around the bowl and a box of crackers while Payne loaded the grill. Cori and her dogs reappeared.

"I didn't expect to see you out this way." Jessie dropped into the chair beside Hugh, vodka-and-orange in hand.

"I didn't expect to see anyone," Hugh said. If he couldn't search for caves, at least he could make nice with Jessie, sound her out before he asked for legal help.

"Still on the lonesome quest, huh?"

"Something like that. How'd you get mixed up with this gang?"

"Cori swung by." Jessie winked at Cori across the semicircle feeding scraps to the dogs. "She figured I needed a break from things. She was right." Jessie gazed down the palm-lined beach. "There was another explosion. Cops're tearing up The Haven again."

"I heard... something about that," Hugh said. "Any idea... Hey! Pea! No!"

The little terrier snatched the burger from Jessie's plate and ran down the beach. Lettuce and Turnip raced after her.

"Get back here with that burger, you little thief!" Cori ran after the dogs.

After more drinks Payne pulled a champagne bottle from the ice and led Anya back toward the Mahogany Row houses. Soon they were out of sight among the palms. The others set their drinks aside, grabbed masks and fins, and ran laughing into the calm water. Jessie hung back, looking doubtful, a battered mask in her hands.

"You really haven't done this before." Hugh stood, wobbled, caught his balance. Was the beer hitting him already?

"Lame, huh?" Her words leaned into each other.

"Here. Let me help."

Hugh adjusted the mask strap, slipped the snorkel on its holder, and they walked to the water. They kicked after the others, Jessie staying close to Hugh, her pale skin standing out against her red bikini, her arm brushing against his.

"Oooh! Cool!" Jessie hooted through her snorkel when a school of blue tang flashed past.

Hugh stayed beside her when she chased after a trunkfish wobbling away from their splashing. Conch were everywhere, their football-sized shells leaving meandering trails where they'd dragged themselves across the sand.

Across the bight they joined Gage, Marina and Alison at the rocky wall sheltering the bay. Waves, driven by the east wind, broke heavy on the ironshore, sending spray flying high. Hugh gazed from the crashing waves back to the beach, feeling more lightheaded than he should have. The ride, the sun, the beer had caught up with him.

"I need to head back," Hugh said. "I'll leave you in good hands." With luck, he would be home before Payne's party left the beach.

"I'll come with," Jessie said. "Buddy system, remember?"

A concerned look went through her eyes. Worry, maybe. Or she was uncomfortable with the others her first time snorkeling.

"Suit yourself. I'm headed home, though."

They swam back slowly, exploring the scattered coral heads as they went. Juvenile snappers swarmed like a hundred golden fireflies around one. Underneath, lobsters waved their spiny antennas. Jessie grabbed Hugh's hand, kept him between her and the lobsters. Near shore, a brown-and-yellow seahorse clung to a sea rod. Jessie's legs flashed pale, slender as she circled for a better view.

Music from the jeep was still blaring when they reached the beach. Hugh shook water from himself while Jessie grabbed a towel. She took off her ring, set it on the truck's lowered tailgate while she wiped sand from her finger. Hugh hadn't thought to bring a towel. Hadn't thought he'd actually go snorkeling.

"Here. Mine's not too wet." Jessie stepped close, held out her towel and her drink.

"No. I'm good. On both counts." Hugh stepped back. The towel smelled of coconut and honeysuckle.

Jessie stepped close again, pressed the towel to him.

"You're not good at hints, are you?" She kissed him slow on the lips.

Hugh took the towel, stared into Jessie's gray eyes. She was pretty. He had been too focused on Mal, on treasure hunting, on hiding his cash to notice that.

Hugh took the towel. Jessie put her arms around his neck and kissed him again. He dropped the towel, kissed her back, feeling sad and wonderful at the same time, seeing Tess walking away in the rain, Mal with Rich Skerritt. He had put that all behind him, though. Jessie was here, and this was good. Hugh wrapped his arms around Jessie's sun-warmed shoulders. Her hands slid to his waist. They stumbled backwards, laughing, and landed on the pickup's tailgate, Jessie's lips still pressed to his. Her necklace was smooth under his fingertips. Breeze off the water swirled cool around them. Waves rumbled in the distance. The palm grove swirled around them, and Hugh didn't care. They had had too much to drink, and he didn't care about that, either. Or about Jessie's ring, still on the tailgate, digging into his back.

Barking exploded beside them. A sand-coated Lettuce leaped onto the tailgate. Jessie spun away, lost her balance, then caught herself on the truck's side. Lettuce pinned Hugh, licking his face and grinding sand into his bare chest.

"Well. You've made friends." Cori stepped around the cars. "Lettuce! Here. Here! HERE!"

She bear-hugged Lettuce, lifted her off Hugh.

"Sorry about that," Cori said to Jessie.

"No, no. It's no problem," Jessie laughed. "For me."

The other two dogs bounded up then, and Lettuce chased them around the cars. Jessie's ring rolled warm between Hugh's thumb and finger and then dropped into his shorts pocket. He stepped to the Mercedes to get his shirt.

"I hate to spoil the fun." Cori downed what was left of her beer. "But I do have to work in an hour."

Gage, Marina, and Alison were wading back in, laughing. Payne and Anya strolled back through the palms, arm-in-arm, an empty champagne bottle in Payne's hand.

They loaded the vehicles, and Cori waved Hugh into the Sand Spit mini truck. He put his scooter and pack in the bed with the dogs and slid into the cab beside Jessie. She leaned against him, warm, as Cori steered a wavering course down the empty road, dogs barking nonstop in the bed behind them. Jessie's honeysuckle scent wrapped around him. Her ring lay warm against his thigh.

A guilty pang shot through Hugh. He had to tell Jessie… something… about his past without giving away too much. He needed her help, but there was no way he could come completely clean. Also, if people came to haul him away when she was with him, she might get hurt. She needed to know that.

At Antonio's Cori herded her dogs inside, leaving Hugh and Jessie alone.

"We need to talk before we go any further," Hugh said.

"Oh. Not a good sign." A worried look played across Jessie's face.

"We're good. But there's things you need to know. About me."

"I know more than you think." Her words slurred.

"Right." Hugh glanced at Cori's apartment. She and Jessie had been way too chummy lately. "How about we do this when we're both sober."

"No. I'm good."

"Let's go inside for a second, then."

Hugh slid open his glass door.

"Look, I... you know I'm lying low and trying to undo some mistakes. What you don't know is if you're with me, you might be in danger..."

A window-rattling snore came from the inner room. Hugh and Jessie both jumped. Hugh peeked through the open doorway. Dermott was splayed across the bed, empty liquor bottle in hand. Rum fumes wafted out the door.

"Oh my God!" Jessie started toward Dermott.

"No!" Hugh stopped her. "He goes berserk if you wake him up. Jerrod walked me through this."

They stepped back out the glass door, and then Hugh slammed it closed. A loud snore from Dermott. Hugh slammed the door again, so hard the glass shook. The snoring stopped. Hugh slid the door back open.

"It sure is good to be home!" Hugh yelled, motioned for Jessie to follow his lead.

"Oh, wow!" Jessie shouted. "What a dump you've got here!"

Rumbling came from the inner room, and then Dermott appeared in the doorway.

"Hugo. Sorry 'bout that. You and…" Dermott pointed at Jessie, tried to focus his eyes, then staggered outside and toward his own apartment.

Jessie smiled at Hugh.

"I know you're hiding out. I…" Her eyes searched his. Her face tightened. "I don't care about that."

"How do you know…"

Jessie kissed him, and then stepped back.

"I've gotta work tonight, too. Doing this later, when we're sober's probably a good idea."

Jessie kissed him long and slow. Then she grabbed her bicycle from beside the house and wobbled down the drive, leaving Hugh wondering what she knew, how she knew. And why her bird ring was in his hand.

14

Thunder woke Hugh in the darkness, set the pans in the cupboard rattling. He checked the bedside clock. Four thirty. His head pounded, and his stomach churned from yesterday's beer. He rolled over, closed his eyes, but couldn't get back to sleep. Jessie's words bounced through his head. She knew more than he had thought, but how much more? And how? She and Mal weren't friends, and Adam hadn't talked with her. Cori had passed Antonio's ramblings on to Jessie? Had to be. Which meant Jessie didn't know as much as she thought she did.

She had said she didn't care about his past, but she had been drunk then. Would she feel the same when she was sober? Would she even remember? Jessie might forget their drunken make-out session. Or worse, regret it. He closed his eyes, tried to sleep.

Jerrod screaming upstairs startled Hugh awake. He jumped, knocked over the bedside lamp. The light bulb shattered on the tile floor. Jerrod screamed again. Hugh rolled off the bed's far side, fumbled for his flip flops so he could clean the mess without cutting his feet. Jerrod yelled again, though not as loud. Hugh flipped on the kitchen light, swept up the broken glass, then dressed for work. If he couldn't sleep, he might as well get something done. He would be early, but he could have the *Skipjack* prepped when Latner and Casey arrived, and the fresh air would help with his hangover. He pressed fresh tape across his door and frame and rode down the hill.

South of the protestors' campsite two men in blue Pelagic Society t-shirts were coming down the road single file. Newcomers, judging by their new shirts, short hair, and their walking the opposite direction from the runway. Both looked surprised to see Hugh.

"Morning, Captain!" the first man said.

Hugh nodded a greeting, kept on.

"Hey, if we wanted to go diving, what's the best outfit?" the second man called out.

Hugh stopped. Blue exhaust enveloped the men.

"You're here for protesting *and* diving?"

"We're not hard core, just lending a hand for a few days." The man coughed from the smoke. "Figured we'd get in a dive or two during down time."

"Any place is good." Hugh hadn't thought of there being part-time protestors. Elena must be pulling in everyone she could. "Blacktip Haven'll probably cut you a deal."

"Roger that," The first man studied Hugh's staff shirt. "Sending us to the competition, huh? Something we said?"

"You guys know the runway's north of here, right?"

"Oh, sure. We figured we'd reconnoiter before things got cranked up this morning. Not much but nature down this way. That cottage on the water yours?"

"I'm inland. Farther down. Why?"

"We'd only seen the one place." The first man held out his hand. "I'm Ike. This is Leo."

"Hugh."

Ike's grip tightened on Hugh's hand like a vise. Hugh tried to pull free, but Ike held on.

"I need to get to work," Hugh said.

"Oh, right. Right." Ike released him. "We'll probably see you around. On the reef."

Hugh rode away, massaging his hand to get its circulation back.

The protestors' campsite was nearly empty, with only one small fire visible. The police had cleared out most of them, whatever they had or hadn't done.

When he reached Eagle Ray Cove, resort staff was gathered out front, talking in low voices. Hugh caught Marina's eye, conveyed a question.

"You feel the tremor this morning?" Marina said. "That was a bulldozer exploding. After it fell in a big sinkhole."

"Another cave-in?" Hugh asked.

Beside him, Gage nodded agreement.

"How'd falling in a hole make a bulldozer explode?" Marina said.

"Ger's pet passing secrets?"

Lee joined them, scowled at Hugh. Hugh raised his middle finger at Lee.

"Rafe said there's a smoking crater in the middle of the track," Marina said. "With scorch marks around it. And buried electrical wires."

"Just came from up there." Dermott wandered up, beer in hand. "Earth's crumbling and smoke's pouring out like all Hell opening up."

"Not a threat to the resort, is it?" Brandon Schaft appeared. "Hell's hard to spin positive!"

"James Conlee was on that 'dozer y'know." Dermott gave Brandon a disgusted look and downed the rest of his beer. "Busted up bad. Flying him to the hospital on Tiperon now."

"You think there's more to come?" Gage asked.

"Dunno," Dermott said. "Smoking like that, no telling what's underground. Rafe questioned all us workers, but we got no reason to burn our jobs. Not natural, though."

Casey joined them.

"Case, you used to prospect up that way," Gage said. "It's eat-up with caves that'd crumble under that machinery, isn't it?"

"I know nothing of caves," Casey snapped. He gave Hugh an angry look. "Or prospecting. The only treasure on this rock is in resort safes."

Mal stood by the lobby steps, listening, eyes locked on Brandon.

"May be duppies cursing the place," Dermott said.

"Rafe swears it's the campers. But he has to link the wiring to them," Marina whispered.

Brandon Schaft slipped behind them, treading light on the balls of his feet, eying each face in the group. Then he circled back to the office feigning nonchalance.

"He's a skulker, that one," Marina said.

Gage and the others made their way to the boats. Hugh followed, wondering if the odd protestors he'd met were connected to the explosion. They had said they were only here for a few days. That was time enough to stage an accident, then fly out again.

"You think it really is just cave-ins?" Hugh asked Casey, trailing behind the group.

Casey stepped in front of Hugh, blocking his way.

"I will say this to you only once," Casey said. "I know nothing of caves, nothing of treasure. The next time you mention it to me, you'll be missing teeth. Or would you rather I tell everyone *you've* been caving, have that bit of information get back to Rafe Marquette?"

Casey pushed on Hugh's still-raw chest.

Hugh winced from pain and from the threat. The constable looking into his exploring would be a catastrophe.

"Exactly right," Casey said. "I don't want a nice policeman tailing me anymore than you want him tailing you. We have an understanding?"

Hugh nodded. Casey stalked to the kitchen for coffee. Hugh cut behind the lobby, hurrying to the *Skipjack*. He nearly knocked Mal down as she stepped from the resort lobby, looking backwards at Brandon by the reception desk.

"Already working the new management?" he said.

Mal looked daggers at him, then her face softened. She let the lobby door close.

"I was harsh last time we talked." She tilted her head, set her earrings flashing. "That wasn't right."

Hugh's insides fluttered again. After everything she had done, how did she still do that to him? Then anger returned.

"You weren't harsh talking to my brother, were you?"

"Please. I was just letting him know you were okay, and letting you enjoy your privacy."

"You were spying on me. Knowing U.S. cops heard every word."

"No harm's come to you. I'm making sure of that."

She put her hand on his arm. Hugh pulled away.

"What are you after, Mal?"

"Spider Bight's lovely, but 'lovely' can hide danger."

"From what, island friends?"

"You can do better than that cook."

"Like you?"

"A disbarred lawyer with money troubles and a drinking problem? There's more to that one than meets the eye."

"Pot, meet kettle."

"What say we forget the last few weeks? Start fresh."

She put a hand on his arm again. Her green eyes were bright, as inviting as they'd ever been. Drawing him in.

Hugh pulled away again. He wouldn't let her do this.

"You're desperate for allies," Hugh reasoned it out as he spoke. "Brown-nosing Brandon to sand bag him, then sweet talking anyone who'll listen so they'll back you when the Schafts go down. Only Skerritt seems taken with Barb."

"You know nothing about Rich, or me." Mal's face went harsh. "Tell your little girlfriend Elena better not be the one tearing up the runway. Rich hired security. And posted a reward. $15,000'll loosen a lot of tongues."

Mal ran a finger down Hugh's chest.

"There a reward for you, Blake? Enough to interest a down and out cook?"

"You're reaching."

"Just friendly advice."

"We're not friends, remember?" Hugh pushed past her.

Hugh climbed on the *Skipjack* with Mal's warning reeling in his head. She had dug into Jessie's past. Or said she had, to rattle Hugh. To Mal he was a chess piece. Or an asset to be kept close and cultivated. He went through the motions of briefing the boat's new divers, two freshly-certified divers on their first dive trip. Retired accountants on a second honeymoon, they said.

"Ernie uses so much air," the wife said. "Our instructor accused him of selling it to the rest of us."

"I'm a heavy breather." Ernie hugged his wife. "But Ginny likes that, don't you, Hun?"

Thoughts of Mal evaporated. New divers who used lots of air could get in trouble fast.

"I'll be with you on the first dive," Hugh said. "Tell me when you've used a third of your air, and I'll get you back to the boat."

Casey nodded agreement.

A north wind made even the island's west side choppy. Casey and Hugh had to steady divers as they rushed to get off the rocking boat.

Twenty minutes into the first dive Ernie waved his hands, jabbed his pressure gauge at Hugh. Half his air was gone. Hugh turned the group, led them back to the *Skipjack*. He surfaced with Ernie and Ginny while the other divers finished their dive.

The second dive, Casey brought Ernie and Ginny back early as well.

"He *is* watching his gauge," Casey said. "They're plonkers, but they're not stupid."

That afternoon Hugh drove the boat through building waves. He stopped at Jawfish Reef, as sheltered a site as they would get in the strengthening wind. Divers hurried off the pitching boat.

Underwater, heavy surge slung the divers back and forth over the reef. Hugh barely noticed, his mind back on Mal. Her warning about Jessie claiming reward money seemed more like a veiled threat. Would Mal turn him in? No. They weren't friends, but they weren't enemies, either. She was reminding Hugh she had leverage on him. That he owed her.

The divers clustered around the coral heads near the mooring pin, the surge and bad visibility keeping them from straying too far. Ernie and Ginny settled in the sand, watching the ghost-like jawfish poke their heads up from rubble burrows.

After ten minutes supervising divers who didn't need supervision, Hugh swam off by himself, mentally playing out possible scenarios with Mal. A parrotfish flashed past him, scales green as Mal's eyes. Hugh pushed that thought aside.

He rounded a coral head, found a stingray skimming the sand, bar jack poised above it. He knelt to watch. The ray glided so close Hugh could have touched it.

A regulator hissed beside him. Ernie and Ginny, closer than the ray. Hugh pointed to the ray, motioned for them to kneel. Ginny shook her head and pointed to Ernie. Ernie slashed a hand across his throat.

Out of air? Couldn't be. Fifteen minutes into a shallow dive, even Ernie couldn't be out of air. Hugh grabbed Ernie's pressure gauge. Six hundred psi. Not empty, but nearly so. A quick check of Ginny's gauge showed she had two-thirds of her air. Had he or Casey forgotten to check Ernie's air in their rush to get divers off the boat? He couldn't remember who had helped which divers. Or was Ernie so nervous he breathed that heavy? They could sort that out later. What mattered now was getting Ernie to the surface.

Hugh signaled Ernie and Ginny to follow him up. They were back under the *Skipjack* in a few minutes, Ernie clinging to the fifteen-foot safety chain hanging from the stern. Hugh checked Ernie's air. Four hundred psi. Plenty for a three-minute safety stop.

Exhaust bubbles from the divers below swirled around them, blinding for a moment. If Ernie's tank was a partial fill, other divers might have one, too. Hugh motioned Ernie and Ginny to finish their safety stop and surface. Both signaled 'okay.'

Hugh dropped back to the reef, did a quick circuit through the group, checking each diver's air supply. All had more than half their air remaining. Hugh glanced up to the boat. Ernie and Ginny were gone. Hugh ascended, rehearsing the 'check-your-air' speech he'd give Ernie. Casey, meticulous about checking every returning diver's gauges, would be chewing them out by now.

Hugh climbed back onboard and found Casey lounging on the upper deck.

"I hope you saved some of his ass for me to chew," Hugh called up. The couple was probably on the bow, smarting from Casey's scolding.

"Eh?"

"The old guy. Ernie. What'd he surface with? Two? Two fifty?"

"You're the first one back, Mate," Casey said.

"Seriously. They on the bow?"

"What have you done?" Casey was on his feet, scanning the water.

"He had a low fill. I left them at their safety stop and went back down to check everyone else's air."

"There!" Casey pointed.

Bubbles welled up at the stern. Two divers were surfacing.

Neither were Ernie or Ginny. Casey barked at them to climb aboard, help look for stray divers.

Hugh dug for the binoculars, cursing himself for not taking Ernie and Ginny all the way up. Why would they wander off when Ernie was damn near out of air?

"Hop back in." Casey's voice was oddly calm. "Snorkeling gear. Search toward shore."

"Why shore?"

"They went over the wall. You won't find them anyway."

Hugh pulled on his mask and jumped off the stern, fins in-hand. He hadn't screwed up, but divers were still missing.

The other guests were coming up now. Still no Ernie or Ginny. Ernie hadn't had enough air to stay down this long, even at fifteen feet. He and Ginny had to be on the surface, just impossible to see among the swells. Hugh swam a broad zigzag course, working closer to shore with each pass. At each turn he looked to the boat, checked his bearings. Checked if Casey was calling him back because Ernie and Ginny were on board after all. Hugh felt sicker with every turning.

The *Skipjack's* upper deck was crowded now, with guests scanning all directions.

The swells became breaking waves in the shallows, tossed Hugh like laundry in a washer. Water went down his snorkel. Hugh gagged, coughed. Twice he waited for a wave to lift him so he could see the boat. A glance at his watch. Ernie had been missing more than twenty minutes.

The water beneath him was four feet deep now. Then less. A wave lifted Hugh, rolled on, dropped him among the broken coral and long-spined sea urchins. He glanced back at the dwindling boat, caught an impression of figures on the boat pointing to his right. Of Casey's silhouette, VHF transceiver in-hand.

The next swell lifted Hugh, and he saw two figures huddled on the beach. He kicked hard. The wave rolled past, and coral rushed up at him. Another wave. He kicked when it raised him from the jagged bottom. The next wave broke over him, pounded him into the rubble. Hugh crawled through the surf, grinding across on the reef, shredding hands, knees, thighs despite his wetsuit. Hugh staggered ashore bleeding, legs rubbery from the swim, praying the figures were beachcomb-ers, picnickers.

Ginny, still in her wetsuit, knelt by two sets of scuba gear. Beside her, Ernie lay on his back. A third figure in green surgical scrubs appeared, crouched over Ernie, doing CPR. Casey's radio call had brought help quickly. Hugh knelt beside Ernie, took over chest compressions. The nurse gave rescue breaths, checked Ernie's pulse when Hugh paused.

The rocky beach blurred. Mist turned to a cold drizzle. Hugh, with a vague awareness of a beach walker arriving, pulling him aside. Of sitting in the rocks, breathing hard. Of Ginny sobbing somewhere behind him. Then he was back on compressions. Another brief rest, then compressions again. Then the nurse - 'Marisa,' her scrub shirt said - stopped him. More people arrived. They rolled Ernie onto an orange backboard. Ernie's hand lay cold against Hugh's arm for a moment. The board was surprisingly heavy despite six people carrying Ernie to a waiting truck. Hugh sat beside Ernie for the bumpy ride to the island clinic.

Then an endless wait while P.C. Marquette talked to the nurse, interviewed everyone involved one-by-one. Hugh squatted under the eaves, waiting his turn, trying to stop his stomach from churning. Someone draped a raincoat over his shoulders. Gage. Marina and the other divemasters wandered by, looked away when Hugh glanced up at them. Alison, teary eyed, put a hand on Hugh's head. Lee smiled like his mouth was full of candy.

"Precious work of art's got a crack in it, eh?"

Hugh looked away.

It wasn't his fault. Hugh had brought both divers to the boat. He'd had eight, nine other divers to look after, divers who might have been low on air, too. Who couldn't surface from fifteen feet?

Hugh's chest ached, as if steel bands were being tightened around him. He needed to run, but there was nowhere to go.

"Hugh. How you doing?" Ger Latner squatted beside him, water streaming off his red rain parka.

Hugh shook his head, tried to stop the blood from pounding in his ears.

"Listen, you work in this business long enough, it'll happen," Latner said. "Usually you get ten years under your belt first, but it'll happen." The words flowed over Hugh. The tightness in his chest eased.

"Hugh," Latner lowered his voice. "Just so I know, you got these two back to the boat, then you went back to round up the other divers, right?"

Hugh nodded, surprised by the question.

"And you knew these two were bad on air, so you stayed close? And made sure they jumped in with full tanks, right?"

"Of course!" Ernie was dead because the man had known he was low on air and swam off anyway, not because of a low air fill.

"Make sure you tell the police that." Latner's eyes bored into Hugh.

Hugh's chest tightened again. If Latner questioned his professionalism, what were the others doing? Anger morphed to shame.

It wasn't his fault, no. But it felt like it was. Divemastering was what he was best at, where he belonged. His last hope. And he had let someone die.

When P.C. Marquette called him inside, Hugh recounted what had happened, answered the stone-faced constable's questions.

Was Hugh *sure* he took the couple to the boat?

Why hadn't he stayed with them?

How long had Hugh been a divemaster?

Where had Hugh been trained?

The constable watched Hugh's face. Watched Hugh's still-shaking hands. Made notes.

Questioning finished, Hugh stepped back outside into a steady downpour.

The sun had set while he talked to the constable. Casey and Latner, rain hoods up, fell silent when they saw Hugh. Latner handed Hugh a dry shirt. Without a word they walked him to the dive truck and drove away, Hugh seated in the middle. Hugh waited for either to say something, anything. For Latner to fire him. For Casey to curse him. Anything would be better than the silence filling the cab.

"Ernie saw a turtle." Latner's voice was monotone. "He chased it into the shallows. Ginny figured they were under the boat, they could get away with another minute or two. Ernie's tank ran dry, he surfaced, couldn't inflate his BC. Waves rolled him and he sucked seawater."

"They knew better than to swim off," Hugh said partly to himself, partly for hoped-for absolution.

Latner and Casey said nothing.

They didn't need to. The police report would say Hugh acted appropriately. But that didn't relieve him of the guilt. Leaving the group for a few minutes and worrying about Mal hadn't killed anyone. But his mental distraction had been part of the accident, even if that were never quantified on a police report or death certificate.

Hugh remembered Casey's speech his first day, what felt like years ago. He had to think like a professional now. Despite that warning, Hugh had relaxed. Ernie was dead. And there was no way to make that better.

At the resort the dining room windows glowed bright. Kitchen staff bustled inside, serving dinner. That seemed wrong, somehow, as if all the lights should be off, meals cancelled in mourning.

"I need to find Ginny," Hugh said.

"Uh uh!" Latner snapped. "*You* don't talk to anyone but our lawyer."

"But I…"

"*I'll* convey condolences and well-wishes and anything else. Period. Anything *you* say could come back to haunt us." Latner's voice softened. "Look, Hugh, I know you want to do what's right. I'll take care of Ginny like she's one of my own. But you'll have zero contact."

Hugh nodded, queasy again. Could he do anything right?

"You made the right choices, Mate," Casey said. "But this is how serious this job is."

Casey walked away, gray rain swallowing him.

"Toss your rust pile in the back," Latner said. "I'll run you home."

"I'm not fired?"

"Only if you talk to Ginny, or anyone else, about this."

15

Hugh dreaded going to work the next morning and facing the other divemasters. He hadn't slept that night, racking his brain over what he could have done differently to save Ernie. The Eagle Ray Diver's staff would be talking about little else. In the pre-dawn light, Hugh pulled on his work clothes and slipped outside. The strange creaking sound came from somewhere overhead again. He was too tired to give it any thought. Hugh had nearly reached his scooter when something crashed to the ground behind him. A stream of obscenity followed. Hugh ran back around the house's corner and found an upended paint can oozing red paint across the dirt. Red splatters covered the teal paneling. Under the eaves, Jerrod hung in his climbing harness, paintbrush dripping more red.

"Sorry. I was trying to be quiet, but the goddamn bucket slipped."

Jerrod belayed himself down, a giant a spider dropping from its web. His harness creaked, like wind in the treetops.

"You're… working on the side now?" Hugh said. It had been Jerrod's climbing rig Hugh had heard every time he slipped into the bushes to search for caves. Had Jerrod seen Hugh sneaking into the jungle?

"Last week or so." Jerrod flashed a crooked smile. "I'm working on Benedict. Patron saint of spelunkers."

Hugh went cold. Jerrod had seen him, all right. But did Jerrod know *why* Hugh was caving?

"Don't worry about me blabbing." Jerrod waved his paintbrush at Hugh's arms. "Those scrapes'll give you away long before I do."

Hugh tucked his arms behind his back, though it was too late to hide them.

"Everybody goes through the pirate treasure phase," Jerrod said. "Nobody's ever found anything, but that's no reason to lose faith."

"A guy has to try." Hugh shrugged, as if ashamed of being found out.

Jerrod's face went serious.

"Sorry about your diver yesterday. Tough situation."

"No one's supposed to... How do you know about that?"

"On Blacktip? Seriously?" Jerrod picked up his paint can. "Don't beat yourself up, Hugh."

"Easier said than done."

Hugh rode away, dreading his welcome at Eagle Ray Cove even more. All the staff knew what had happened with Ernie, down to the last detail. Would they be as understanding as Jerrod? Would the resort's attorneys? Despite Latner's warning, Hugh needed to talk to someone about what had happened, someone with legal experience and no connection to Eagle Ray Divers, who would never talk to Latner. Another reason to get with Jessie. After work. He could sort out what she knew about him then, too.

He was jolted out of his thoughts south of Captain Vic's by two figures crouched in the weeds to the right of the road, as if looking for something. Ike and Leo. Hugh didn't have the energy to say hello to the chatterboxes, or the patience to get into one of their question sessions. He'd have to interact with people at work soon enough. He kept his head down, steered to the left edge of the road to avoid them.

"Howdy, Captain Hugh!" Ike stepped onto the road as Hugh neared. Leo followed suit, motioning for Hugh to slow.

Hugh cranked the scooter's throttle wide open. The engine spluttered like a dying weed wacker.

"Hey, we just had a quick question!"

Leo reached for Hugh's handlebars. Hugh swerved, wobbled on the road's unpaved shoulder, but kept himself out of the ditch. He recovered his balance and continued on. Dead weeds from the roadside stuck in his flip-flops. What was it with this island, with someone always forcing him off the road?

Eagle Ray Cove's entrance was thankfully deserted when Hugh arrived. He made for the dive shop, bracing for the accusing stares from the dive staff. For the questions about Ernie from the guests. At the staff lockers, though, he found the other divemasters watching Barb Schaft tacking a memo to the wall, pounding staples into each corner as if she were hammering shingles. Barb stepped back to let the staff read.

> *All staff drink discounts are hereby discontinued.*
>
> *Resort staff are not to be at the resort bar except for official functions requiring their attendance or if invited by a guest.*
>
> *If invited, staff may enjoy a maximum of two drinks with guests in* any twenty-four-hour period.

"I'm sure everyone understands," Barb said. "Our cocktail area has taken on the air of a roadhouse, what with so many of the staff camping there every evening. And drinking more beer than they pay for!"

Barb waddled away, humming to herself.

"That pair know how to build morale, don't they?" Gage whispered when Barb was out of earshot.

The others nodded but didn't dare speak. They all headed for the pier. Marina put her arm around Hugh's shoulders.

"Chin up. Don't let yesterday snowball."

The wind had shifted south. At the pier's end, Latner and Casey stood shoulder to shoulder, studying the waves rolling across the cut, talking over whether the boats should go out. They spoke quiet, so the others couldn't hear.

Lee gave Hugh a smug grin.

"Hope we don't have to go out," he said. "It'll be harder than ever for us to keep track of divers. Well, some of us, anyway."

"It'll be harder than ever getting guests back on the boat in one piece." Alison gave Lee a nasty look.

"Yeah, our guests aren't the sharpest light bulbs," Gage said. He saw Hugh. "Oh, crap. I didn't mean…"

Hugh waved him off. He deserved it, though Gage hadn't meant it as criticism.

"You did all right," Marina said. "Most of *them* have no clue how we keep them alive."

She jerked her thumb toward the dive shop. There, a dozen eager-faced dive guests waited for a sign from the crews. Latner and Casey walked back to the boats.

"We're up, Mate." Casey said.

The dive staff groaned. The guests whooped.

Across the dock Lee made a show of yelling out roll call, watching Hugh as he shouted out each name. Lee's divers chuckled. Guests on the *Skipjack* looked uneasy. Hugh gritted his teeth and cast off their dock lines.

"It'll be fine today," Casey said when Hugh climbed to the bridge. "None of our punters'll be wandering off too far, or taking their eyes off you." He gave Hugh an odd look.

"What?" Hugh said, expecting sarcasm or insult.

"You don't rattle easy," Casey said. "Experienced staff have panicked over less."

Hugh was speechless. Casey had complimented him for the second time in as many days. The more he screwed up, the more respect the captain seemed to have for him.

Before the first dive, Hugh briefed the safety procedures, maximum depth and time, reminded everyone to check their air before jumping in. He needn't have worried. As Casey had predicted, the divers stayed close to Hugh. Hugh, in turn, stayed close to the boat, checked everyone's air time and again and brought the divers to the surface as a group.

The second dive brought more of the same, with the divers' bubble trails clustered together in a single boil where Casey led them around the reef. Once all the divers were back onboard, Hugh felt himself relax.

When the boats returned to Eagle Ray Cove at midday, more notices from the Schafts had been tacked up around the resort. Staff-owned cars, scooters, and bicycles were not to be parked on resort property. Staff were not to use or cut through 'guest areas' unless instructed to by management or invited by a guest. Staff were not to wear sunglasses when talking to guests. Staff would police the grounds for litter and fallen foliage. Staff would wear a new uniform of khaki shorts and bright yellow Hawaiian shirts with 'Eagle Ray Cove' embroidered on the front.

"Sure we wouldn't've been better off with Mal?" Alison flipped through the sheaf of notices.

"No. The Schafts 're just idiots on a power trip," Marina said. "Mal'd eat people alive."

"Or turn 'em to stone," Gage said.

"This used to be fun." Alison shook her head.

"We stick together, we'll ride this out," Casey said. "Watch each others' backs."

Hugh ate lunch quickly, eager for the day to be over so he could track down Jessie. He was nearly finished when Marina joined the staff on the deck, slipping her phone in her pocket as she sat. She leaned over the table, motioned the others close.

"That was Rafe," she said. "It *was* a bomb at the runway site. Some kind of diesel-and-fertilizer something or other. They've jacked the reward to $50,000 and…"

Hugh didn't hear the rest, his pulse was pounding so loud. He knew where fertilizer was hidden. Near where a vehicle to haul it and diesel fuel could park out of sight. If he could find out who was going to the cave, he could claim the reward and have the cash he needed. He could call Adam, have him ask the Feds about a deal, then have Jessie act as the go between and stop mangling himself caving. All he needed was proof of who the bomber was. Or bombers.

Ike and Leo. It had to be. They didn't look or act like the other protestors, or even hang out with them. And with their vaguely military bearing, they probably had the training to build a bomb. He had to check in with Jessie this afternoon, see if she would act as a mediator without giving too many specifics, then stake out the cave on his way home.

After work Hugh raced to Blacktip Haven, hoping to catch Jessie during a lull. At the bluff-top retreat, he followed the main pathway through the sea grapes to the resort's central building, a twelve-sided single-story with screen porches all around. Voices murmured inside. Hugh stepped through the door and saw familiar faces. Elena Havens. Frank and Helen Maples. Dr. Someone from Payne's party. Payne himself, shaggy head in the middle of the group. Across the room Jessie was stacking wine glasses. She smiled when she saw Hugh and motioned him over.

"Skerritt has a stake," Payne was saying, "and the Bottoms have more. They're the ones forcing Rafe's hand. Both families stand to make a fortune."

"But no one here would blow anything up," Helen Maples said. "The question is who would?"

"Conspirators plotting their next move?" Hugh whispered when he reached Jessie.

"Oh, Payne and the Maples came for drinks. The rest just showed up. They're jumpy. The cops hauled off a bunch of Earth Federation people today."

"Which ones are Earth Federation?" Had Hugh's reward been sent packing before he had a chance to turn them in?

"Green shirts."

"Oh. Good." Blue-shirted Ike and Leo were still on island. Jessie gave Hugh an odd look.

"Come on," she said. "I have a couple of minutes before I have to prep dinner."

Elena saw Hugh and broke away from the group.

"You're not leaving, are you?"

"I stopped by for something else."

"Oh, but we need all the help we can get to fight for Mother Earth. You do love your Mother, don't you?"

"Absolutely. But right now I need to talk to Jessie. It's kind of important." Hugh pulled Jessie onto the back patio, let the screen door clap shut behind them.

"Kind of important?" Jessie said.

"Important I didn't get sucked into whatever's brewing in there. Where can we talk privately?"

Jessie led him on a winding course through the sea grapes, away from the main building, ducking under low mangrove limbs and around shrubs. The trees ended abruptly with a bluff-top view across the island's northern half. Boobies circled over the green-brown pond, and beyond, black smoke rose from the construction site. A rotted vegetation stink rose from the pond. Jessie sat on a wooden bench facing north.

"I'm glad you stopped by," she said. "Sorry I was so presumptive the other day."

"No. I'm, we're good..." He wanted to know what she knew about him, and how she knew it, but that had to wait.

"It sounds like you made the best of a bad situation yesterday." Jessie cut him off.

"*You* heard about that?" He'd make time for this, since she'd brought it up. "Any idea where I stand with that? Legally?"

"You followed procedure? Stuck to standards? You're solid. That your important question?"

"No. totally unrelated… honest to God, you really a lawyer?" Hugh didn't have time to ease into it. He had to know if she would help, then get to the cave on the off chance Ike and Leo showed up this evening.

"I… um… used to be." Jessie looked puzzled.

"So… You could help me with a legal something?"

"I can't practice in the Tiperons." Jessie stared across the pond. "Or the States anymore, for that matter." She turned back to Hugh, face guarded. "What kind of legal something?"

"I don't know exactly. Not yet. And licensed doesn't matter. I mainly need advice and someone who can speak legalese with some people in the U.S." Hugh waved a hand at the smoke rising from the construction site. "That out there may have set a ball rolling."

"Hugh, I have to tell you…"

"No. I trust you. I'll fill you in when I know more. You'll help?"

He was losing light and still had to bike to the cave.

"I'd love to, but there's something you need to…"

"Thanks! We'll talk later, but I have to run right now."

Hugh jogged down the pathways back to his scooter, leaving Jessie open-mouthed on the bench.

The sun was setting when he reached the cave. A truck's fender was barely visible through the screening mangroves. Hugh's heart jumped. Someone was here. All he had to do was see who it was and the reward was his. He rode past, rounded the next curve, and stopped. He stashed the scooter in the bushes and doubled back on foot. There no sound or movement from the cave. Hugh wriggled into the underbrush across the road and waited, ignoring the thorns jabbing at his arms and legs. Whoever was in the cave had to come out eventually.

He had never seen Ike or Leo with a vehicle. They could have borrowed a truck. From Elena. Maybe that was what the impromptu meeting at Blacktip Haven had been about. It didn't matter. As soon as Hugh had proof, he was a phone call away from putting cash in his pocket.

The shadows lengthened. Mosquitos swarmed in the underbrush, buzzing around Hugh and boring into any flesh he left exposed. He tucked his arms inside his t-shirt, squatted to cover his bare legs. Orange lights flickered in the undergrowth around him. Will-o'-wisps rising from the swampy ground? More winked across the road and clustered by the cave entrance.

If Elena were involved in the bombing, working through Jessie might be difficult. But Hugh didn't have a choice. He would collect his reward and deal with any blowback later. Jessie would understand. This wasn't an attack on her or Elena, it was him doing what he had to do to stay free. Hugh worked a hand out of one of his sleeves, swatted at the mosquitos swarming around his ears.

White light flashed faint inside the cave, so brief Hugh thought he had imagined it. Then again, quick, a flashlight bouncing off cave walls. The light brightened, then snapped off. A shadow detached itself from the cave mouth, a darker spot in the post-dusk gloom. A lone figure worked its way down toward the hidden truck. Was one of the men still in the cave? Or waiting in the truck? Hugh kept himself stone still, ignoring the mosquitos gnawing at his forehead.

The figure neared the road. A man, his walk and outline familiar. Ike or Leo? In the dim light, it didn't look as muscled as either protestor, or as tall. The man reached the road, looked both ways as if checking for anyone watching, then flipped up the hood of his sweatshirt.

Casey!

Hugh stayed squatted, stunned, as Casey walked back to the truck. A moment later came the rumble of a diesel engine starting, then the Eagle Ray Divers flatbed pulled onto the road with its lights off. It headed up the road, back toward the resort. A hundred yards later its lights clicked on, then were lost around the curve.

Hugh leapt from the bushes, swatting the mosquitos from his face, and ran for his scooter. Casey was the runway bomber? Looking back on Casey's rants on the boat and his face-off with Dermott, Hugh should have suspected him. Casey's hands and knees were scraped from crawling underground setting up bombs. And Casey had come late to Payne's party, reeking of diesel, after the boom people had taken for thunder the night of the first runway explosion. Had it been Casey who had tossed Hugh's place, after all? Had he had time to ransack an apartment at one end of the island, then set off a bomb at the other end and still get to Toad Hall? No, Hugh's home invasion and the bombings couldn't be related.

Hugh wheeled the scooter onto the road. A dead bougain-villea branch, covered in thorns, clung to the rear tire. Hugh brushed at it. The branch stuck to the rubber, as if a thorn were stuck in it. He plucked it off. Air hissed from the tire where a thorn had punctured the tire. Great. The resort was the closest place to swap out a tire, and he needed to get home now. Hugh shoved the bike back in the bushes and set off south on foot, alternatively walking and jogging to get home faster. His mind raced. Hugh had Casey dead to rights. He could be rid of the condescending son of a bitch with a word.

But that would cost him his job when Latner found out. And the reward money that had sounded good when Hugh thought he was exposing two annoying strangers now felt wrong when he thought of claiming it in exchange for Casey. Casey was an arrogant ass, sure, but being an ass didn't justify Hugh ruining Casey's life.

But if Hugh turned a blind eye and Casey blew up something else, someone might get hurt, or worse. Then Hugh would be as responsible as Casey.

Headlights flickered ahead of him, then the *bwop-bwop-bwop* of a misfiring engine. Hugh waited for Antonio to pass. Instead, the Jeep creaked to a halt beside him.

"Hugo" Antonio leaned out of the driver's window. "You taking exercise?"

Jerrod grinned from the passenger seat.

"Hoping for a ride home," Hugh said.

He climbed in the back seat, and Antonio turned the Jeep and headed back south.

"You seem troubled, Brother Hugh," Jerrod said. "Underground got you down?"

Hugh scowled at the caving reference, tried to change the topic.

"Nope, just kicking around doing something that hurts somebody or not doing anything knowing someone else'll get hurt."

"'Hurt' being either Mal or the Schafts?"

Hugh didn't respond. He had said too much. But if Jerrod thought he was talking about Eagle Ray Cove politics, that was fine.

"Damned if you do and damned if you don't, eh, Hugo," Antonio said. "Best to pick the one damns you the least."

"'Course, anything you do, or let happen, that thing's on you," Jerrod said. "Whether you mean it for good or evil. Karma's unforgiving that way."

"Karma?" Hugh said. "From a reverend?"

"Former," Jerrod said. "Kinda for that reason."

"Anything you can do to get rid of those Schafts, do that," Antonio said. "Nothing that gets rid of them can be too evil. Right, Jerrod?"

Jerrod laughed.

"Well, someone had to tell Brandon to piss up a rope."

"I missed something," Hugh said.

"Brandon up and fired Jerrod, not an hour ago," Antonio said. "We were headed back in to pick up his stuff."

"Fired for what?"

"Insubordination." Jerrod grinned. "He told me to move my scooter, so I tore down his rules and suggested an anatomical impossibility for him to do with them. I didn't know a person's face could turn that color."

"So… you're leaving the island?" As odd as Jerrod was, Hugh had grown accustomed to him being around.

"Nah. It's a blessing, really," Jerrod said. "It's depressing at The Cove with B. & B. holding sway, and Polly's been wanting me to come up to Scuba Doo for a while."

"Getting on Brandon's bad side not going to mess up your karma, Rev?" Hugh said.

"The bad side's the only acceptable side of that douche to be on." Jerrod laughed again. "That help with your problem?"

"Not even close," Hugh said. "But I wish I'd seen Brandon's face."

Hugh closed his eyes, slowly relaxed despite the bumpy ride. He didn't have to do anything about Casey that night, or even the next day. There had been days, weeks between explosions. Casey would let the police clear off the site before he struck again. Hugh could maybe talk to Casey privately, let Casey know Hugh knew, without being confrontational. If Casey knew his secret was out, that might stop any more bombing. But if Casey refused to stop, was Hugh willing to turn him in? He would talk to Casey first thing tomorrow and hope for the best.

"Earth to Hugo."

"I'm good, Antonio," Hugh said. "I just need to sleep on things, see what kind of harm I feel like doing in the morning."

"That's the spirit!"

16

The next morning Hugh found a knot of resort staff blocking the walkway behind the lobby. Barb and Brandon Schaft walked a tight circle at its center, glaring at the staff surrounding them. Casey stood with Marina and Gage on the crowd's near side. Across the crowd, Mal leaned against a deck post.

"I won't tolerate disloyalty!" Barb shook her finger at the group. Brandon, arms crossed, nodded agreement. "Sneaking behind our backs! Undermining our authority! Then to find out one of you is planning a heist, and only one of you came forward to tell us, well, that goes far beyond disloyalty."

Hugh joined Casey and the others.

"What's going on?"

"Not a clue, Mate. Just got here."

"You!" Barb jabbed a pudgy finger at Casey. "I'm wise to you, Mister."

"What are you on about, woman?"

Hugh's stomach sank. Barb and Brandon knew about Casey's bomb making. The Schafts would collect the reward and Casey would go to jail.

"Those scrapes. You sneaking off all the time." She waggled her finger at Casey. "Yes, I've seen you. You won't be burrowing into *this* office, my little gopher! I'm two steps ahead of you."

"You're two steps closer to the loony bin."

"Oh, I have all the details! On good authority!" She glanced at Brandon. "Consider it a kindness I'm nipping it pre-bud, letting you walk away rather than having you arrested!"

"Let's have these details, then. Here in front of everyone." Casey laughed. "Did you actually use the word 'heist?'"

"You think there's gold in the resort safe. You plan to tunnel in and steal it, then hide the loot in caves!"

Hugh tried not to laugh. The Schafts knew nothing about Casey and his runway bombs. Across the crowd, Mal was smiling. Brandon smiled back at her. Had she put this squirrely idea in Brandon's head? To have the Schafts publicly humiliate themselves? If so, she was playing a dangerous game.

"Tunnel with what?" Casey said. "This is solid limestone."

"Oh, that was the beauty of your plan, wasn't it? The cave only you know about. Impossible for us to find the entrance, what with all the uncleared jungle out there. But we know your end game, Mister! Resign quietly we won't involve the police."

Oh, involve them." Casey's smile turned nasty. "Marquette will pack you off to the nut house. And my attorney will make certain you stay there."

"I'll not be spoken to that way!"

"I'll speak to you any way I please. You've slandered me in front of twenty witnesses. I own you, you daft cow!"

Casey stalked down the boardwalk.

Mal's smile broadened.

"You come back this instant!" Barb started after him. "You're fired!"

"Barb." Ger Latner's voice was a whip crack. "A word."

Latner walked to the lobby without looking back. Barb followed. A moment later Latner and Barb's shouting echoed through the closed doors. Then silence. Latner walked out, looking like he was enjoying a morning stroll. The silent staff watched him go. Brandon, eyes wide, started toward Latner. At a quick look from Latner, Brandon veered off, scuttled for the lobby.

By the bar Mal could have been a child delighted by an unexpected magic show. Hugh raised an eyebrow at Gage and Marina to see if they knew what was happening.

"Ol' Barb may run the resort," Gage said, "but Ger just made sure she knows he runs dive ops," Gage said.

On the pier Casey glared at anyone who tried to talk to him. Hugh left him alone, readied the boat, helped the guests to board. He needed Casey in a good mood before he mentioned fertilizer or the runway. After work, maybe, before Casey skiffed out to his boat, when it was just the two of them.

Hugh spent the day mentally debating how best to pull Casey aside, rehearsing how he'd start the conversation. He would approach Casey as a friend. Or as a not-enemy, anyway. As much as he needed the money, the only way he could turn Casey in was if Casey refused to stop and left Hugh no other option.

At the day's end, though, instead of heading for the *Bident*, Casey stalked up the boardwalk toward the resort's center. Hugh hurried after him. He was even with the dive shop when footsteps sounded beside him. Lee. Mirroring Hugh's gait.

"What's the hurry, Blake?" Lee stuck his grinning face at Hugh. "Lose another guest?"

Hugh's fist hit Lee before he realized it, popping the little divemaster in the nose so hard Lee dropped to his knees, clutching his face. Hugh yowled at the pain lancing through his hand and wrist and forearm. Hugh hopped on one foot, then the other, shaking his hurt hand.

Blood flowed through Lee's fingers. He stared at Hugh in stunned disbelief.

"You hit… I thing you broke by doze!"

"You broke my hand!"

"You're godda be so sorry…"

Hugh stepped toward Lee. Lee crawled backwards, stood and half-ran past Ger Latner and into the dive shop. Hugh's mouth went dry. Latner had seen him hit Lee. He had broken Latner's cardinal rule with Latner looking on. He was fired. It had been worth it, seeing the look on Lee's face and watching the little rat scurry away, but Hugh was done at Eagle Ray Divers. And his hand ached.

"Took you long enough," Latner said. "Go get someone to show you how to throw a proper punch."

Latner stepped back into the dive shop.

Hugh stared at the door. Latner had expected him to hit Lee sooner or later. Then he remembered Casey. Hugh hurried up the boardwalk to catch up to the captain.

As Hugh neared the resort lobby, though, the door flew open and Brandon bounced out like a wide-eyed jack-in-the-box and pulled Hugh aside, away from the reception desk and the guests there.

"Hugh. You're not like the other dive staff. I've noticed that." Brandon whispered, tucking in the red Hawaiian shirt he'd adopted as his uniform. "You know what I'm talking about."

Hugh's annoyance turned to fear. Brandon seemed to be a self-absorbed buffoon. Had Hugh misread him? Was Brandon the one spying on him?

"What do you mean?" Hugh kept his voice even.

"You've been a professional. You have that air about you. We professionals need to stick together among these dive gypsies." Brandon gave Hugh a knowing wink. "One professional supporting another. Making the resort is run, well, professionally. If you take my meaning."

Brandon gripped Hugh's arm, spoke lower.

"No telling when the diving department might need new management, hmm?"

Hugh laughed with relief. This was a clumsy power play? Then anger surged up.

"That 'unprofessional' dive staff saves lives every day," Hugh said loud enough for everyone in the lobby to hear. "You want to get rid of Ger, you're on your own."

Brandon's face paled. His wispy moustache quivered. His eyes darted to see who had heard Hugh.

Hugh pulled free of Brandon's grasp, stalked out the front door. Casey wasn't in the parking lot. Great. He'd lost Casey and publicly defied Brandon. Latner could shield the dive staff from the Schafts, but he couldn't stop the Schafts from digging into Hugh's background. They would focus on Hugh now, look for weaknesses. Find out there was a reward to be claimed.

Hugh went to the parking lot, then remembered he had left his scooter in the roadside bushes the night before. He would have to use a resort one-speed bike to get home. Hugh cut around behind the resort office, headed for the guest bikes by the laundry room. Voices came low and angry from the laundry, became clearer when Hugh reached the bikes.

"You know damn well it's not Hugh," Casey growled low.

"We know damn well it's someone." Mal hissed. "I, or Rich, find you know anything…"

"Cross me or anyone I work with, it's the last thing you do on this island."

"One of your buddies is trashing Rich's runway, you'll go down with him."

"Not as quickly as Miss Mallory LaTrode will go down. Or is it Mallory Black? Or Molly Black. Whoever, she's still wanted for trafficking stolen antiquities. And for her partner's disappearance. Probably a different person, but the authorities would be the best ones to sort that out. Don't you think?"

Silence. Hugh pulled the nearest bike from the rack and ran, wanting to be gone before Casey or Mal stepped from the laundry. Mal couldn't think he was the bomber. She had thrown that out to see what Casey knew. But she had never talked of betraying Hugh before. This may have been a ploy, but was she really thinking of turning Hugh in, after all?

The bike was too short for him, and soon Hugh was gasping for breath, his legs aching despite going little faster than a brisk walk. An unexpected relief washed over him as he pedaled, though. He had spent the month worried about being found out, and all this time Mal was in hiding, too? For smuggling? Now he had something on her. There was a twinge at that, remembering those first days with Mal. His insides still jumped when he thought of her. That shouldn't be, but there it was. He could no more expose her than he could expose Casey.

And Casey shielding him was unexpected. Reassuring, too. It also gave Hugh a lead-in for the fertilizer conversation they still had to have.

The sun was below the tree line when Hugh finally reached the edge of Antonio's clearing. Brandon, Casey, and Mal, the slow bike ride had him home later than usual. Cori's dogs were barking, but thankfully from inside Cori's apartment. A Skerritt Construction pickup truck was parked by Dermott's place. Hugh barely saw it.

A bulky man in a light blue t-shirt was sliding Hugh's door closed from the inside. Hugh leaped from the bike and ducked behind a tree. What would Ike, or Ike and Leo since they were always together, be doing in his place? Had they heard rumors he was hiding something and wanted to search while he was gone? No. They knew his schedule, knew he was usually home now. Hugh shivered despite the heat. He was an idiot. They were bounty hunters here to haul him back.

A roar came from his apartment. Then a thud of a body slamming into a wall. The sliding glass door shook, as if from an earthquake. Another roar, and the sound of furniture breaking. Ike yelled. Leo's face pressed against the kitchen window for a moment, then he was snatched back, shrieking in terror. Cori's dogs howled. The walls shuddered, sending dust and leaves falling from the eaves. The bedside lamp crashed through the kitchen window, taking blue mini-blinds with it. Then the sliding door flew open and a bloody-faced Leo stumbled outside. Dermott charged out, tackled Leo, hit him twice and Leo lay still. Dogs howled louder.

Dermott scanned the clearing. His eyes, red from booze and disturbed sleep, locked on Hugh.

"Sorry, Hugo," Dermott said before Hugh could speak. "Don't know who they are. I clean up the mess."

"What happened?" Hugh ran to Leo, checked for a pulse. He was alive. Good.

"Don't know, rightly." Dermott sat back in the dirt, shook his head. "Sleeping when these two grabbed me. Tried to put a bag over my head…"

Hugh slipped past Dermott, into his apartment. Ike lay sprawled facedown on the floor, arm at an unnatural angle. Thick black cable ties were strewn like pick-up sticks on the floor around him. An empty pillowcase lay beside him. Ike's pulse was ragged, but he was alive, too. Dermott's feet shuffled behind him.

"They're gonna hurt like hell when they come to," Hugh said.

The men had studied Hugh's daily routine to find the best time to abduct him. They had probably wanted to grab him on the road the day before, when he had refused to stop. Then they'd come here knowing he was usually home by now. Had mistaken Dermott for Hugh in the dark room.

A worried look crossed Dermott's face, was quickly replaced by the dangerous look Hugh had seen at the runway before Dermott hit Casey.

"They jumped me, no warning," Dermott rumbled. "Self-defense. Don't even know who they are."

"I believe you."

"Not going back to jail." There was an edge in Dermott's voice. "Not you or anybody else sending me back to jail."

Dermott loomed over Hugh, blocking the doorway. The unconscious bounty hunters were suddenly a minor worry compared to Dermott.

Then an idea sprung into Hugh's head fully formed, an idea that might solve multiple problems at once.

"Dermott, instead of going to jail, how'd you like to split $50,000?"

Dermot paused, his fists half balled.

"Constable Marquette's looking for whoever's blowing up the runway, right?" Hugh said. "Now here's these two, up to no good, attacking innocent people. I've seen these guys sneaking around a cave up by the resort. What do you bet these are our trouble makers?"

Dermott looked doubtful, but his hands unclenched.

"How you know they the ones?"

"The cave they were in has stolen fertilizer inside. We put them in the cave and call Marquette. You stay out of jail, and we walk away with cash in pocket."

Dermott's eyes narrowed.

"How you know about caves and fertilizer, Hugo?"

"I've... been searching on my own. Look, no one's gonna believe I did this to two guys, and I can't move these jokers by myself." Hugh held up his hurt hand for Dermott to see. "Dropping them somewhere else, then splitting the money makes sense."

Dermott smiled, nodded.

"Great," Hugh said. "They're not gonna be out forever. We need to get them hog tied and onto your truck."

Hugh handed Dermott a handful of cable ties. Soon they had both men's hands and feet bound. Leo started to come to as they tied him up. Dermott whacked him again and stuffed a washcloth in each man's mouth. They laid Ike and Leo in the truck's bed like felled logs and set off north up the coast.

"Those two after you," Dermott said after a few minutes. "No other reason them to be in your place. And you not surprised to see them."

"They're protestors who went too far. Probably out to rob me. All of us."

"Uh uh. Came straight to your place. And you want them gone, no one the wiser. What you been doing, Hugo, to have men like that after you?"

"Let's just say I don't want to go to jail, either, Dermott, and it's got nothing to do with that damn runway."

Dermott laughed, a deep rumble like the beginning of a rockslide.

"You got layers to you, Hugo. Knew you was playing something close. How you know I won't turn you in?"

"Will you?" Hugh heard himself say. This plan had come together so fast, he hadn't thought beyond framing Ike and Leo.

"Oh, no worries about that, Hugo. We do stick together on Blacktip."

At the cave, Hugh showed Dermott where to park behind the roadside bushes. Ike and Leo had regained consciousness during the ride and were yelling as loud as their washcloth-filled mouths allowed. Dermott smacked both of them both and they lay unmoving, unconscious again. Fireflies flashed thicker than ever in the underbrush. Inside the cave Hugh clicked on his light, and they propped the men against the fertilizer bags.

"You have a knife?" Hugh asked.

Dermott gave Hugh a surprised look, but handed him a pocketknife. Hugh slit open a bag, rubbed the fertilizer on Ike and Leo's hands, then poured a handful over their clothes. Dermott gave his rumbling laugh again.

"You don't miss a trick, Hugo."

"Sure. Call Marquette. You saw suspicious-looking protestors going in this cave, then heard them fighting. I'll cut their ties."

Dermott went outside to call. Hugh cut the cable ties, tucked them in his pocket then joined Dermott. They reached the truck. A distant siren wailed.

"Dermott, you mind running me up to Parrett's Landing?"

"Parrett's...? Oh ho, you busy tonight, Hugo." Dermot studied Hugh again. "And don't want to talk to any policemen, huh?"

"I *really* need to talk to a friend there right now." Dermott might sell Hugh out, claim all the reward, but Hugh had to chance it.

Jessie's place glowed above the trees when Dermott dropped Hugh off beside the road. Hugh climbed to the upstairs deck, not sure whether the stairs were swaying or if his legs were still shaking from the encounter with Ike and Leo. Jessie answered his knock, looked surprised to see him.

"We need to follow up on our talk," he said before she could speak.

"I need to clear something up..."

"If you help me, you need to get up to speed on things. Fast."

Jessie opened her mouth, but Hugh cut her off again.

"Let me get it out. I was a bonds trader, and I made a mistake and lost some people's money. Then I tried to make the money back, and I lost even more. A lot more. I sold everything I had and mostly paid it back, but I still had to run to keep out of jail."

Hugh paused to let Jessie take that in, expecting shock or a cascade of questions.

"I know," Jessie said.

"How could you know?"

"When we met… Here, sit down. The day before I left the U.S., some people asked me to keep an eye on you. For a weekly paycheck."

Hugh sat stone still. Jessie was the spy. And he had recruited her to help him. Idiot!

"I was coming here anyway," she said. "In debt after the divorce. Through the legal grapevine I got the offer to keep tabs on you, call if you went anywhere else. Not a ton of money, but it covered expenses that first month. Then I realized I liked you and stopped checking in."

"So, when I felt paranoid, I was right to?" Hugh's jaw clenched.

"No. I mean, yes. But I'm not helping them anymore. I took their money and did squat."

Jessie's gray eyes were fixed on his now. She chewed at her lower lip. Hugh fought back a blinding anger.

"So were you going to split the take with Ike and Leo?"

"Who?"

"The bounty hunters who broke in my place with cable ties and pillowcases."

"Oh my Gawd! I knew nothing about that! I would've warned you!"

"I'm supposed to trust you?"

"Yes." Her eyes were angry now. She tugged at her pendant. "I didn't have to volunteer any of this. And if I was reporting back, I'd've known about them sending people, and definitely wouldn't have come clean tonight." Jessie's voice shook. "I tried to tell you a couple times before, but…"

It made an odd sort of sense. But blindness to Mal's conniving had landed him in a big mess. He wouldn't let Jessie play him like that.

"You lied to me."

"Technically, no. I was friendly for the wrong reasons, but that's not lying. That's two-faced. And I stopped."

"That's better?"

"I'm sorry. What would convince you? Ask me anything and I'll tell you."

"Why the switch?"

"I'm making plenty now." Jessie fingered her cross again. "And I don't want to ruin… whatever this is. You don't run into many questing knights these days, no matter how rusty their armor."

Hugh wanted to believe her, and part of him did.

"Any more bounty hunters on their way?"

"Probly. As bad as folks want you, I'd count on it."

Hugh was back in his no-win situation. He could ditch Jessie and take his chances, or he could trust her and maybe find another solution. She already had contacts with the people he needed to deal with.

"If I hired you, would we have any kind of attorney-client privilege?" Hugh said.

"We'd have accomplice-criminal privilege." She chewed her lip again. "But what d'you have in mind?"

"Any way the people you were working with would cut a deal if I paid all the money back, including interest?"

"You committed a felony." Jessie stifled a laugh. "And last I heard you were still about twenty grand shy of paying it back."

"I'm about to be $25,000 richer."

"How on Earth…"

"Right about now Constable Marquette's arresting two bounty hunters in Pelagic Society shirts for bombing the runway site."

Jessie's eyes went wide.

"Long story," Hugh said. "I found the fertilizer while I was exploring. The two guys grabbed Dermott in the dark by mistake. Big mistake, for them. I needed to make them go away, and Dermott didn't want another assault conviction. All in, like, the last hour."

"So… these're the bombers?"

"Doesn't matter. Marquette'll seize all the makings, there won't be any more explosions, and I can pay everyone back. Yeah, I committed a crime and the Feds still want me. But if the damage is fixed, would they maybe want me a little *less*? Maybe enough less to make bringing me in not worth anyone's time?"

"Doubt it, but I can ask. Recovering the funds is a big deal to them, but…" her voice trailed off.

A thought struck Hugh, blinding, obvious. He was an idiot.

"You're the one who tossed my place. The night of Payne's party. You showed up at Toad Hall sweaty and out of breath."

"Guilty." Jessie winced. "It was when I started going through your stuff that things changed. It… wasn't right. I left after a couple of minutes, then stopped spying on you and got to know you."

"You're ahead of me there."

He should be angry, Hugh knew, but somehow he wasn't.

"Hey, I'm sorry," Jessie said. "Weird, huh, sitting next to someone you thought you knew, but who feels like a total stranger."

Hugh nodded. If Jessie helped him, she would be implicated right along with him, whether her attraction to him was real or not. He wanted to trust her. If he was reading her wrong, though, he was screwed. He wished they could start over, but how?

"I'm Jessie." She smiled, took his hand. "I'll probly see you around."

17

The next day the island buzzed with news of Rafe Marquette arresting two runway saboteurs.

"The gentlemen had no passports," P. C. Marquette said to the locals crowding the Eagle Ray Cove deck. "There's no record of them entering the country via any immigration point. Their boat in Spider Bight never cleared Customs and was packed with illegal weapons and surveillance equipment. We're still sorting out what to try them for first."

Marisa the nurse had people laughing at her stories about treating the men's wounds.

"Crazy talk, from them both," she said. "Fertilizer fumes made them goofy, or they beat each other silly in that cave. Kept talking about an animal attacking them. One said a bear, the other swore it was Bigfoot."

"Duppies got 'em, right enough," Antonio said. "Ol' May Cow protecting its own from foreign craziness. Lucky Dermott found 'em."

Dermott nodded at Hugh from across the bar. Casey's gaze went from one to the other, but he said nothing.

The next day the extra policemen left for Tiperon, taking the bandaged Ike and Leo with them. That afternoon Jessie pulled Huh aside at the Eagle Ray Cove entrance.

"The prosecutor says no-go." She spoke low so no other homeward-bound divemasters could hear her. "You're kind of a big fish. Embezzling $500 grand doesn't just go away."

"It was worth a try," Hugh said. Great. He was back on square one.

"Your stunt with the bounty hunters didn't help any, either." Jessie laughed.

"What happens when the real bomber strikes again? You and Dermott'll give back the money?"

"It won't come to that," Hugh said. "Trust me."

Land clearing at the runway site resumed the next day. Rich Skerritt held court at the Eagle Ray Cove bar at lunch.

"The hippies are gone," Rich Skerritt crowed. "We're back to making this island into a thing of beauty."

"That's right, Mr. Skerritt." Brandon Schaft bounced beside Skerritt, shoulders back and belly jiggling. "And we'll get these slack workers back to being useful, too."

Brandon strutted across the deck, shooing the dive staff back to the pier. The divemasters wandered down the boardwalk in ones and twos.

"Wild week for caves," Alison said. "First, B. and B. are ranting about caves under the office, now bombers get arrested in a real cave."

"That story about Casey's tunnel was a hoot," Gage said.

"Like to know where the punter came up with it." Casey gave Hugh a long look. "And why Dermott's splitting the reward with an F.N.G."

Hugh slowed to let the others get ahead of them. Casey slowed with him, eyes never leaving Hugh.

"Casey, I stumbled across that cave looking for... other stuff," Hugh murmured. "Then Dermott got in a jam and it was an easy way to get rid of two guys Dermott beat up."

"In your house. Why?"

"Does it matter?"

"Whether they're guilty or not, you'll get your money, that it?" Casey's voice went cold.

"Those guys weren't good people," Hugh said. "And I won't sell out the person who hid fertilizer."

Casey stopped, his face stone. His eyes bored into Hugh's. Hugh took a half step back, expecting a punch.

"But I was worried someone else might get hurt, or worse, the next time a bomb went off," Hugh said. "This way the bad guys are gone, there's no more fertilizer for bombs and everything's good."

"You're playing with fire," Casey said. "And butting in where you shouldn't."

"I'm playing the hand I'm dealt, as honestly as I can."

Hugh kept on to the *Skipjack*, not caring if Casey followed.

The wind had strengthened during lunch, was now blowing hard from the southwest. Hugh pivoted the *Skipjack* from the dock, studied the cut as he idled out. A deck-high wave crashed across the reef.

"This'll be fun," Hugh said.

"Wait 'til later, Sherlock," Casey said. "That shite'll be on our stern. We get our divers back safe, you and I will have a long talk."

Casey pressed his sunglasses to his nose and cinched his sweatshirt hood tight around his face.

They wallowed up the west coast, beam seas setting the *Skipjack* rolling. Past The Pinnacle they turned to the island's lee. There, the sea spread flat as any lake. They tied off at Hammerhead Wall, in sight of the East Sound and its World War Two-era pier. Casey briefed, and they dropped the divers as quick as they could. The guests, many still queasy from the ride, stayed close to the boat. One elderly couple spent the dive in the shallows under the *Skipjack* and were the last ones back aboard.

"How was the dive, Tommy?" Hugh helped the gray-haired man take off his dive gear. Nicotine stains yellowed the man's fingers and moustache.

"Great!" The man looked to his wife. "That stingray came right up to Mary and me, close enough to touch."

"He's the Stingray Whisperer," Mary said.

"I got so caught up with Mr. Ray I just…"

Tommy stopped mid-sentence.

"Hon, what's up?"

Tommy didn't move.

"Tommy? You okay?" Hugh put a hand on the man's back.

Tommy stared, unblinking. His lips trembled, trying to speak. Hugh leaned close to hear. No sound came out. Hugh waved his hand in front of Tommy's face. No reaction. He grabbed the man's hands.

"Tommy? Can you squeeze my hands? Squeeze my hands!"

"Bloody hell!" Casey snatched the oxygen kit from its rack.

These symptoms, so soon after surfacing, it had to be an embolism - an air bubble in the bloodstream, blocking blood flow to the brain. But that made no sense. Tommy hadn't made a rapid ascent or held his breath. A stroke? Had heavy smoking made his lungs so fragile they couldn't stand up to diving's pressure changes? Didn't matter. On the boat the treatment was the same: pure oxygen to counteract the bubble. Get him to a doctor and a recompression chamber.

That flashed through Hugh's mind in an instant. Casey pressed the oxygen mask to the man's face.

"Get us out of here!" Casey yelled.

Hugh was already leaping to the helm. He started the engines, called Eagle Ray Cove on the radio and shoved the throttles forward. Casey's training echoed in his ears: 'if someone's hurt badly, redline the engines. They can take it.'

But where to go? With an embolism, every second counted. Brutal waves on the west side meant a forty-five-minute ride to the resort. They had maybe fifteen minutes of emergency oxygen onboard. And Tommy couldn't take the rough ride. Hugh saw Ernie on the beach again. He pushed that image aside.

"Headed for The Cove?" Ger Latner's voice on the VHF crackled over Hugh's head.

Hugh hesitated. The crumbling Civil Defense pier was just down the coast.

"Ger, can a car get to that old eastside dock?"

A long pause, then:

"You know East Sound, Hugh? Nasty coral in there, and it's silted damn shallow."

"We get to that dock, he has a chance."

"I'll meet you there."

A guest's head popped up from below.

"Casey says to make for the east side dock."

"Already on it!" Hugh snapped.

"Casey says the guy just squeezed his hand!" The guest yelled.

There was no way. Casey was keeping everyone's spirits up. Tommy was unresponsive. Casey knew as well as Hugh did Tommy had minutes to live. If he wasn't dead already. But they had to try, hope for a miracle.

They came even with the East Sound cut. On the fringing reef, dead branches jutted upright in the coral where fishermen had marked the entrance. More handmade stakes marked a winding channel through the lagoon. Hugh lined up on the cut, hoping the stakes weren't just random sticks, and ran full throttle between them, keeping his propellers high as possible. Once inside he steered a slalom course around the dark hulks of lurking coral heads toward the cement pier.

The props hit sand, set the *Skipjack* shuddering. Shouts came from below. Hugh backed to idle. Running aground where help couldn't reach them would kill Tommy as surely as the long ride down the west coast.

Fifty yards ahead the Eagle Ray Divers flatbed pulled onto the rust-and-concrete pier. Latner and Marisa climbed out.

At a shout from Casey, guests lowered the *Skipjack*'s fenders. Hugh pivoted the boat, reversed the engines and the *Skipjack* settled alongside the pier, props throwing gouts of sand in the shallow water.

The pier, designed for larger Navy vessels, rose even with the helm, six feet above the main deck. Tommy was strapped to the backboard, oxygen tank tucked between his knees. Casey barked directions, and the guests lifted the backboard over their heads and slid it onto the pier. Tommy's lips moved. He was still alive, somehow. Mary clambered up after him. Latner signaled 'okay' and waved Hugh away.

Hugh idled back through the maze of stakes, gripping the chrome wheel tight to steady his hands.

"Good job." Casey dropped onto the bench seat beside him.

Hugh nodded. Now he had to get the other guests and the boat back to the resort safely.

They rounded the island's northern tip. The first wave crashed on the bow, sending spray over the helm, soaking Hugh and Casey. The shoreline to Hugh's left was visible only when the *Skipjack* crested each wave. Hugh fought into the southeast swells to keep the waves off the *Skipjack*'s beam, angling farther and farther from the island.

"It may've been better putting everyone off with Tommy." Hugh yelled through the crackling wind.

"Still can." Hugh couldn't tell if Casey was testing him, but as scary as these seas were, the thought of running through East Sound again was scarier. He was committed. Hugh angled south, well outside the west side mooring balls.

The island was far off their port side when they drew even with Eagle Ray Cove. Salt stung Hugh's eyes, made it hard to see anything but the wheel and the gauges. He would be able to see the channel markers when they were closer. He hoped.

"You know if you bollock this up we're all dead, right?"

Hugh ignored Casey, cranked the wheel to port, tried not to think of getting sideways in the cut.

The boat swung up one wave face, then down, then back up as the next swell caught them. Hugh matched boat speed to the wave, perched the *Skipjack* high on its shoulder. Through the haze he made out the green and red channel markers. The waves grew, bunched together over the shallows. Hugh pushed the throttles forward. The wave ahead rose high as the bridge. Another behind pulled at them. Hugh nudged the throttles forward again. The *Skipjack* inched back up onto his wave's shoulder. The wave slowed. Hugh adjusted his speed. The wave behind closed the gap, pulled at him again. The stern started to lift. Hugh jammed throttles all the way forward. He saw, peripherally, the channel marker tops going past on either side. Then the wave died and they were safe inside the reef.

Cheers erupted from the guests below.

Hugh released the wheel, tried to straighten his fingers. He gasped at the pain.

At the dock, they offloaded guests, then went to the dive shop. Hugh dreaded another grilling from Constable Marquette. He pressed his arms to the table to keep his hand steady enough to write his accident report. He was finishing when Ger Latner came in from the clinic.

"You guys did good," Latner said. "Guy's still alive. Shouldn't be, but he is. On his way to the chamber on Tiperon."

Hugh leaned back, his body trembling in relief. Casey stood, stared down at Hugh.

"We're still due for a talk," he said. "But later."

Casey left the shop, headed for the *Bident*. Hugh went to the tiki bar, hoping a beer would calm his jangling nerves.

"Vicious out there," Marina was saying. "Never seen Lee so quiet. It was nice."

"I never heard Gage cuss like that," Alison said.

"There's a reason I wear brown shorts on days like this." Gage drained his beer.

"And you." Marina pointed at Hugh. "You docked in the East Sound? Holy cow!"

Ger Latner settled into the chair next to Hugh.

"Hell of a run you made," Latner said. "I know coxswains with fifteen years experience who wouldn't've done that."

"Now you tell me." Hugh tried to laugh.

"I know Casey'll never say anything to you, but you should know…"

Hugh braced for the criticism.

"… he said, 'Hugh's perfectly fine with the boat.' Never heard him say that about anyone else he's trained."

Latner pounded Hugh on the back again and left. Around Hugh the other dive staff nodded, raised beer bottles in toast. An anvil lifted from Hugh's shoulders. Today didn't make up for Ernie's death, but he had saved a life. From behind the bar, Mal watched Hugh with narrowed eyes.

A yell came from the resort office. Barb Schaft stormed toward the crowded deck, red plastic gas can in one hand and a box of kitchen matches in the other. Rich Skerritt followed in her wake.

"You people think this is a joke?" She shook the can at the nearest cluster of staff. "Leaving this outside our door for the police to find?" Barb rounded on the dive staff, jabbed her finger at each one in turn. "When we find who did this, you'll be on the next plane to the Tiperon jail!"

Barb's eyes blazed scanning the surrounding faces.

"If anyone knows anything, you come forward now and there'll be no punishment. One chance only! Who knows something?"

Mal stepped from behind the bar. Barb jabbed her finger at her.

"You, your highness! You seem to be in the know about everything."

Mal gave Barb her poisonous smile.

"Nothing to say?" Barb stepped toward Mal.

"Just a question," Mal spoke soft, but her voice carried across the deck.

"Well?"

"Have you met Portia?" Mal stepped aside for a heavyset woman in a red silk dress, wrists sheathed in gold bracelets, coifed hair and perfect make up. "Rich's wife. Just in on the last flight. Portia, *this* is Barb Schaft."

Rich Skerritt's face went pale. He backed toward the resort office.

In the same instant Barb's mouth dropped open, Mal stepped back, and Portia hit Barb with an open hand that snapped Barb's head sideways.

"I'll show you what a wedding ring means!" Portia hit Barb again, dropped Barb to her knees.

Staff and guests scattered. Portia grabbed Barb's hair, pulled her upright, hit her again, then dragged her down the boardwalk. Barb screamed for help, swatted at Portia, clawed at Portia's hand in her hair. She grabbed a post, dug in her heels. Portia yanked Barb's hair. Barb howled, released the post, and launched herself at Portia. As Barb clutched for Portia's waist, Portia held her aside, raised Barb's head and smacked Barb's face hard with her open hand. The impact echoed through the courtyard. Blood flowed from Barb's mouth and nose.

"Ooo! Portia with a wicked left hook!" Gage said.

Another blow. Then another. Barb swayed, upright only because Portia was holding her.

"Someone should stop them." Hugh took a tentative step toward the women.

"You want to get whacked, go right ahead." Marina stepped back from Hugh.

"Hey! What the hell?" Brandon Schaft ran from the office. He grabbed Portia's hand, tried to pry her fingers from Barb's hair. Portia, half spun, backhanded Brandon, her hand barely slowing as it made contact. Brandon's head rocked back. He staggered, then his legs bucked and he crumpled on the wooden decking, hands splayed wide and head shaking, eyes trying to focus.

"I'll give you the same as I give your whore wife!" Portia Skerritt's voice thundered through the grounds. She smacked Barb again.

Then Ger Latner was there, grabbing Portia's backhand mid-swing. Prying Portia's fingers from Barb's hair. Pulling her away from Barb, who collapsed, tufts of hair settling around her.

"Portia. Enough." Latner's voice was low, forceful. "You made your point." A quick nod toward Barb trying to pull herself to her knees, face covered in blood.

Portia swung at Latner. He caught her hand again. Held her at arm's length.

"You hit her again, you may kill her."

"She did it bold-faced," Portia said. "All but rubbed my nose in it. What was I supposed to do?"

"This." Latner's voice stayed calm. "Now let it go."

"She needs to understand what she did…"

"Barb won't even look at Rich again without her teeth rattling."

"I'm filing charges!" Brandon, struggling to his feet.

"You'll go away and not cause a fuss." Latner towered over Brandon. "Or should I let go of Portia?"

Brandon's face went white. He stepped to Barb, helped her to her feet, guided her toward the parking lot.

"We're going to the clinic. And we'll see what the constable has to say about this."

"I'll call Marisa," Latner said. "But I wouldn't count on too much sympathy from Rafe Marquette. Portia's his aunt."

A glare from Brandon, then he was gone. Latner smiled at the stunned guests.

"We apologize for the commotion, folks. Drinks are complimentary this evening."

Latner led Portia into the office, arm around her shoulder, head close to hers, whispering.

Hugh went to the bar to pay for his beer, suddenly exhausted. Mal watched him approach.

"I need a word with you," she said low. Her smile sent a chill of fear down his spine.

"What, you burn your bridge with Skerritt and now want to be friends with me?" Hugh said.

Hugh didn't care what Mal was plotting. He wanted to pay for his beer and go home.

"I'm a little short on cash this month." Mal's teeth flashed white.

"Well, your manager's salary'll solve that soon enough."

Hugh slid a $10 bill across the bar.

"I was thinking more along the lines of $25,000." Her teeth flashed again. "You'd be amazed what Dermott'll say when he's full of free beer. Something about kidnappers in your apartment."

"So tell Marquette." Hugh tried to sound confident. Mal had finally turned on him, after all. He had been naïve to think that would never happen.

"Then I wouldn't get $25,000. And I'd have to figure out where you hid all that cash you brought down with you. Rafe's my Plan B."

"He arrests me, you'll get nothing."

"Just the reward for Blake Calloway. Then I could rent Antonio's nice master suite, maybe remodel it a bit. The money still stashed in your place, Blake?"

Hugh's face, hands were numb.

"That's what I thought," Mal said. "Now, I think a payment plan would be best, don't you?"

"It's always been about the money, hasn't it?"

"Please. Everything's about the money," Mal said. "You're here because of money. And as soon as I get enough, I'm gone. Your stash should be enough."

Hugh staggered from the bar. Idiot. Mal's eyes, her tone said she would bleed him dry, then still turn him in. With Skerritt alienated, he was her golden ticket. Why had he ever trusted her? He rode home trying to think of some way out of this mess. If he turned her in, she would still have him over a barrel. And he had no proof she had stolen anything or smuggled anything.

At Antonio's Hugh barely noticed Dermott sitting outside the old tool shed, waving a drunken greeting. Inside, Hugh sat, willed his heart to slow. Mal's pawn still sat on his bedside table, the heavy game piece holding down loose notes in the ceiling fan's draft. At least he had ruined the chess set she cared about more than money. Mal's sole trace of sentimentality. A vague suspicion crept over him at that thought. He took the pawn to the kitchen, scraped a knife blade across its black lacquered bottom. Paint flaked off, a small fleck at first, then larger bits as Hugh kept scraping. He held the pawn to the sunlight streaming through the broken window. The pawn's base gleamed bright yellow. Gold, not lead, gave the pawn its weight. The other painted pieces had been just as heavy.

Hugh stuffed the pawn in his pocket and raced outside.

"Dermott! I borrow your phone?"

"I...sure, Hugo." Dermott looked dazed.

Hugh snatched the cell phone from Dermott and stepped back inside his apartment. He photographed the pawn, then punched in the number for Blacktip Haven. Jessie answered.

"You said I'm a big fish, right?" Hugh blurted.

"What? Yeah."

"Well, would prosecutors go easy on me if I could give them a bigger fish?"

"It'd depend on the how big the fish is."

"How about one that smuggles stolen antiquities and maybe offed her partner in crime?"

"That might do it. This bad girl have a name I could float?"

"See what a search for Mallory LaTrode, or Black, or Molly Black turns up. And a gold chess set. I'm sending you a photo. I don't need my charges to go away, I just need for no one to come after me here."

There was silence on the phone for so long Hugh thought he had lost the connection. Then Jessie spoke.

"You know I won't be able to go back to the States either, right?"

"But you'll make the call?"

"Soon as you hang up."

18

Two days later a pounding on his sliding glass door woke Hugh. He rolled across the bed, peered through the inner doorframe to the glass door beyond. Casey stood outside, glaring in. Hugh pulled on shorts and a shirt and went to the door, but didn't open it. Casey had never been to Hugh's place, and now here he was and looking angry. It was time for their reckoning.

"You open up, Mate? Or should we shout at each other?"

"Depends on why you're here."

"Détente. Open."

Hugh slid the door open. Casey stepped inside.

"You're a cheeky one," Casey said.

Hugh said nothing.

"First, I can't fathom why Mal's so taken with a numpty. Then I suss that out and find you're blind, stupid, and deserve whatever happens to you. Then you do me a good turn, out of the blue."

"You weren't a threat," Hugh said. "Not like that." This was about the fertilizer, but what had Casey 'sussed out?'

"That's weakness on Blacktip," Casey said. "Weakness can be deadly. And you're a threat to me, eh? Next time anything happens at that bloody runway."

"Marquette seized all the makings. Nothing *can* happen." Casey was here to threaten him. What else had he and Mal talked about in the laundry room, that Hugh hadn't heard?

"You've got it all reckoned, eh?"

"If anything else happens, I'd have to…"

"You won't have to anything," Casey said. "I've given Ger my notice. I leave in three days."

"Because of this?" Casey couldn't be so angry at the new runway that he would leave his beloved Blacktip.

"It's a different island than I moved to," Casey said. "The place I loved is gone. I can't turn back the clock, so I'll find someplace new and enjoy it until some Skerritt-type ruins it, too."

"And you're telling me this why?"

"We're allies, however temporarily. You're an F.N.G., but you're a decent mate. Whether you mean to be or not."

Hugh sat, stunned. But Casey wasn't through.

"I also pay my debts. There's things you should know about your friend Mal. She's gunning for you."

"I heard," Hugh said. "The other day. At the laundry."

Casey looked surprised. Hugh hadn't thought that was possible.

"That why she's M.I.A. since yesterday?" A calculating look crept across Casey's face. "She with your bounty hunters?"

"I… no…" Hugh kept his voice even as he could. How did Casey know the arrested men were bounty hunters? And more important, what had happened to Mal? If she had bolted, any deal he might have with the Feds was shot. "You sure she's not just sick at home?"

Casey studied Hugh for a long moment.

"I'm here for me, not Mal," Casey said. "I'm off, heading east for the Windwards. If I'm not betrayed."

"No. No reason to. How'd you know about the two guys?"

"Cheers, Hugh."

Casey slid the door closed behind him and was gone.

Hugh sat a moment longer, letting Casey's news settle. His personal tormentor was leaving. Work would be happier. An unexpected sadness crept in then. There had been respect in Casey's voice. An exchange between equals, or nearly so. They had finally reached that point, and Casey was leaving.

Casey had taken a fair way out, leaving the island without putting Hugh in a position of having to tell the police what he knew. Casey may have been a minor demon, but he was an honorable one.

Mal's absence was worrisome, though. Skerritt had promoted her to manager the morning after Portia had whacked the Schafts, and she had spent the day strutting around Eagle Ray Cove, terrorizing the staff. Her disappearing after her greatest triumph made no sense. She couldn't be gone. He needed information. Once again, Hugh missed having a phone. He kicked the scooter started and sputtered up the coast road, headed for Blacktip Haven.

Hugh caught Jessie cleaning up after the morning rush. She smiled when she saw him, set aside the dirty dishes she was collecting.

"You missed breakfast," she said. "But… this isn't a social call, is it?"

She motioned Hugh out to the resort's pool deck, deserted with all the guests off to the dive boat.

"You hear from any of your friends?" Hugh said before the screen door closed.

"Uh uh." Jessie sounded concerned. "Last word was they were looking into details. No promises, but they were interested. And they haven't said no."

"Mal's missing since yesterday. Any way she could've caught wind people are on her trail?"

"Oh." Jessie grimaced. "Yeah, that'd screw the pooch."

"Her hiding on the island's best-case. Her cutting a counter deal's worst."

"I'll call. Now. It may be a while before I hear back, though. I'm on it."

Hugh stopped by Mal's cottage on his way home. There was no answer when he knocked and no signs of stirring inside. No one at the resort had seen her, either.

The next morning there was still no sign of Mal. The Eagle Ray Divers staff, though, was focused on Casey's leaving.

"He's part of the island," Alison said. "I figured he was waiting for Ger to move on. Guess he got tired of waiting."

"Leaving this sudden? Island rot snapped him," Gage said. "Gets everybody, they stay too long."

"Uh-uh, something's squirrelly," Marina said. "Casey up and quits the same time Mal goes missing? That's not coincidence."

"Right. She's probably hiding on Casey's catamaran," Gage laughed. "They've just pretended to hate each other all these years to throw us off."

"No great loss, on either count." Lee's voice was muffled by his bandaged nose.

"Casey's been sitting on 'g,' waiting on 'o' for years," Gage said. "And Mal played one card too many with that Schaft business. I bet Rich had her taken out and shot after she called Portia in."

Hugh gritted his teeth, anxious about bad news from Jessie. Where, or why, Mal had gone made no difference. That she was gone meant he was cooked.

Ger Latner stomped in, cutting off conversation.

"New crews starting today," he boomed. "It's Gage with Lee On the *Barjack* and Hugh with Alison on the *Skipjack*."

"Jeez, Ger…" Gage started.

"By default," Latner growled. "Marina's training the new hire. No way I can put Hugh and Lee together. And Lee'd run roughshod over Alison."

"As long as Captain Grumble's leaving, we're good," Marina said. "And Ali gets her own boat."

The strange sadness washed through Hugh again. Working with Alison would be fun, but in an odd way he didn't quite understand, he would miss Casey.

And still there was no word of Mal.

That afternoon Rich Skerritt called the resort staff together. Jerrod stood beside him.

"I'll make this quick," Skerritt said. "Jerrod's Eagle Ray Cove's new daddy rabbit. He knows the resort, he knows you all, and he knows how to keep his nose clean. Anybody got a problem with that, or wants to talk about previous management, there's two flights off island each day."

The gathered resort staff exchanged glances. Mal was gone for good, then. Hugh ran for his scooter. Jessie had the day off. She would be at her place, reading whatever medieval gobbledygook she was into these days. Maybe he could use her computer, find a non-Interpol country Tiperon Air flew to.

Hugh had barely reached Parrett's Landing's raised deck when the cottage door burst open and Jessie bounced outside.

"Mal's in custody!" she said. "Whatever she did, the Tiperons waived extradition. Marquette nabbed her and that chess set and shipped them north."

"And me?" Hugh said.

"You're good. Ish. You're still wanted, and they'll arrest you if you go back to the U.S., or anywhere, really. But they dropped the bounty so low you're not worth anyone's while. Oh, they need that pawn, too."

"I'll go get it now." Relief washed through Hugh.

"Sounds like they wanted her dead-to-rights before they cut you loose. That's what took so long."

"I can't thank you enough. For everything," Hugh said. "Celebratory drink?"

"No. I'm done with that. Starting over."

Something in Jessie's tone made Hugh pause.

"You okay, not being able to go home after…" He wasn't sure what to call what Jessie had done.

"'Aiding and abetting,' they said." Jessie flashed a thin smile. "I knew what I was doing. When I came here I wanted a new life and was willing to do whatever it took. But there's cash in my pocket now. To hell with them. I'm on a quest of my own. You're a basket case, but I like basket cases. We'll get you back together."

Jessie smiled, set her eyes crinkling.

"And if that doesn't work out?" Hugh said. This, whatever this was with Jessie, was new and untested and fragile.

"We'll burn that bridge when we get to it. Whatever happens, I'm moving forward. So are you, with Mal *and* Casey gone."

"You have no idea. If you're not drinking, you mind if I do?"

"Sit. Stay."

Hugh and Jessie were on the Eagle Ray Cove pier at dawn the next day to watch Casey sail away. Hugh still didn't fully believe Casey was leaving. They sat side-by-side watching the *Bident* motor between the flashing red and green beacons. Once past the reef, the catamaran sails went up and it turned south, sails stained red with the sunrise.

The pier shuddered then, setting the water around the pilings rippling. A moment later came a succession of low booms, like far-off thunder. Jessie looked to Hugh. Black smoke boiled above the northern tree line.

"Oh, no…" The sound of his own voice surprised Hugh. Casey must have left a last round of explosives at the construction site and triggered them from his boat, a grand goodbye for Blacktip Island.

"That at the new runway?" Jessie said.

"Where else."

"So… you'll have to give that money back."

"Doubt it," Hugh said. "Ike and Leo could've timed bombs to go off later."

"Who's the bomber, Hugh?" Jessie's voice was icy.

"A ghost. That'll be the last of it."

Jessie studied the retreating *Bident*, then studied Hugh.

"Right," she said.

Jessie's ring felt red hot in his pocket. Hugh looked away.

That evening, Dermott grabbed Hugh at the Eagle Ray Cove bar, pulled him aside so Jessie couldn't hear.

"Who set that bomb, Hugo?" Dermott stuck a finger in Hugh's chest, pushing Hugh backwards.

"Someone who'll never set another one."

"My money's already spent, y'know." Dermot loomed over Hugh. "Anybody wants it back, you paying for us two."

"Not a worry, Dermott. The cops'll figure it was bombs our boys set before they left. Got caught, I mean."

Dermott studied Hugh for a long moment.

"You living on a razor's edge, Hugo."

They were cut off by Antonio's shouting, beer in hand.

"Dark thing in a dream told me be at that site this dawn,'" Antonio yelled. "Just got there when Whoom! Ground shook and flames shot up and smoke boiled up from all over."

Antonio paused, making sure he had everyone's attention.

"Then Whoom! Whoom! Whoom! Bunch more times, all in a line, dead center down that track. Black smoke swallowed everything, like that clearing never happened. Island reclaimed its own."

Hugh left Dermott, rejoined Jessie.

"One big trench now, with all that rock crumbled down deep into sink holes," Antonio kept on. "Don't think even Mister Rich got the money to fight the island itself."

"I surely do hope that's it." Dermott's eyes were locked on Hugh. "For couple people's sakes."

Jessie was watching Hugh, too. Across the deck, Lee and Alison had their heads together, whispering. Glancing at Hugh and Jessie.

"You up for a beach walk?" Hugh said to Jessie.

Jessie looked puzzled, but followed him down the boardwalk. They eased down the steps to the wet sand. The stars littered the sky like exploded sequins. Heat lightning flashed on the western horizon. If Casey had really sailed southeast, he'd be in those storms by now. Hugh was certain Casey had changed course once Blacktip Island was out of sight, though, disappeared with a new destination and a new name. It didn't matter. Casey was gone. Mal was gone. It was as new a world for Hugh as it was for Jessie.

"The more I think about it, the more I think I don't want to know any more about those bombs," Jessie said.

"Probably not."

"So we're back to 'aiding and abetting.'"

"You aren't."

They were even with Mal's cottage.

"You feel like sitting?" Hugh said.

"On the sand?"

"There's a hammock up here."

Hugh walked up the slope toward the low cottages, slowing when he neared the two palm trees.

"Careful," he said. "It can be hard to see in the dark."

Hugh guided Jessie to the hammock, and they sat sideways in the netting.

"I don't want to know how you knew that." Jessie's voice came sharp.

"My bed that first night back on the island," he said. "Long story."

"Just you and a pawn?"

"I *was* the pawn," Hugh laughed.

He had come full circle since that night. He was over Mal and back in this perfect beach scene with someone who honestly cared for him. Will-o-wisps flickered near the cottage, mirroring the heat lightning over the sea.

He had no formal lease with Antonio. He could move into Mal's place. It was nicer than Antonio's and had no nosey neighbors. There was also no telling what Mal might have left hidden there. He had the next day off. He would rent Mal's cottage, start searching high in the attic and work down, see what he could find. Then he would tackle the grounds outside. If anything were hidden, he'd find it. There was no hurry. He had the rest of his life to look. And hopefully Jessie to watch sunsets with.

"I... found... something of yours." Hugh slipped Jessie's silver ring into her hand.

Seconds passed while Jessie rolled the ring between her fingers. Then she gasped when she realized what it was.

"Where'd you...?"

"It must've fallen in with my snorkeling stuff," Hugh said. "At Spider Bight, I guess."

There was a long pause before Jessie spoke again.

"So... that missing cash. It was in your place all along, right?" Jessie's voice was a caress in the darkness.

"Yeah."

"Still is?"

Why?"

"A girl could live comfortably on that."

CPSIA information can be obtained
at www.ICGtesting.com
Printed in the USA
LVHW041034280720
661664LV00007B/464